Hani and Ishu's guide to Fake Dating

BY ADIBA JAIGIRDAR

The Henna Wars

Hani and Ishu's Guide to Fake Dating

Hani and Ishu's guide to Fake Dating

Adiba Jaigirdar

First published in Great Britain in 2021 by Hodder & Stoughton Limited
First published in the United States in 2021 by Page Street Publishing Co.
Published by arrangement with Page Street Publishing Co.,
c/o Macmillan Publishing Group, LLC. All rights reserved.

7 9 10 8

Text copyright © Adiba Jaigirdar, 2021

The moral right of the author has been asserted.

Book design by Julia Tyler for Page Street Publishing Co.
Cover illustration by Nabigal-Nayagam Haider Ali

A CIP catalogue record for this book is available from the British Library.

ISBN 978 1 444 96224 6

Printed and bound in Great Britain by Clays Ltd, Elcograf S.p.A.

The paper and board used in this book
are made from wood from responsible sources.

Hodder Children's Books
An imprint of
Hachette Children's Group
Part of Hodder & Stoughton
Carmelite House
50 Victoria Embankment
London EC4Y 0DZ

An Hachette UK Company
www.hachette.co.uk

www.hachettechildrens.co.uk

To all the Bengali kids who grew up never seeing a reflection of themselves

content warnings:
This book contains instances of racism, homophobia
(specifically biphobia and lesbophobia), Islamophobia, toxic
friendship, gaslighting, and parental abandonment.

chapter one

~ishu

I'M WRAPPED UP IN BIOLOGY HOMEWORK WHEN MY phone buzzes. Once, twice, three times before swiftly buzzing off the corner of my desk and into my bin.

'What the fuck?' I mumble to the air, shutting my biology book with a thud and diving into the bin full of nothing but used makeup wipes and torn-up pieces of paper. I didn't know that my phone was a) that desperate to be trash and b) that sensitive to receiving texts.

To be fair, getting texts is not really something that I'm accustomed to, so I guess my phone isn't either. It is, after all, a cheap three-year-old thing that takes at least a whole minute to load anything up any more.

The phone is still vibrating when I finally find it. This time, with a call, of all things.

I don't remember the last time I received a call. It was probably from Ammu or Abbu calling to let me know they would be home late or something. This time, though, the phone screen is flashing my older sister's name: Nikhita.

'Nik?'

'Ishu, thank God!' Nik's voice sounds so weird over the phone – way higher than I remember it to be. Maybe it's just been that long since I spoke to her. She left two years ago to study at University College London, of all places. Talk about setting the bar high.

Nik has been back exactly once since she waved goodbye to us at the airport two years ago, for a two-week holiday. She spent the whole time poring over her medical books before swiftly boarding her return flight with bloodshot eyes, looking as if she hadn't been on a holiday at all. Such is the life of a medical student at UCL. She rarely even calls Ammu and Abbu, but they're mostly OK with it because Nikhita is making the family proud. She's making her dreams come true.

'Um, why are you calling?' I only register that it's kind of a rude question when the words are already out of my mouth. The thing is, Nik never calls me. In all our years of being sisters, I'm pretty sure she has never called me once. She only occasionally texts me on WhatsApp when Ammu and Abbu aren't available, to ask when they will be available. Never to have a chat with me, or to check up on me.

'God, Ishu, I can't just call my little sis? Why did it take you so long to pick up?' Her voice comes across as frustrated, but I can sense something else there too. Some kind of nervousness that she's trying to hide. What does perfect Nikhita have to be nervous about?

'I was studying. Leaving Cert coming up, you know?' She

can't have already forgotten about the state exams that decide what universities we get into.

'Oh, ha. Yeah, the Leaving Cert. Wow, I remember those days. Wish I could go back to that.' She wants to sound biting and sarcastic, I can tell. But it comes across flat. Like her heart is not quite in it. 'So, um. Are Ammu and Abbu in yet?'

There it is.

'Um, yeah, I'm pretty sure they are.' I turn in my chair to face the window – it's already pitch black outside. I was so absorbed in my work I didn't realise that it's well into the evening. The clock hanging up on my wall reads 8:33 p.m. 'They're downstairs, watching something on TV, I think.' I can hear the low hum of the television, the words of a Hindi natok floating up through the small crack in my bedroom door.

'Cool, cool. Well, listen. I really need you to do me a favour, OK?'

I sit up straight. A favour is definitely a first. I'm not sure how I'm supposed to respond to that. Should I demand she tell me what it is before agreeing to it? Should I demand a favour in return? Before I've made up my mind, Nik has already launched into what she needs from me.

'Basically, I'm coming back home for a few days to surprise Ammu and Abbu. But I left my keys with them last time I visited, so I just need you to let me into the house tomorrow after school. You can do that, right?'

'You're surprising Ammu and Abbu?' I can't wrap my head around the word 'surprise.' You don't 'surprise' Bengali parents unless you want a thappor to your face. Not that Ammu and Abbu are the kind of people to go around giving thappors willy nilly – or ever – but still. Surprises and Bengali parents do not go together.

'Don't say it like that.' Now Nik sounds offended.

'Like what?'

She sighs. 'Never mind. Can you just help me, please?'

'You know it's the middle of the school year, right? Why are you coming tomorrow? Is everything OK?'

'Everything is fine,' Nik says in a voice that suggests that everything is definitely not fine. I hope when she's a doctor she'll be better at reassuring her patients. 'I just haven't seen you guys in so long, and…I have some news. Will you help me or not?'

'Well, I'm hardly going to slam the door in your face.'

I can hear an exasperated breath on the line, as if Nik has been trying really hard to keep her exasperation to herself but I've made it impossible. 'OK. Thanks, Ishu. Um. I'll see you tomorrow, I guess.'

'See you tom—' Nik has already hung up.

I know I should probably worry more about whatever's going on with Nik, but I figure we'll deal with it the way we always deal with things – each on our own. My responsibility here is to open the front door and let her in. I can definitely do that.

Plus, I still have an entire chapter of biology I want to make notes on. So, I toss my phone on my bed and flip open my biology book once more, putting Nik out of my mind.

It's a good thing I spent last night studying because Ms Taylor springs a surprise test on us as soon as we walk into double biology in the afternoon. Surprise tests are her absolute favourite thing, even when she hasn't actually taught us half the material she's supposed to have covered. At least once a fortnight we start biology class with a test – if not more often. I have a feeling these are about to become even more frequent the closer we get to our Leaving Certificate.

Somehow, my classmates are still surprised by the test. I just roll my eyes, pick up my pen and dig in.

Most of the questions are on the chapters I was making notes of last night, so I'm feeling pretty confident. On the other side of the aisle, Aisling Mahoney is biting her lip so hard that I'm surprised she hasn't drawn blood. When she looks up and catches my eye, she gives me a nasty look. I shoot her a wicked grin in return.

It seems to get under her skin, because she scowls and goes back to her test – which is more blank space than anything else. Maybe if Aisling spent more time paying attention and less time snapchatting in class she would actually know some of these answers.

Humaira comes around to our row at the end of the test, collecting up our papers.

'How'd you do?' she asks Aisling.

'Bad.' Aisling casts me a glare as if it's my fault she didn't do well. 'I hate these surprise tests. I can never keep up with biology; there's way too much to study.'

'Don't worry, I'll help you out, yeah? We can go over some stuff during lunch,' Humaira offers with a smile. She's the only other Brown girl in our class – the only other South Asian girl in our year – and because she's been in this school for longer than me, sometimes I think people expect me to be exactly like her. But Humaira is the most annoyingly helpful person I've ever met, so everyone was a bit disappointed to learn that I'm the most annoyingly unhelpful person they'll probably ever meet.

'Thanks, Maira.' Aisling flashes her a smile, like it isn't her own fault for not paying attention, for not studying. I notice my fists are clenched on my desk. I unclench them slowly, trying to rid my body of the tension it has built up in the last few minutes, and open up my biology textbook.

Humaira doesn't need my help or protection, no matter how much I want to shake her and say *For God's sake, stop!* She's way too eager to lend a listening ear, to be the person that everybody goes to for help. She doesn't see the way they're leeching her of everything she has and giving back nothing in return. Sometimes I wonder how Humaira has lasted this long. Sometimes I wonder how much longer she'll be able to last.

But it's none of my business.

It's not like Humaira and I are friends.

When I first moved to this school in second year, Humaira was the one tasked to show me around and guide me. I had no doubt it had to do with the fact that we were both Brown girls and everyone assumed that we would get on. But Humaira and I couldn't be more different, even if we are both Bengali.

Humaira shuffles towards me next, surprising me with a smile. 'How'd you do, Ishita?' I don't know how she can code switch so effortlessly. Because our parents are Bengali, we have two names – I'm Ishu to family and most Bengalis, and Ishita to everyone else. But Humaira has so many names at this stage that it's difficult to keep them straight.

'Fine, probably.' I shrug. If I'm being honest, I'm pretty sure I aced it. Like I've aced every single test since I started at this school – As all around. But Aisling is already glaring daggers at me and she might actually murder me if I don't show at least some humbleness.

'Nice.' Humaira sweeps my test away into her bundle.

'How'd you do?' I ask.

She gives me a small smile and taps the side of her nose before moving on to the next row of seats.

I roll my eyes. I'm pretty sure if Aisling had asked, Humaira would have been more than happy to share.

But whatever.

chapter two

WATCHING ABBA SPEAK IS KIND OF A SURREAL experience. His voice envelopes the whole room, and even though he's speaking to everyone at this rally it seems as if he's speaking *only* to me. In some ways, he doesn't seem like my Abba at all. In other ways, he's all of the wonderful things that make him my Abba.

Beside me, Aisling slips her phone out of her pocket. The glare of her screen is uncomfortably bright. I feel a prick of annoyance, but bite it down.

On the other side of me, Deirdre holds up her own phone to me. The top right reads 6:35 p.m. Dee raises an eyebrow like she's asking me a question. I shake my head, hoping that answers her, but she's frowning now.

Before I know it, she's leaning forwards until her shoulders bump against mine. 'I thought you said we could leave at six thirty?' She says it like being here is some kind of punishment.

'Just wait a few more minutes…' I mumble, staring straight ahead at Abba. Trying to tune back in to his speech. I have –

of course – already heard it many times. I could probably give the speech myself, if I didn't absolutely hate speaking in front of people.

Still, I can't ignore the way Dee leans over me to exchange a pointed glance with Aisling. Like being here an extra five minutes is truly painful for the two of them.

I chew on my lip, trying to decide the best course of action. On one hand, I don't want to leave Abba here mid-speech. On the other hand, I don't want Aisling and Dee to keep disrupting him.

'Come on,' I find myself whispering as I motion for the two of them to follow. In a few moments, we've weaved through the throng of people outside the mosque and are outside the gates. I can still hear the murmur of Abba's speech here, but it's not loud enough to decipher the words.

'If your dad gets pissed, just tell him that you had plans with us,' Aisling says when she glances at me. Like she can see the tension in my expression, and she's mistaken it for fear of repercussion from Abba.

'He won't get angry,' I mutter, following Aisling and Dee towards the bus stop.

'We don't have to go to *all* of his speeches, do we?' Aisling asks. There's a sneer in her voice, though she tries – and fails – to keep it out of her expression.

I have to stifle a sigh. I'm wishing that I had never told Aisling and Dee about this. When they asked me to hang out today, I should have said I was doing anything else – anything other than helping Abba with his political campaign.

Even hearing that it was going to take place outside the mosque hadn't stopped Aisling and Dee from wanting to tag along. I had even felt a beat of excitement that I could show them our mosque. After all, I've spent so much of my time there – Eid, and jummah on the holidays when I don't have school.

But it was obviously a mistake.

'I thought it was kind of interesting,' Dee says. Aisling turns to her with surprise written all over her face. She obviously doesn't think anyone is capable of being interested in Abba's political campaign, in the fact that he might be the first South Asian and the first Muslim to be elected to the county council.

'My dad says he's so proud of how progressive Irish politics have got. That even someone whose English isn't…' – Dee glances at me – '…so great has a shot at winning.'

I can only settle Dee with a frown. 'My dad's English is perfect.'

In fact, his English is probably even better than mine. Unlike us, Amma and Abba spent their childhood learning all the mechanics of the English language. Abba sometimes uses so many big, obscure words that I'm sure he's memorizing a dictionary in his spare time.

'Yeah, but…you know.' Dee raises an eyebrow like this is some kind of inside joke.

'I know…?'

'He has an accent,' Dee says. 'Like, kind of a thick one.'

'Everyone has an accent,' I insist. I want to press on about it more. Abba being in the running for the county council elections is a big deal, after all.

But Aisling and Dee don't get it, and I'm not sure I can make them understand.

'I guess, yeah. It was kind of boring…' I cross my arms and lean against the glass of the bus stop, trying to ignore the uncomfortable gnawing in my stomach.

Moments later, the bus pulls up in front of us, and the three of us pile on. Aisling and Dee slip after each other in the same row, and I slide into a window seat on the other side. My eyes take in the mosque passing by us as the bus begins to pull away. There's a crowd of people going towards the mosque now. I know Abba planned to join everyone for Maghrib prayer after his speech – even though he rarely prays at home.

I wish for a moment that I had insisted on staying until the rally was finished. But we did make plans to leave at six thirty, and I guess it's not Dee and Aisling's fault that Abba's speech went longer. Or that Maghrib prayer isn't until much later. I doubt Aisling and Dee even know what Maghrib prayer is – never mind when it takes place.

'So, when we get to mine, Dee and I want to catch up on *Riverdale*,' Aisling says. She had originally suggested that I go over to watch a movie – like old times, when the three of us spent our days holed up in each other's rooms. But it feels like we haven't done that in months.

'I'm not sure I want to watch *Riverdale*,' I say, regretting the words immediately as I watch Aisling's eyebrows furrow.

'Well, it's two against one, sorry,' Dee chimes in.

I heave a sigh. 'You know…it's getting late. I should probably just get off at my stop and go home.'

'Seriously?' Aisling crosses her arms over her chest, examining me with a glare. 'You said you would come over today if we went to your dad's thing.'

'I said I was going to my dad's thing, and maybe after I'd come over. *You* wanted to come to my dad's thing.'

Aisling just rolls her eyes, like I had somehow forced her into the mosque against her will – like anybody could force Aisling to do anything she didn't want to do.

'Tell your parents that you want to stay over. *I'm* staying the night,' Dee says.

'You know I can't.' I sigh, turning away from the two of them. I don't know how many times I've had this same conversation with Aisling and Dee. They still keep insisting.

'I just don't understand,' Aisling says. 'Your mam knows me. She's met me. You're always going to be safe and comfortable in my house. Why can't you just sleep over?'

'There's no logical reason for it, Aisling.' I'm tired of having to explain this over and over again. Especially because one day I'm afraid Aisling and Dee are going to be tired too, and their tiredness won't lead them to accepting me as I am, but to finding someone else who can do all of the 'normal' things they want to do. Like sleep over. 'It's just part of being Bengali and Muslim. It's just…the way things are.'

'So you're just going to go home?' Aisling doesn't look happy from the way her lips are pressed into a thin line. I hate it when Aisling looks at me like that. She seems to do it more often than not these days; it feels like I can't do anything to make her happy. I remember when we were in primary school – before we even knew Dee – and we used to do everything together. Back then Aisling didn't mind so much that I couldn't stay out late, or do sleepovers, or go drinking (which of course she didn't do back then). Now Aisling seems to notice all of the little things that make us different. And she hates them all.

'I have to. It's…going to get dark soon, and…yeah.' The truth is that Amma won't mind if I stop by and watch a few episodes of *Riverdale* with Aisling and Dee and am home a few hours later. She probably wouldn't even mind if I slept over at Aisling's. But if I go to Aisling's, I'll definitely miss Maghrib, and watching *Riverdale* with the two of them is not worth missing that. Going over to Aisling's means I can't pray at all, because the one or two times I've mentioned prayer to Aisling and Dee they've got so uncomfortable that it made *me* uncomfortable. So it's better that I just keep that part of my life wrapped up and hidden away in my own home.

'You're coming tomorrow, right?' Dee asks, and I look away from the window and towards her. She's wearing a bright smile. 'After school…bring something to change into!'

'I don't know…' Aisling and Dee invited me to the cinema, and I already know that their boyfriends, Barry and Colm, are going to be there. I'm not sure if I want to spend a whole afternoon listening to them shift in the movie theatre, being the fifth wheel. Before I can make an excuse, Aisling leans forwards and shoots me a glare.

'Don't you dare back out!' she says. 'Come on, Maira. We came to your dad's thing. And you promised!'

It's the last thing I want to do after a whole day of school, but I nod. 'Sure, yeah. I'll be there.'

Aisling still seems a little annoyed at me the next day at school. I try to appease her with bright smiles all day.

But at lunchtime, while I'm slipping books out of my locker, Aisling shoots me a strange look.

'Everything OK?' I ask.

She leans her back against the locker next to mine and says, 'Are you really friends with Ishita Dey?'

Dee stops secretly scrolling through her Instagram by her own locker next to mine to give me a once over at Aisling's question.

'Why would you ask that?' Ishita and I are definitely not what I would call friends. I wouldn't even call us friendly. Honestly, I'm not sure what I would call us. Complicated, I guess.

'This Instagram picture you put up last weekend has her in it?' Her statement comes off more like a question, even as she's holding up her phone to show me the picture. Aisling must have really been analyzing the picture well, because you can only see Ishita in the very corner and she's not even very clear.

'She's like…a family friend, kind of. Or like…a Bengali friend. I don't know. I was at a Bengali thing.' I shake my head. I don't know how to explain myself. The whole Bengali thing is so different from anything my white Irish friends have ever dealt with – there's no way to explain it without getting into the nitty gritty of it. And even then, they don't get it. Or don't want to get it, I suppose. There's just no Irish equivalent of dawats.

'It looks like fun,' Dee says, tucking her phone into her breast pocket and away from the prying eyes of the teachers. 'How come you never invite us to your "Bengali" things?'

'Um.' I hesitate, unsure of exactly how to answer that. *Because you're not Bengali* seems a little too direct. But it's also the truth. I'm not sure why they would even want to come. They would fit in about as well as an elephant in the middle of a poultry farm. 'I guess…it's just a thing that…my family does. It's not really for…friends.'

'Ishita isn't your family,' Aisling points out.

I have to stifle a sigh. I also have to stop myself from rubbing my nose in frustration. And I have to keep my tone in check, ensuring none of my annoyance seeps in. 'Yeah, Ishita is like…a family friend. So it's a little different. It's complicated.' Aisling and Dee look like they still have a million questions. Questions I don't have answers to. Questions I don't want to answer. So I zip up my bag and swing it on to my back and say, 'I'm starving. Can we have lunch please?'

By the time the last bell rings, I am exhausted. Somehow, Aisling and Dee are the exact opposite. They seem to be even more energised by the fact that it's Friday afternoon.

'We're going to get changed in the bathroom,' Aisling tells me. 'You coming?'

'I have to get my stuff from my locker first. I'll meet you guys there.'

As I'm getting my things, I notice Ishita glaring at her locker on the other side of the hallway like it has somehow wronged her. I swing my P.E. bag out of my locker at the same time that Ishita shuts her locker door with a thud. Nobody else seems to notice just how loudly the door hits home. *What did that locker ever do to you, Ishita?*

'Hey,' I call over, even though I know I shouldn't. Ishita isn't exactly known for being happy-go-lucky, but I don't think I've seen her this angry since last year, when she got a B+ on an English essay. She tried to contest the grade by talking herself up to Ms Baker, the English teacher, but Ms Baker had smiled wanly and said she'd made up her mind and the result couldn't be changed. Ishita threw a fit and got a week of detention.

'What?' Ishita turns her glare to me.

'Everything OK?' I lower my voice so she knows we can have a private conversation.

'What do you care?' Ishita asks.

'You just seem…angry? Bad test result?'

Ishita blinks at that, like a bad test result shouldn't have come into my mind. Even though that's literally all Ishita ever seems to think about.

She shakes her head. 'No, it's nothing. Whatever.' Then she turns on her heel, swinging her bag over her shoulder, and disappears out of sight.

'Yeah, bye to you too, Ishita!' I mumble under my breath as I swing my own locker door shut. 'You have a great weekend too, Ishita!'

'Who are you talking to?' Dee turns the corner, looking around me at the nearly empty corridor. She's already changed into jeans and a crop top, her hair is out of its usual ponytail, and I'm pretty impressed at the amount of makeup she's managed to put on in this short amount of time.

'No one.' I shake my head, getting Ishita out of it. She's been nothing but a burden since the day she moved to this school. Before Ishita, I was whoever I wanted to be. After Ishita, it was like our shared culture painted us with the same brush. If Ishita did something, Aisling and Dee would ask, 'Why does she do that?' If Ishita said something, 'Why does she say that?' I know it's not her fault that people think our culture must be why we act and say the things we do, but still.

'I need to get changed,' I say. 'I'll be back.' I try my best to forget about Ishita. I have other things to worry about.

chapter three

I am literally going to catch pneumonia and die.

I roll my eyes at my phone even though Nik isn't here to see – it's just me rolling my eyes at a non-sentient object. Nik has been texting me for the past hour about how she's at home and I need to let her in. Even while I was in the middle of class! I guess because Nik has spent so little time thinking of anyone other than herself it didn't occur to her that I can't open the door for her while I'm in school. She didn't even remember what time school ends, even though she was attending the same school as me just two years ago.

Ishu!!!

Her texts are getting more and more frequent and more and more annoying. They're making my blood pressure rise. I can hardly do anything for her from the bus, and her texting repeatedly isn't going to change the fact that there's a downpour, or that I still have fifteen minutes on my route before I reach home.

I tuck my phone into the front pocket of my bag, cross my

arms over my chest, and glare at the rain-drenched window. If I don't get my anger down to at least a simmer I'm sure I'll say something to Nik that I'll regret later. I probably shouldn't start her first trip home in months on the wrong foot.

Nik tries to give me a smile when she sees me coming through the pouring rain. I can tell her heart's not in it, but whatever. I guess I can't really blame her – the rain *is* cold.

'Hey.' I slide past her and slip the house key into the front door. I twist it just once before it clicks open. Slipping inside, I leave the door open for Nik to come in. She does, with a slight shudder, taking in the house as if she's seeing it for the first time.

'You've had the walls repainted,' she says.

I look at the walls when she says this. That feels like so long ago; it's a memory that's already blended together with others.

'I guess.'

'It looks nice.' Nik lifts a finger to touch the wall, like somehow it will feel different too.

We both slip off our shoes, and as Nik walks from room to room, taking in all that's changed since the last time she was here, I take her in. Because it's not just the house that's changed; Nik has too.

Her hair is much shorter than it used to be. Her thick black locks that she used to proudly grow out have been cut up to her shoulders, and even has brown highlights. She's put on weight too. Before, Nik was all skin and bones, and I'm pretty sure the only thing she consumed regularly was buckets of coffee. Now she and I could fit into the same clothes.

Ammu won't be happy about that at all.

'When did we get this fancy coffee machine?' Nik exclaims from the kitchen.

I sigh, slipping inside to see Nik admiring the coffee machine I convinced Ammu and Abbu to get by insisting that I needed it if I was going to ace my Leaving Cert. I'm pretty sure Ammu and Abbu would buy me an army of unicorns if I told them it would help me ace my Leaving Cert.

'Like two months ago,' I tell Nik.

'Wow, Ammu and Abbu have really been spoiling you, huh? Their babu.'

I roll my eyes. Babu is a nickname that Bengalis sometimes give to the youngest child in their family; it literally translates to baby. But I used to throw a fit whenever anybody called me that, so it never really stuck. Only Nik uses it, to tease me. Like Ammu and Abbu haven't been doting on her, their perfect, favourite child, for our entire lives.

'Why are you here?'

Nik halts her excited examination of the coffee machine and eyes me with some disdain.

'I'm not allowed to come back to my own house without having to explain myself?' Her voice is huffy.

'You haven't been back here in more than a year,' I say. 'You barely even call.'

'Doesn't change anything,' Nik says. 'I just wanted to see you guys. See Ammu and Abbu…' She trails off for a moment, before adding, 'Well, I have something to tell them as well.'

'So you couldn't tell them that you were coming?' I ask.

'It's a surprise, like I said. They'll be happy to see me unexpectedly.' Nik smiles as she says this, and everything clicks into place.

Nik doesn't just have a surprise for Ammu and Abbu – she has a bad surprise that will make them mad. But if they're delighted to suddenly see Nik back home, will they let their anger get in the way? That must be what Nik is banking on – their happiness overriding their anger.

The news must be pretty bad for her to fly all the way here to tell it to them.

'Well, they probably won't be back for a few hours still, just so you know.'

'That's OK. I can catch up with you, right? How's school? Got a boyfriend?'

I sigh. 'I have to go study.'

'Seriously? I haven't seen you in a year.'

I want to say, *And whose fault is that?* She's the older sister. She's supposed to come visit. She's supposed to spend Christmas and New Year's with us. She's supposed to call and text to let us know what's going on with her life. But she never has.

It's not like we were ever close anyway, but ever since Nik left, it's like an emptiness has opened up in our house. The lack of her presence has always pressed on us.

'Your surprise visit isn't going to stop my teachers from giving me tests.'

'It's Friday,' Nik insists. Like she didn't use to spend her Fridays locked up in her room, studying for the Leaving Cert. You don't get into UCL by taking time off studying whenever you feel like it.

I sigh. 'You know what will make Ammu and Abbu even happier to see you?'

Nik's face brightens at the question. 'What?'

'If they come home to a home-cooked meal prepared by their two daughters.'

By the time Abbu and Ammu arrive home, Nik and I have managed to cook a pot of biryani. Neither of us are exactly skilled chefs, but with the help of a packet of Shan Masala we managed to make something halfway decent. Something Ammu and Abbu will definitely appreciate.

When the click of the door sounds, a shadow passes over Nik's face. It's only there for a moment, and then she's pasting the kind of smile on her face that she reserves for our parents – the one that tells them she's the star daughter. I finish setting the table while Nik goes to greet my parents.

While I set the plates and pour the water, I can hear the squeals of delight Ammu and Abbu let out at the sight of Nik.

'What are you doing here?' Ammu's voice is brighter than

I've heard it in a long time. 'You didn't call!'

'It was a surprise…' Nik is unexpectedly stoic in her responses. 'Come in the kitchen, Ishu and I cooked you dinner.'

Abbu catches my eye as soon as he steps into the kitchen. 'Ishu, you knew Nikhita was coming? And you didn't say?'

I shrug. 'She just called me yesterday…she said she wanted to surprise you.' For a moment, I'm afraid they're going to reprimand me for keeping the secret. Instead, Abbu and Ammu both break out into smiles – which grow wider when they spot the table laid out and the bowl of biryani in the middle.

'You made this?' Ammu breathes in the aroma as she sits down, eyes wide. Abbu takes the seat opposite her, already piling biryani on to his plate.

'Ishu helped.' Nik gives my shoulder a little nudge, like I'm supposed to be grateful that she's given me some credit. Even though I didn't 'help' her – we made it together.

In fact, it was my idea to make it in the first place. So if anything, *she* helped *me*. But whatever.

'It's so good,' Abbu says between mouthfuls. Even Ammu seems to be enjoying it. I have a feeling they would say it was amazing even if it tasted like shit, just because their favourite daughter, Queen Nikhita, made it.

When I sit down to eat, though, I have to admit that it isn't bad. It's not quite as good as Ammu's biryani – but she's had years of practice, and Nik and I have had none. We've kind of outdone ourselves.

I'm bubbling over with pride and good biryani when Nik drops the bombshell.

'Ammu, Abbu…' she says. 'I didn't just come home to see you. I have some news.'

'Oh?' Ammu leans forwards. No doubt, she expects something good: Nik has won an award, she has an internship, she's somehow graduating early. Something worthy of a star daughter.

Nik takes a deep breath and says, 'I'm taking a year out of uni. I've…met someone.'

Suddenly, it's like someone has sucked all the air out of the room.

chapter four

'WHAT DO YOU MEAN YOU'VE MET SOMEONE?' ABBU
asks, at the same time that Ammu shrieks, 'A year away
from uni?'

Everybody's forgotten about the biryani now. It sits
untouched in front of them.

Well, I haven't *forgotten* about the biryani, but I can hardly
dig in while we're having a family crisis.

Nik isn't looking at either of our parents. Her eyes are
trained on her plate, like that'll somehow dig her out of this
hole. Of all of the bad news I could have imagined Nik sharing,
I would have never imagined this.

'It'll just be for a little while,' Nik says. 'We're…I mean,
we've been seeing each other for a while. And…well, we want
to get married, and I can't really study and manage wedding
planning at the same time. And—'

'Are you pregnant?' Ammu interrupts. 'Is that what this is
about?'

'No!' Nik finally looks up, and I can see unshed tears in

her eyes. Confessing all of this must really be taking a toll on her. Seeing her like this sends a little pang through my heart. I don't think I've ever seen Nik cry before. Maybe when we were kids, but not in years and years. Nik is made of stone. Nik is invincible.

At least, that's what I used to think.

'I just...' Nik mumbles slowly. 'Isn't that something you want from me? To get married and start a family? Isn't that what you did, Ammu?'

Ammu shakes her head, even though that *is* what she did. She got married just before her final year of university, barely pulling it together to scrape a pass in her final exams. She's only ever used her degree to help Abbu with his grocery shop – never to find a job that's all her own. She's always wanted more from us. Both Ammu and Abbu always have.

'Not yet,' Ammu says. 'You're at UCL, Nikhita. You're studying medicine. This is your dream. You can't give it up for some man who obviously doesn't want you to achieve your dreams if he's asking you to take time off.'

'He's not asking me.' Nik's voice is firm now. 'I'm the one who wants to take time off. I...I need it for myself. For us. We're getting married. It's a big commitment. It's a lot. And taking time off, it's not forever. Just a year, and then I'll go back. It'll be like I was never gone. I promise.' There's a whine in her voice as if she's a child asking her parents for a birthday present, not an adult who is apparently about to get married.

Shit, Nik is about to get married.

'Who is this guy?' Abbu demands. 'Some Londoner?'

Nik shakes her head. 'His name is Rakesh. He's Indian too. He graduated with his engineering degree last year.'

I look to Abbu and Ammu. Surely, an Indian engineer will make them satisfied, if not happy. You can't really ask for much more, can you? Nik chose the kind of guy that Abbu and Ammu would have chosen for her. Still, my parents are wearing twin expressions of disgust, like Nik has just told them she was planning to marry a shada guy with no prospects.

'I can't believe after everything we've done to make sure you get into a good university, to make sure you get the best education…' Abbu trails off, shaking his head. He stands, his chair scraping loudly against the tiles of the kitchen floor. For a moment, he looks at Nik like he has more to say, before turning around and storming up the stairs. Ammu follows after him a minute later.

Nik just sits in her chair, silent tears sliding down her cheeks. I don't know what to say or do.

How could Nik be so…foolish? How could she come here after months and months and declare that she is going to leave uni to get married? Why would she leave uni to get married?

'They'll…come around,' I offer, placing my hand on Nik's shoulder in what I hope is a soothing gesture. She shrugs me off, like my touch burns her.

'They won't,' she says. 'God, I don't know why I thought there was even a chance they'd understand.'

'It's big news,' I say defensively. 'You can't really blame them for being angry. You've worked so hard to get into UCL, and to throw that away—'

'I'm not!' Nik exclaims. 'I said…I said I'd go back and finish the degree. Just…right now isn't…it's not a good time. I need time…' It sounds more like she's trying to convince herself than me.

'Can't you marry him and finish off the year?' I ask. 'I mean, it's just a wedding—'

'I can't.' Nik's voice is stone. 'You wouldn't understand. You've never…' She shakes her head, like even trying to explain is beyond her. 'I should go. Rakesh got us a hotel room in town—'

'He's here?'

'Yeah…I thought I would introduce him, you know. But… maybe not. I don't know. I have to think about it. Can you…' She finally turns to me, her eyes wide and pleading. It's an expression I've never seen on my sister before. 'Try to persuade them that I'm doing the right thing?'

How can I when I know she's definitely doing the wrong thing? But how can I deny her when she's just been crying?

'Sure, I'll try,' I promise half-heartedly.

It's enough for Nik, because she actually smiles. 'Thanks, Ishu.'

I keep my door slightly ajar that evening, listening to the sound of Ammu and Abbu discussing the events that unfolded earlier today. They're always so sure that I'm busy with my studies, so used to my quiet self, that they would never imagine I could be listening, or even paying attention.

'We have to find some way to get her back to university,' Ammu says, like it's her decision and not Nik's. I'm sure my parents could find a way to convince Nik to go back. They're pretty persuasive.

'I'll talk to her. One-to-one. She's young. She's just caught up with this idea of being in love.' Abbu sounds convinced. 'It'll be OK.'

'What if it isn't?' Ammu's voice sounds desperate. 'What are you going to do if you can't convince her? We've spent our entire life trying to make those two into human beings, and now—'

'Nik will go back to university and finish her degree and become a doctor.' Abbu's voice carries a tone of finality that makes me wonder who he's trying to convince. 'And…Ishu… she's doing fine. She's on the right path, right?'

I sit up, nearly dropping the maths book I was pretending to study.

'We thought Nik was on the right path too.' Ammu sighs,

like Nik's decision to take a year away from university is somehow contagious. 'Nik was always so…on track. I don't understand what could have happened.'

'I'm going to call her and figure things…' I close the door to my room softly as Ammu and Abbu continue trying to solve the Nik problem.

Setting my book down on the desk, I slump down in my seat, not sure what to think. I always thought that if I kept my head down and studied and did my best and went to the best university I could also study medicine, and Abbu and Ammu would be proud of me. This is what we've been working for my whole life. Not just me, but them too. They moved us here, to this country, to have a better life. To have a shot at all of the things that they didn't have a shot at.

Now, just because Nik is a screw up, that suddenly means that I might be too? My parents have always seen us as a unit, though Nik and I have little in common. Now I realise that they had just two shots at getting it exactly right, and since Nik is screwing up her shot, I have to show them that I'm willing to do whatever it takes.

I just have to figure out a way to prove it.

chapter five

I DON'T KNOW WHY, BUT ISHITA AND HER PUCKERED-UP angry face follow me all the way to the cinema. If Aisling and Dee find it strange that I hardly say a word on the bus, they don't say anything. They're too busy exchanging glances and giggling together. This is usually how things go when I'm the fifth wheel at their dates.

When we get to the cinema we're greeted by Aisling and Dee's boyfriends – Aisling's Barry and Dee's Colm. And there's a third boy there too. A boy I've never met before.

'This is Fionn.' Barry introduces him with a grin. From the way Dee and Aisling glance at me with bright eyes and smug smiles, I know this is some sort of a set up. I groan inwardly, even while putting on a smile outwardly.

'Hey, Fionn.'

Fionn has dirty blonde hair, pale white skin, and electric blue eyes, and even though he's half a head taller than me, he slouches in a way that makes him look much shorter.

He's definitely not my type.

I know it even more when Aisling and Dee pair off with their significant others and I'm left to shuffle next to Fionn, who mumbles things about school and exams and how his favourite film is *Midnight In Paris* because Woody Allen is a genius director. I have to physically stop myself from both rolling my eyes back into my head and running away from the movie theatre. Instead, I clamp my hands together and say, 'Wow, interesting,' like I'm really interested in hearing about films by paedophile directors.

I keep looking over at Aisling and Dee during the film, trying to catch one of their eyes to say, *Get me out of here please!* but they're too busy sucking faces with their boyfriends to notice. At one point, Fionn even tries to slip his fingers into mine. That's the point where I leap up, announce 'bathroom' under my breath, and rush out.

'Well? What did you think of Fionn?' Aisling asks after the film is over and I've told them – insisted – that I need to get home. Thankfully, they didn't let me go off on my own, even though I know they'd rather spend more time shifting their boyfriends. It's a cool and clear night, so the walk to the bus stop is actually pleasant – except for all the talk of Fionn.

'Seems like you two were chattering away for the entire film,' Dee adds.

I smile tightly, not sure how to break the news to them. Fionn was definitely chattering away during the whole film. So much so that I barely have any idea what the movie was about.

'He's OK, I guess,' I mumble.

'Just OK?' Dee asks. 'I thought he seemed really nice. He's one of Colm's best friends, you know.' That's funny, considering Colm and Dee have been dating for a whole year and I've never heard of or seen Fionn before.

'I don't think we really clicked,' I say. 'I mean…we didn't have much in common. I don't know.'

'He seemed to fancy you.' Aisling smiles. 'You can say it if you fancy him too, you know.' She nudges me with her shoulder like I'm just being too shy to confess my feelings for him or something.

'Was this supposed to be a set up?' I ask. 'Because I don't really appreciate that.'

Aisling rolls her eyes now, while Dee casts me a nervous glance.

'Come on, Maira,' Aisling says like I'm being unreasonable for not wanting to have a random set up with a random white guy sprung on me. 'Fionn is well fit. And you haven't had a boyfriend in ages.'

'Is it because you're Muslim?' Dee asks in a low voice. 'Your parents will disown you or something if they hear you've been on a date with a boy?'

I bite back a retort that I know will cause tension, and instead heave a sigh. 'No, my parents wouldn't mind…it's just…' I can't even remember the last time I've been into a guy like that. Right now, all men seem overwhelmingly unattractive – except the ones on the Netflix shows I watch.

Sometimes I think that maybe I like guys more as a concept than a reality. And girls more as a reality than a concept.

I've spent the better part of the last year trying to figure out how to say that to Dee and Aisling.

'You should give Fionn a proper shot,' Aisling says. 'You're just too resistant. He fancies you, and you…haven't even tried with him. At least try shifting him before you make up your mind.'

The idea of having to shift Fionn to make up my mind about him sets my stomach roiling. If not Fionn, though, I bet there'll be other guys. I wouldn't be surprised if Aisling and Dee have an entire roster of guys they plan to set me up with. They've been talking about it for a while now, and since I've been less than enthusiastic about the idea now they've just gone ahead and done it without my permission. I doubt there's an end to this.

'The thing is…' I say slowly. 'I'm not…really into guys right now. I mean—'

'You're a lesbian!' Aisling says, looking at Dee with delight. 'I said so, didn't I?'

I have to pinch myself to keep from saying something I'll regret.

'I'm…bisexual,' I say. 'And I mean…I don't know…I guess I don't really find boys all that appealing right now. Does that make sense?'

'No,' Aisling says, at the same time that Dee nods and says, 'I guess.'

They exchange a glance, and I'm not sure what exactly it means. Then Dee sighs and says, 'Hey, I'm sorry we flung the whole Fionn thing on you without asking. We didn't know you were…bisexual. Just…we thought…'

'I know. I'm not mad or anything.' Even though I am a little bit mad. 'I just don't really want to do the dating thing right now, you know?'

Aisling sighs. 'So why say you're bisexual instead of just that?'

'Because…I *am* bisexual,' I say. 'And I also don't want to date right now.'

'Have you even kissed a girl?' Aisling asks.

'No,' I mumble. Unfortunately, I have kissed way too many boys – most of them unpleasant experiences.

'Then how can you say you're bisexual?' Aisling asks.

I rub the sides of my arms, even though it's not cold, before answering. 'That doesn't mean I can't know. Liking someone isn't about kissing. I mean, you don't only like Barry because he's a good kisser, do you?'

Aisling shrugs, like maybe she does. I feel a little bad for Barry then, even though I barely even like him.

Dee stares at the ground instead of looking up at either of us. I'm not sure whose side she's on here – though it seems she isn't on mine, because she's letting Aisling just go on and on.

'I just don't know how you can turn down guys like Fionn when you don't even know how you feel about girls. And when you've kissed plenty of guys who aren't even as fit as him.'

She says this as if Fionn is some great catch, like he didn't spend half the film worshipping Woody Allen.

'I do know how I feel about girls,' I insist, because that seems like it holds more weight than the Fionn thing. He's just some guy, at the end of the day. If it wasn't him, it would be another guy – though ideally someone with less problematic taste in film directors.

Aisling rolls her eyes, looking like she definitely doesn't believe me, but she doesn't say anything else for a few minutes.

Dee's the kind of person who likes to keep the peace, so she lets us peter out into silence as we walk. Pretty soon, we're at the bus stop. According to the Real Time Information, the bus is only five minutes away.

'Look…' I say as we come to a stop. Normally I would let things go, but this feels too big. Other than my parents, I haven't told anyone I'm bisexual…until now. Aisling can't just pretend that I'm not because I haven't kissed any girls. 'I would really appreciate if you guys could just give me some space about this. I'm still trying to figure stuff out, how to tell people, and what exactly I feel and—'

'How can you know and still be figuring stuff out?' Aisling folds her arms together and raises an eyebrow. Like everyone who has *some* knowledge has figured all things out.

'Because—'

'Aisling, I think you're being a little insensitive.' Dee finally speaks, interrupting me. Aisling takes a step back, turning her raised eyebrow to Dee. If she expected Dee to take anyone's side, it was probably hers. 'But…Maira, you have to admit, Aisling is kind of right, even if she hasn't said it in the best way. It just sounds like you're confused and you don't even know what or who you want. You can't really take out your frustration about that on us.'

'I'm not—'

'I know.' Dee's voice is soothing, like she's speaking to a child who has acted out. 'And I get it. But…you probably shouldn't go about telling people you're bisexual when you don't have any experience. Hell, even I've kissed a girl, and I know I'm not gay. It's just a little demeaning if—'

'Actually, I have kissed girls. A girl, I mean.' For a moment, I don't even know who spoke those words. I only realise it was me from the stunned expressions on Dee and Aisling's faces. The words came out of my mouth, and Dee and Aisling definitely heard them. I just don't know where they came from. 'I…am actually seeing someone.' This time, I say it slower. Choosing my words. Not letting my heart – or rather my anger – speak for me. 'It's just…new, so…we're not really telling people.'

Aisling's expression changes from shock to anger. 'And who is this girl you're dating?'

I search around in my head for names. If it's someone they don't know, someone they can't search up on Instagram, they'll know I'm lying, and then I'll be back to square one.

Before I can think too much about it, my mouth forms the words, 'My girlfriend is Ishita Dey.'

'You're home early for a Friday,' Amma says when I slip inside the house later that evening. 'I thought you were going to a movie with your friends?'

'I was…I did. I wasn't feeling great, so I came home,' I mumble, taking my shoes off and hanging my coat up.

I'm about to go up to my room when Amma reaches out a hand to stop me. She takes me in with a frown on her lips.

'Are you OK, Hani?'

Coming home to my mother's voice saying Hani after a whole day of being called Maira always feels strange. Like stepping out of a skin that belongs to me but doesn't quite fit. Hani is the name that Amma and Abba have been calling me for as long as I remember. It's the name that feels like *me*. Humaira is just the name on my passport, my birth certificate. The name given to people who aren't family, who aren't Bengali. And Maira…that's just what Aisling decided to call me on the first day we met in junior infants. And it stuck.

'I'm OK, Amma,' I say.

'Did you get into a fight with your friends?' I don't know how she knows. It must be a mam-sense thing. 'I'll make us some cha and we can talk about it?'

This is something that Amma and I do sometimes. When she's feeling down or I'm feeling down, we make cha, sit in a bed under the covers and talk about what's bothering us. Or sometimes about nothing much at all, really.

'OK,' I say. 'Let's have some cha.'

After changing into our PJs, Amma and I get into my bed with warm cha in our hands. Abba is already sound asleep since he has a meeting early in the morning and has to be up at the crack of dawn. He's been working so hard to be elected councilor that I feel like I hardly see him.

'So…are we talking about it or are we not talking about it?' Amma asks, sipping her tea with one hand and wrapping her other arm around me. 'Because we can just drink cha in silence, if you want.'

I heave a sigh. I trust Amma with my life. Even though I tell Aisling and Dee that they're my best friends, it's really Amma who's my best friend. She gave up her job when she was pregnant with me – and she never went back to it. She says she has no regrets. Instead of working, she spends her time leading the PTA, which she says she does mostly because she wants to keep me close.

But if I tell Amma that I've lied to my friends about dating Ishita, she'll probably say I should tell them the truth. Fix things with honesty and integrity. Rubbish that I definitely don't want to hear – or do.

I take a slow sip of my tea before clearing my throat.

'I went to the movies with Aisling and Dee, but they were trying to set me up with some guy their boyfriends know.'

Amma takes a strand of my hair in her fingers and tucks it

behind my ear gently. 'And…that made you upset?'

'A little, I guess. I tried to explain to them that I don't really want to date boys right now…and that brought up the whole bisexual thing and…they were weird about it.'

'Maybe they just need more time?' Amma offers. 'It can take people time to process things.'

'You and Abba didn't need time to process,' I say. 'You hugged me and told me that you loved me and were proud of me and—'

'We did need time to process, Hani,' Amma says slowly. 'We just processed on our own, not in front of you.'

'So…you were upset when I told you?' They were so accepting – like they had never expected me to be anything but bisexual. I never imagined that's how things would go for us.

'We weren't upset, but…we had to change our perceptions a little bit.'

'What does that mean?'

'It means that…we had these ideas in our head about how things would look for you, and us, down the line, and we had to shift those ideas and make room for new ones.'

'Like…instead of a husband some time in the future, I might have a wife?' I ask.

'Yeah, things like that. And…about how we would deal with telling other family members. How they might react. But…we wanted to deal with that ourselves. Process it all with each other, so you didn't have to worry about it.'

I never imagined that Amma and Abba had to go off and have conversations about these things. That they would be affected by my coming out in our community, and with our family.

'We could process on our time because we're adults and we have three kids. We know how things work now. Your friends might need a little bit more time to figure these things out. Just…give them time and space. They'll come around.'

'OK.' I nod. After all, if my slightly conservative Bengali Muslim parents can get onboard with my bisexuality with very few questions asked, why couldn't my white Irish friends?

chapter six

~ishu

SATURDAY MORNING, I WAKE UP TO A LOUD *PING!* FROM my phone.

Reminding myself that I need to start setting that thing to silent – since Nik has decided she actually needs a sister now – I lean forwards and pick up my phone from the bedside table.

The notification tab at the top of the phone shows that I have a message on Instagram. I shoot up to a sitting position, rub my eyes, and look at the screen a little more closely.

I don't even remember having Instagram on my phone. I'm pretty sure the last time I put up a photo was at least a year ago, if not longer. I don't use Instagram because I don't care to see all the 'aesthetic' photos that people put up there.

I pull down the notification tab expecting that a troll has managed to get through whatever filters Instagram has, but instead there's a message from Humaira Khan, of all people.

Mairaisdreaming: hey, what's up?

I stare at the message for much longer than I need to. Trying to process the fact that Humaira sent me a message.

And that *that* is the message she sent. We barely ever talk. We're definitely not friends, or even anything resembling friends.

I have a bad feeling in my gut even as I accept her message request.

Umm, what's up with—

Before I can finish typing my message, a call request from Humaira starts up. Has she just been waiting around for me to see her message? Why is she calling me?

My finger hovers over the green accept button, slides to the red reject button…then back to accept.

Humaira's face fills up my phone screen.

'Hey!' Her voice is too bright – like she's putting it on for me. And she's sitting by a window, where the sunlight filtering in makes her glow a little too much. She looks like an angel, with the sunshine forming a kind of halo around her cascading black hair.

'What the fuck do you want?' I rub my eyes again, stifling a yawn. I can only imagine what Humaira is thinking of me. I'm in my PJs with bed head.

'Good morning to you too, sunshine,' she says with a frown on her lips. 'Has anyone ever told you that you curse a lot for a Bengali?'

I fix her with a small glare. 'What does that even mean? Bengalis can curse a lot. Plus, I'm Irish too. Maybe I curse just the right amount for an Irish person, ever think of that?'

She rolls her eyes, but I can tell that she's amused from the way her lips are twitching at the corners. 'I'm calling because I…' She tucks a strand of hair behind her ears and looks to the side of my head. '…need your help.'

'Well, obviously. Help with what? Did you fail your biology test?'

'No!' she exclaims, finally meeting my gaze. 'We didn't even get back our results yet, but I'm pretty sure I did well on it.'

'Then what subject do you need my help with?'

She actually does smile this time. 'Do you think everything is about school? Do you even have any hobbies outside of studying?'

'Studying is not a hobby,' I point out. 'And if you want my help, you're not doing a great job of warming me to your cause. Which I still don't know anything about, by the way.'

Humaira sighs. For a moment, I think she won't even tell me what kind of help she's looking for, because she just looks around herself. Like she's trying to kill time, or find an excuse or something. I'm just about to tell her to either hurry up and get on with it or hang up the damn phone when she finally starts speaking.

'Look. Before I tell you, I just want you to know that this is a weird situation and I just thought of you because…I talked to you at your locker the other day, and…in the moment, I couldn't think of literally anyone else.'

'OK…' I have to admit that she has piqued my curiosity, even if I am a little offended at how much she emphasised 'literally anyone else.'

She takes a deep breath and says, 'So…yesterday I kind of

came out to my friends.'

'Oh.' That certainly isn't what I was expecting. She doesn't seem happy to be sharing this news with me, either. She rubs at her arms and stares downwards.

'Yeah…it didn't go as well as I'd hoped. They were…really dismissive. I told them I was bisexual and they basically said I couldn't be because, well, I've never kissed a girl.'

'OK…'

'Well, so. I had to tell them that I have kissed a girl, because…y'know.'

'Right…' My piqued curiosity has turned into a kind of cold anxiety. Because I'm afraid I know exactly where Humaira is going with this.

'So I told them that we're together,' she finishes off in a rush. 'They already found it weird that we were kind of talking in biology, and I guess there was like a weirdly pixelated version of half of you in one of my Instagram photos from last weekend at that dawat, so it was just like…the natural conclusion, and now—'

'You want us to stage an elaborate breakup?' I offer, already knowing that's not what she's asking me.

'More like…an elaborate relationship, followed by a breakup?' She's looking at me with so much hope sparkling in her that I almost – almost – feel bad about the fact that I'm going to crush her.

'You realise that this would be the most complicated thing ever?' I ask. 'Have you even considered the implications? We would have to come out to the school, to our families, to the community! It's a big ask, Humaira.'

'You can call me Maira,' she mumbles.

'I do not want to call you Maira.' I sigh. 'Look. I'm sorry your friends are assholes, but…I can't help you. I'm not out to my parents yet.'

'I didn't know you were—'

'Yeah. Because you didn't think about me, or how pretending to be in a queer relationship would affect me, right?'

Humaira at least has the decency to look embarrassed. She shakes her head and says, 'I'm sorry. I should have…thought about it more. I was just…' I can hear a waver in her voice. 'My parents are so accepting of my sexuality and my friends were…awful. I guess I was just so overcome with how terrible I was feeling. I didn't really think—'

'Whatever.' I cut her off. Humaira is the kind of girl who definitely thinks she'll get what she wants by turning on the waterworks. Her friends are, after all, white feminists. 'If that's all, I have to go. I haven't even had a cup of coffee yet.'

'OK…bye. Have a good—'

I hang up before she can finish. Leaning back on my bed, I heave the kind of deep sigh of relief that makes the bed reverberate. Dating Humaira Khan, or even pretending to, would have been…a lot. I'm not even sure why her friends would believe for a moment that it's actually true. We're so different.

Too different.

chapter seven

~ishu

AMMU AND ABBU ARE QUIETLY ANGRY FOR THE WHOLE weekend. I know I should broach the subject of Nik and her boyfriend (fiancé?) with them, especially since Nik keeps texting me day in and day out to see what the situation is. But after seeing their anger, I decide to leave it for a bit. Maybe in a few days they'll calm down enough for me to try and put in a good word. Though I'm not even sure what I could say to warm them to the idea of their apple-of-the-eye daughter going against everything they've worked for by dropping out of university.

The only good thing to come of it all is that Abbu and Ammu have started to pay more attention to me all of a sudden. They both take the day off from work on Sunday so that we can sit down to have lunch together.

'I'm sure the news from Nik has got you thinking,' Ammu says midway through our meal of rice, chicken curry, and daal. I knew it was coming but it doesn't stop my heart from plunging into my stomach with nerves. Ammu speaks slowly, like she's really picking her words. 'We just want to make sure you know that sometimes…people make mistakes like this.'

'When they're young and think they're in love.' Abbu sighs like the very idea of love is preposterous. 'There are more important things than love, Ishu. Or what young people think is love.'

'You can't survive on love,' Ammu adds. 'You survive on security. Money. A good job. And with that everything else will come too: happiness and love and a family.'

'And the most important thing is keeping your eyes set on your future goals,' Abbu says firmly. He holds my gaze with a hardness in his eyes. 'Do you understand?'

I nod my head. 'Yes…I mean, I'm on track! I have good results, and I'm sure I'll get into a good medical course in university…'

'Yes…' Ammu nods, though my good standing in school doesn't seem to be bringing her much satisfaction. 'Your sister was getting good results too. She was prefect, remember?'

Abbu nods fondly, his face softening. It's like he's remembering a memory from a long time ago, even though Nik is only three years older than me. 'She should have been Head Girl. Maybe she would have got into a better university then. Cambridge, Oxford…Maybe then she would be…'

I'm not sure that being Head Girl would have changed the trajectory of Nik's life. Then again, I guess you never know, do you?

Ammu and Abbu look so devastated, like they're mourning

something as they chew their chicken curry and rice slowly.

I don't know why I say it; the words just tumble out of me: 'I'm going to be Head Girl.'

They both snap to attention at that. Ammu with bright eyes, Abbu with a flicker of suspicion.

'They don't choose Head Girls until later in the year,' Abbu says.

'Yes...' I say slowly. 'But...I'm pretty sure I will be. I mean...because I have the best results and everyone likes me? I'm definitely a top contender.'

Ammu smiles wider than I've seen her smile in a long time. 'Why didn't you tell us before?' She leans forwards and squeezes my hands for a moment, before glancing at Abbu. 'We don't have to worry about our Ishu. I told you.'

My heart fills up with a mixture of pride and guilt. Pride that Ammu is finally seeing me as the daughter that can succeed – that can fulfill her hopes and dreams. But the guilt? It grows deeper with every passing moment. Because I'm pretty sure I could never be Head Girl.

There are prefect and Head Girl applications at the office. They've been there since last week, and I haven't even thought to pick one up. Why would I?

Being Head Girl is not about results or studies, it's basically a popularity contest. I don't think I'm about to win one of those any time soon.

But if I'm not Head Girl – if I'm not even prefect – that'll be another blow to Ammu and Abbu's expectations. Another thing that we couldn't do for them, despite everything they've done – they're still doing – for us.

I pick up both the prefect and Head Girl applications from the office during lunch. The school secretary – Anna – gives me a curious look as she hands them over to me. Like she already knows that I'm not winning any favours with my classmates.

Maybe I can turn things around? It can't be that difficult. If Aisling Mahoney can be popular, why not me? I just have to put on a smile and turn on the charm.

I can do that.

I think.

I try it as I walk into our base classroom with the applications tucked into my backpack. I paste a smile on my lips, as bright as can be, and stroll in.

Nobody notices me. Since we don't have a dedicated cafeteria for the school, most of the girls from our year gather in this base classroom during lunch and breaks. The classroom is split into different groups of friends, each of them crowded around desks. The mixture of their laughter and talk fills the air. It's already giving me a headache, but I'm determined to try this being sociable thing.

I approach a group of girls who are sitting at the front

of the room: Hannah Flannigan, Sinéad McNamara, and Yasmin Gilani. I've never spoken to Sinéad or Yasmin before, but Hannah has been sitting beside me in economics all year.

'Hey!' I put on the brightest voice I can. It comes out a little too high pitched. I try to ignore that. The three of them turn almost simultaneously, questions marks on their faces.

'Um, hey,' Yasmin says in a tone that isn't exactly oozing friendliness. But I'm willing to look past that.

'That economics homework was really hard, right, Hannah?' I ask, leaning against the desk in what I hope is a casual gesture.

Hannah shares a look with Yasmin and Sinéad. 'Yeah...I guess,' she squeaks.

'So um...can I join you guys for lunch?'

They share another look with each other.

'We don't really have any space.' Sinéad says, even though there's an empty chair right beside her. When I look at it pointedly, Hannah adds, 'We're saving that for someone. Sorry, Ishita.'

'OK, whatever.' I roll my eyes, before remembering that I'm trying to be popular so I probably shouldn't do that. 'Um. Maybe another day?' I smile, even though I hate how desperate my voice sounds.

'Yeah, maybe,' Yasmin says in a voice that tells me there will definitely not be a day when I'm sitting next to them for lunch.

I turn away and look over the rest of the classroom, broken up into cliques: I belong in none of them, and I can't see that changing in the future either.

I'm about to turn around and go back to my usual lunch spot at a dark corner by the lockers when I spot the group at the back of the room: Humaira, Aisling, and Deirdre are joined in a hushed discussion.

My strange conversation with Humaira from Saturday morning had almost completely dissipated from my mind, despite the strangeness of her request. Now it comes to me again. Humaira's desperation.

Maybe Humaira's desperation is exactly what I need right now. Usually, I would write a pro/con list before making a decision like this, but seeing the three of them right there, deep in conversation, I know I don't have the time for my carefully curated decision-making process.

Before I can talk myself out of it, I'm strolling to the end of the room, hoping against hope that Humaira hasn't come clean to her friends yet.

'Hey, Humaira.' The three of them blink up at me. 'Um… do you think I could talk to you for a sec? Uh, privately?'

'Oh…' For a moment, Humaira's eyes travel to her two friends, before she turns to me with a smile that takes up her whole face. 'Sure!' She's up in a flash, almost like she was expecting to see me. 'Be right back!'

hani

Ishita leads me away from the classroom and to a deserted corner of the hallway lined with lockers.

'So…' She folds her arms over her chest, like I'm the one who dragged her here and not the other way around.

'So…'

'Did you tell your friends the truth?'

'Not yet.' I sigh. 'Sorry…I mean. I was just going to.' That probably doesn't make me sound any better, considering I leapt out of my seat as soon as Ishita appeared.

'Don't.' Ishita's voice is stern. 'I mean, look. I was thinking, and maybe we should give your plan a try.' She shrugs, her voice sounding so casual that it makes me suspicious.

'And what made you change your mind?'

'I just had a change of heart. I want to help you out.' She looks at me like she's doing me a huge favour.

If it was anyone else, I would believe that they were doing it out of the goodness of their heart. But Ishita?

'Right.' I scoff. 'Cough up the real reason. Come on. What's in it for you?'

She finally drops her arms to her sides and says, 'I need to be Head Girl.'

It's so unexpected that I can only blink at her for a full minute. 'What?'

'Head Girl. I want to be Head Girl.'

'Since when? You've never cared about that stuff.'

'Yeah, well. I care now. And…people…like you.' She frowns at me, like she doesn't quite understand why they do but she's willing to entertain it. 'You're like, friends with everyone. So if we pretended to date and you put in a good word for me…?'

'And you would play along with my friends?'

'Yes.' Ishita nods. 'Totally. Like, whatever you— well.' She stops herself before she can finish her sentence. 'Not whatever you want. Within reason, obviously.'

'You know you're going to have to pretend to like me, right?' I ask. 'And…if you want to be Head Girl, you'll also have to pretend that you like other people.'

Ishita scrunches up her face as if she's in pain. 'Yeah,' she grunts. 'I know.'

I want to ask her more, but I doubt Ishita will answer. She looks like she barely wants to be having this conversation with me now.

'Should I…come over after school? We can figure out all the logistics, and—'

'No.' Ishita cuts me off. 'I mean…maybe I should come over to yours? You said you're out to your parents, right?'

'You know we're just going to talk, right? Figure this out? Not—'

'Just give me your address.' Ishita is already taking her phone out of the pocket of her shirt. She looks up at me expectantly.

I sigh, wondering for a moment if this is worth it. Ishita Dey is not exactly a ball of sunshine. We're so far from friends that I'm not sure how we'd go about doing this thing together.

I rattle off my address anyway.

This may be the only way to convince everyone that I know who I am, and what I want.

'Ishita Dey is coming over today,' I tell Amma as soon as I dash into the house. 'Is that…OK?'

Amma is in the sitting room, tapping away on her phone. She blinks at me slowly with her eyebrows furrowed together. Like she needs a few moments to process the information.

'Ishita…like, Aparna and Dinesh's daughter?' There's so much confusion in her voice. I don't blame her. Ishita has never come to our house without her parents before, and even when she has come here we haven't exactly chatted it up.

'Yeah, that Ishita,' I say.

'Is this something to do with you avoiding your friends?'

Amma asks.

I shake my head – maybe a little too quickly – and say, 'We're just…hanging out.' I shrug nonchalantly, even though I know that Amma can see right through me. She knows I'm lying.

She doesn't press me though. Just shrugs and asks, 'She'll be having dinner?'

'I'm not sure…'

'She'll have dinner.' Amma's voice is firm. 'I'll call Aparna and tell her.'

'OK, OK.' The thing about Bengalis is that they don't let you leave their house without having some kind of food. Visiting someone and not eating is basically one of the biggest insults to Bengalis.

When I get upstairs, my room is a mess. I haven't cleaned it in a whole week, and in that time the floor has accumulated enough dirty laundry to fill up the washing machine twice over. My desk has a pile of unreturned and unread library books that is half as tall as me. And my dressing table has so many bottles and vials and brushes that I could probably start my own beauty line.

I pile all the clothes into my wardrobe and shove the books and makeup into whatever drawers have remaining space. The room smells a little funky – probably from all the dirty clothes – so I throw open the window before changing out of my uniform.

The doorbell rings just as I pull on my trousers. I rush

downstairs, hoping to beat Amma to greeting Ishita. No luck; Ishita is already inside when I get to the door. She's smiling at Amma, and her smile is so awkward that it looks as if she's in pain.

'Hey, you made it!' I try not to let on that I'm panting a little from running down the stairs so fast.

Ishita raises an eyebrow. 'I did.' I can tell from the pained expression on her face that she's trying to be nice – even if she's failing pretty badly at it.

'Well, um. We should get upstairs?' My eyes flicker between Ishita and Amma – because Amma is looking at me with a bemused expression.

'Do you two share any classes?' she asks.

'No!' I say, at the same time that Ishita says, 'Yes.'

'I mean…' I shoot Ishita a small glare. 'We both do the core subjects…obviously. So…um.'

Amma nods, like what I said actually makes any kind of sense. She turns to Ishita and says, 'I called your Ammu and said you'll be staying over for dinner.'

'Great, thank you, Aunty.' Ishita shoots her another polite smile before following me to the stairs.

'What the hell was that?' she whispers as soon as we're out of Amma's earshot.

'What the hell were you doing?' I ask. 'Why couldn't you have just stayed quiet and let me handle it?'

'Um, maybe because you looked like a deer in the fucking headlights. We do have a class together. Biology, remember?'

I stop at the top of the stairs, fixing her with a glare. 'No cursing at my house, Ishita.'

She rolls her eyes. 'You can't be serious.'

'If I wasn't serious I wouldn't say it, would I?'

For a moment I think she's going to fight me on it. Instead, she closes her eyes, takes a deep breath, and says, 'Fine. No cursing in your house.'

I smile. I really hadn't expected to her to give in that easily. This is Ishita Dey after all.

I lead her into my room and she takes it in with narrowed eyes. Even with everything hidden away from her eyes, I can almost see her bite back a comment.

'Your room is…nice.' She says it like it's a struggle to say the word *nice*.

'Thanks….you can sit.'

While she perches on the bed like she really doesn't want to touch anything, I take the comfy chair by my desk, facing her.

'So.'

'So.' She holds my gaze for a long moment, before turning away and saying, 'First of all, you have to tell your mom that we're together.'

'What?' Lying to Amma is the last thing I want to do, and I've already done it way too much these past few days.

'Otherwise you're going to give everything away,' Ishita says. 'You were a disaster down there. Your mom definitely suspects something is up. Just easier to say that we're dating, right?'

Would Amma even believe that? She knows me better than anyone else in the world and…Ishita is not exactly my type. Though I guess Amma doesn't know that. There have never been any girls before.

'You weren't much better, you know.' I shoot back at Ishita. 'You shouldn't have even rung the bell. You could have just texted me so I could open the door—'

'You didn't even give me your number,' she points out. And I know it's true but the fact that I'm even partially at fault for the disaster downstairs makes me even more annoyed at her.

'Well, you didn't ask for it.' My voice comes out more like a snarl than anything else. It even takes me aback. I haven't heard that kind of anger in my voice – or even felt this constant itch of irritation – since before Polash left for London.

Ishita raises her palms up in front of her, like she's surrendering. 'This is not how couples act, just so you know.'

'Because you know a lot about what couples act like?' The words are out of my mouth before I can take them back.

She observes me with narrowed eyes for a moment before shaking her head and standing up. 'OK, this is obviously a waste of time. I should just go home and find someone else to fake date. I didn't commit myself to anyone yet.'

There's a sinking feeling in my chest and it grows wider and wider with every step she takes. And she's taking mighty slow steps like she doesn't really want to leave.

I imagine Aisling's smug face at lunch today, and Dee's

words from Friday echo in my head. That helps me swallow down my anger.

'I'm sorry.' Ishita halts in her tracks. I bite my lip, wishing that I didn't have to do this. 'I…need you. More than you need me, I guess.'

Ishita turns to face me. There's a flash of something in her eyes that I can't quite make out. 'I'm sorry too.' The words take me aback. Ishita Dey apologising instead of gloating in her win? 'We both need each other to make this work. So…we should both try to make this work. Right?'

I hold her gaze for a moment before taking a deep breath and nodding. 'Right. Sorry. I should have given you my number.'

'You should have.' There's a hint of smugness in Ishita's voice as she sits down. There's the Ishita I know.

'So…I guess I can lie to Amma,' I say. It'll be hard but Amma will definitely figure out something is up if I don't. 'But…then you'll be outed to my parents. And to the school. Are you OK with that?'

Ishita shrugs. 'It's not being outed if I out myself, you know. As long as it doesn't get back to my parents – and it won't – I'm good.'

'OK…so…you should probably call me Maira from now on. It's what my friends call me. Nobody calls me Humaira.'

'I'm not calling you that,' Ishita scoffs. 'That's a bastardisation of your name. Why do you let them call you that?'

'It's difficult to say Humaira.'

'It's literally one extra syllable. Plus, they say Maira wrong. They say it like Máire, which is a different name!'

I can't help the smile that bubbles up inside me. I don't think I've ever seen anyone get worked up over a name before.

'Look…you can't keep calling me Humaira. It's…weird.' I insist. 'Nobody calls me that. Maybe you should call me Hani.'

'Fine,' Ishita says like that's the last thing she wants to call me. 'Then, I guess…you should call me Ishu.'

'Cute.' My smile widens. Ishita is definitely not an Ishu.

'Shut the fuck up.' Ishita rolls her eyes, but I can see the corners of her lips twitching with her attempts to bite back a smile. 'It's what my family calls me, OK?'

'I said no cursing.'

'Sorry.' Again, the apology. Those words out of Ishita's – Ishu's – mouth sound blasphemous. I stifle my surprise for it as fast as I can. If I say anything, she'll probably take it back. So I just change the subject.

'If you want to be Head Girl, you'll have to do stuff you probably won't want to do, you know. School events, parties, talking to people, being…a pleasant human being.'

She frowns but nods. 'Yeah. I can do it. I was pleasant to your mom downstairs.'

'You looked like you were constipated,' I say. 'I don't think anybody wants a constipated Head Girl.'

'My constipation wouldn't stop me from doing a good job so that's just fucking – shit – fuck.' She clamps her hand over her mouth, her eyes widening as she looks at me. She looks so adorably terrified – in the most un-Ishita way I've ever seen in my whole life – that I can't help but burst into a fit of laughter.

A moment later, Ishita joins me until our laughter melds together into one large guffaw.

If someone had told me Ishita Dey and I would be laughing our asses off in my bedroom today, I would have never believed them in a billion years.

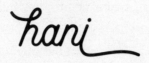

chapter nine

AFTER OUR LAUGHTER DIES DOWN, ISHITA – ISHU – AND
I settle down into a strange silence. It's not exactly awkward,
but it's not comfortable either.

I grab hold of the laptop on the top shelf of my desk and
open it up. If we're going to do this, we need to do it properly.

I sign into my Google Docs and create a brand new
document. *Untitled Document* glares up at me brightly from
the screen.

I turn to find Ishu looking at me with a question mark on
her face.

'If we write down our lies, then we won't get caught,' I
explain. I've never really lied to Amma or Abba, and I don't
really want to start lying to them now, but I guess I don't really
have a choice. So if I'm going to lie, I might as well make sure
I'm doing it well.

I type *Hani and Ishu's Guide to Fake Dating* into the title
space, stifling a grin of satisfaction at having come up with
that all by myself.

'So…how did it start?' I ask.

'What?'

'You know…' I turn to her slowly. 'How did we start… dating?'

Ishu shrugs. 'Is it anyone's business?'

I heave a sigh. I should have known Ishu would be like this. '*You* can answer people like that,' I say. 'I can't. That'll just come off as defensive.' *Not everyone is as abrasive as you, Ishu,* I want to say, but I keep that little thought to myself.

'Make something up. I'll go along with it.'

A prickle of annoyance crawls up my skin at her nonchalance. I narrow my eyes. 'You said we both need to make this work, Ishi— Ishu.'

I can almost see her stifle a sigh of her own. She shifts, the bed creaking under her weight. 'Maybe…we started hanging out during one of the Bengali dawats? They'll be so confused at the concept of a dawat that they probably won't even ask any more questions.'

I smile, thinking back to Aisling and Dee's confusion about Bengali parties just the other day. If I had mentioned the word *dawat* to them, I'm not sure how they would have reacted – with even more confusion, I'm pretty sure.

I turn back to my laptop and the blank white page in front of me.

Started dating: after hanging out together at Bengali dawats.

I frown at the sentence for a moment, before turning back to Ishu. 'How long have we been together?'

Ishu scrunches up her face a little, like this is the last question she wants to answer. I have to bite back a smile. At school, Ishu always seems so controlled. Completely put together. I don't think I've ever seen her…let go. Ever seen her at ease. I've definitely never seen her scrunch up her face like this before.

'It can't be for very long…' she finally says slowly. 'Because…I mean, that would be suspicious, right?'

'Right…'

Started dating 2 weeks ago: after hanging out together at Bengali dawats.

'We should have some rules,' I say. I type *RULES* in big bold letters.

'What kind of rules, exactly?'

'Like…we can't tell *anyone* the truth,' I say, meeting her gaze with my own. 'Not our parents, not our best friends. Nobody.'

Ishu shrugs. 'It's not like I have anyone to tell anyway.'

RULES:

1. Hani and Ishu can't tell <u>anyone</u> the truth about their plans.

2.

Almost as soon as I stop typing, Ishu clears her throat and says, 'We need boundaries.'

'What kind of boundaries?'

'Well…how long is our relationship going to last? When will we break up? Who breaks up with who?'

I shake my head because it should be obvious, right? 'We

break up when our goal is complete. When you become Head Girl and…Aisling and Dee understand that I am who I am.'

Ishu is watching me, almost unblinking. There's something uncomfortable in her scrutiny. I can almost feel the judgment through her gaze. I shift around in my chair, avoiding her stare. I expect her to say something condescending or mean about what I've just said.

But she finally just says, 'OK. That makes sense, I guess. I should break up with you, though.'

I scoff, turning to her with narrowed eyes. 'What? Why?'

'Because if *I* break up with you then people will think I'm cool. Plus, then your friends will feel sorry for you.'

I can only blink at Ishu for a moment. 'Oh. I guess…that makes sense too.'

RULES:

1. Hani and Ishu can't tell <u>anyone</u> the truth about their plans.

2. Hani and Ishu will break up when Ishu is Head Girl and…

I pause, not sure how to phrase the last part of the sentence.

2. Hani and Ishu will break up when Ishu is Head Girl and Hani's friends accept her for who she is.

An inexplicable lump is forming in my throat, but I gulp it down and keep typing.

3. Ishu will break up with Hani when their goals are completed.

'OK.' I spin my chair around all the way this time to look at Ishu. 'Anything else?'

Ishu seems to consider the question for a moment. She

looks down at the baby blue duvet on the bed, picking lint off of it with her fingers. 'You know, I've never dated anyone before.'

If I didn't know any better, I would think Ishu actually sounded…insecure? She suddenly seems smaller – like admitting that little thing about her has somehow diluted the…intensity of her. Even though I assumed she had never dated anyone before, and I know she knows I assumed that.

'It's not a big deal,' I say. 'Dating is like…' I lean back in my chair and stare up at my ceiling as if I have spent an eternity studying the intricacies of dating. Really I've been in one relationship with a boy who was kind of horrible. And I went on a few dates after which that amounted to absolutely nothing. 'It's…not a big deal. When you're dating someone for real, I mean. It's just about having fun, right? About being with someone who makes you happy.'

'What if I do something wrong?' From the little ridge that appears on Ishu's forehead, I know that she's not joking. She's actually worried about getting dating *wrong*. I'm not sure if that's possible.

'You won't get it wrong,' I reassure her. 'That's why we have this to help us.' I point to the document open on my laptop. 'To help us get everything right.'

I lean towards the laptop and click a few buttons until I can type in Ishu's e-mail address.

I can hear the tinny beep of Ishu's phone. She slips it out of her pocket and snorts. 'Cute title. Not obvious at all.'

I roll my eyes and open my mouth to retort, but Amma's voice floating up the stairs interrupts my thoughts completely.

'Hani! Bring Ishita down to eat dinner!'

'OK, coming!' I call back, hoping she can hear me through the closed door.

I turn back to Ishu. 'You don't speak Sylheti, do you?'

Ishu shakes her head. 'I understood a little, though. Food, right?'

I smile, nodding, a strangely pleasant feeling bubbling up in my stomach that I don't quite understand.

'You're going to tell your mom, right?' Ishu says, as she stands from where she was sitting on my bed.

'Tell her…'

'That we're dating,' Ishu says, like that should be obvious.

'*Now?*' My voice sounds a little more shrill than I had anticipated.

'When else?'

'I'll tell her…later. After you're gone.'

She raises an eyebrow, like she actually doubts me. 'You'll chicken out.'

'I won't chicken out. I promise, I'll tell her. I just need to… prepare. Let's just go to dinner, yeah?'

Ishu still doesn't look like she believes I'll actually tell Amma, but she follows me downstairs silently anyway.

chapter ten

THE BUS RIDE HOME FEELS STRANGELY PEACEFUL, EVEN though agreeing to do this whole fake dating thing *should* be making me panic. After all, it's a big lie. And it's going to take a lot to spend all that time with Hum— Hani and her friends.

Still – there was something peaceful about having dinner in her house. Aditi Aunty made chicken curry, and it was the best chicken I've *ever* had. Even better than Ammu's – though I'll obviously never tell her that. I can see myself getting used to Aditi Aunty's cooking…to sitting at that dinner table opposite Hani, who gave me the warmest smile when I complimented her mom's cooking…

I'm still thinking about the chicken curry when I get off the bus. On the horizon, I can see the dipping sun. The sky is a cascade of colours, slowly getting darker and darker the closer I get to my house.

I spot Nik when I'm still a few minutes away. Suddenly, I feel like I've been transported back in time to Friday afternoon. Except there's none of that impatient air about her today.

'Did you call me?' I ask as I approach her, slipping my phone out of my pocket to check. Just in case. But Nik shakes her head.

'I was just around the neighbourhood…'

'How long have you been waiting?'

She sighs. 'A little while. I just wanted to see how Abbu and Ammu are doing.'

I push past her and open the front door. She steps into the house after me, and there's such a marked difference between how she enters today and how she entered on Friday, that I feel a pang of worry in my chest. On Friday, Nik just felt like Nik, my older sister who has been outshining me my entire life. Today, Nik seems small. Defeated. Like someone I don't even know.

'Do you think they'll be up for meeting my fiancé?' she asks. 'We're supposed to go back to London next week, so—'

'They're still mad,' I interrupt her. 'I don't think that's just going to go away…Nik, I don't understand. Why don't you just go back to university and put off your marriage to this guy until you finish your degree? You don't have long to go.'

'Two more years is a long way to go, Ishu.' Nik's voice is heavy. Her decision is finalised, I know. There's nothing I can do here to change her mind. 'I already handed in my paperwork anyway. I can't change my mind. Not until a year later, at least.'

'If he loved you, would he not wait until—'

'Ishita.' Her voice is somber. Reprimanding.

I hold my palms up to show that I mean no harm. 'I'm just trying to understand your logic. I'm having a hard time wrapping my head around it.'

'Have you even talked to Ammu and Abbu about me and Rakesh?'

'It's been difficult,' I say. Still, I feel guilt wrap around me. I've been so concerned with myself that I haven't really thought about Nik. Then again, should I really feel guilty about it? Nik has been my sister for my whole life, and in all that time she has never put me over herself. So I don't know why she expects me to put her and her fiancé over me. 'Ammu and Abbu have been taking out their frustrations on me, you know. Like they think if they don't give me enough attention I'll become a fuckup too.' I pause, catching Nik's eyes. 'I mean—'

'They think I'm a fuckup, huh? Or is that you?'

'Not me,' I say in too much of a rush.

Nik shakes her head. 'Ishu, one day you'll realise that…that living up to Abbu and Ammu's wild expectations of us is not all that it's cracked up to be.'

'What the hell does that mean?' The more she talks, the less Nik seems like my sister. If someone told me that the real Nik was abducted by aliens and replaced with this version, I would fully believe them. Or maybe it could even be a clone situation. Anything other than this really being Nik. These words really coming out of her lips. So different from the sister I have known for my whole life.

'It means that…' She sighs and shakes her head like I'm not worth sharing her thoughts with. 'Don't worry about it. I should go.'

'You're not going to wait to talk to Ammu and Abbu?' I check my watch – it's seven o'clock, which means at least one of them should be home soon. The South Asian grocery shop we own in town usually closes at six on the weekdays.

'Not today,' Nik says. For a moment, as she hovers by the front door, taking her leave, I notice that Nik looks aged. Like the past few days, telling Ammu and Abbu about her plans, have made her older than her years. Like they've taken something from her.

I wonder for a moment if I've contributed to it too. By focusing on myself instead of trying to help her. I wonder if I should tell her that I will – somehow – find a way to make Ammu and Abbu come around. If I should promise to keep my word this time.

Instead, I say, 'OK…see you, I guess.'

She holds my gaze for a long moment. Then, mumbling, 'See you, Ishu,' she disappears out the door.

chapter eleven

We should go on a date
Like...a fake one...

I wake up the next morning to Ishu's message brightly glaring at me from my phone screen.

It's six o'clock, a whole hour before I usually get up for school, so I'm a little cranky as I sit up and hit the video chat button on Instagram.

'Hey!' Ishu looks ready for the day, with her school uniform on and her hair perfectly brushed. 'Good morning.' She smiles that half-pained smile, and it looks better than it did yesterday – so that's...something.

'You know it's six o'clock, right?' I try to fix my hair. 'Like... dawn.'

Ishu's smile widens. 'Sorry. I didn't mean to wake you up. You have bed head.'

I click the camera off and crawl out of bed. 'What do you mean we should go on a date? When?'

'Like...today? After school? People have to know that

we're together, right?'

'And how will they know if we go on a date?' I prop the phone up on the top of my sink as I begin brushing my teeth.

'I mean, we would have to show them. Photos and stuff.' She shrugs. 'Isn't that what people do?' She seems like she's genuinely asking, like Ishu doesn't really know what people do.

'Aa-gesh,' I say through a mouth full of toothpaste. Somehow, Ishu seems to understand me, even though she rolls her eyes.

'So...? We could go to a fancy restaurant or something?'

'And you're going to pay for me?' I ask.

'I said a fake date, Hum— Hani.' She catches herself at the last minute. 'If I'm paying for it, then we're going to McDonalds.'

I sigh. 'Sure, we can go somewhere 'fancy,' but like... within a limit and with some vegetarian options, please.'

'Are you...vegetarian?' Ishu narrows her eyes, like vege-tarianism is something unheard of.

'Not...exactly, no.' I don't remember the last time anyone questioned me about this. I've got used to just saying I'm vegetarian because it's much easier than having to have a discussion about halal and haram. When I mentioned it to Aisling, she started going on about animal cruelty and how religion wasn't a good reason for killing animals in such cruel ways. She wouldn't listen to me, no matter how many times I tried to explain that the way Muslims kill animals for halal meat is no more cruel than the way non-Muslims do it.

'I eat halal.' I finally spit it out. 'That's like—'

'I know what halal is,' Ishu says. 'I'm Bengali, remember?'

'Yeah, but you're not Muslim.'

'I'm also not ignorant,' Ishu retorts. 'You could have just said we should go somewhere that's halal.'

'There aren't a lot of halal options in Dublin.'

Ishu shrugs. 'I don't mind…I don't want us to go somewhere that you don't like…'

'Right…'

'I mean,' Ishu adds. 'I'm trying to look like a nice person. Caring that your girlfriend can eat the food at the restaurant you're going to is like…compassionate, right?'

I have to bite back a smile. 'I would definitely say that falls into the category of compassion.'

'Good!' Ishu smiles, sitting straight with her shoulders back like she's proud of herself for managing this very minimal form of compassion all by herself. 'So…I can research some places we can go and…I'll see you at your locker at three o'clock. OK?'

'OK.'

'Have you told Aditi Aunty yet?' I knew this was going to come up. I meant to tell Amma last night, after Ishu had left and she had curiosity plastered all over her face. Since she didn't ask me any questions I decided to just leave it be for the moment. But if Ishu and I are going to make it official all over our social media profiles, then I definitely need to tell Amma before that happens.

'I'll tell her today.'

'Don't chicken out.' Her voice is firm, like she's a teacher scolding me.

'I won't chicken out!' I exclaim. 'Why are you up so early in the morning anyway? Nightmares about not making Head Girl?'

'This is when I'm normally up,' Ishu says. 'I wake up early to study. Mornings are like…the time when I focus the best.'

'Oh.' I wonder for a moment if Ishu does anything other than study, because that's all I've ever heard her talk about. She must have some hobbies, right? Some interests other than constantly studying? Even if she's lacking in the whole friendship department…

Before I can ask – before I can even formulate a question – Ishu looks at the watch on her wrist and declares, 'I should get to that. Tell Aunty. And I'll see you later. Bye!' And then the screen is blank.

'You woke up early today,' Amma says as soon as I descend the stairs. There's a question in her voice, though she doesn't ask it.

'Yeah.' I pick my words slowly, because I'm not sure how to say this. Lying to Amma is definitely not something that comes easy to me. 'Ishita called me and woke me up.'

'Oh…I didn't know you were that kind of friends,' Amma

says with a raised eyebrow.

I take a deep breath and admit, 'Actually, we're not. We're not really friends at all. I mean…we are, but like…not friends like…like…' Amma is staring at me as if she knows exactly what I'm about to say. So I just say it. 'Ishita and I are kind of seeing each other.' The words come out in a rush. Somehow, Amma seems to understand me, because she looks taken aback. So maybe she didn't know what I was about to say at all.

'Oh,' she says after a moment of hesitation. 'That's…not what I expected but…I'm glad. I'm happy for you!' She sounds happy – but in a clipped, fake way. I look down, instead of at the fake smile on her lips.

'It's just, like…new,' I explain. 'I'm sorry I didn't tell you earlier. I was just…figuring things out?'

'Hani.' Suddenly, Amma's arms are wrapped around me in an embrace. I can smell the scent of her coconut shampoo and sweet, rose-tinted perfume. 'I'm happy for you. Really happy for you.' She sounds sincere this time. She sighs once we've parted and says, 'It's just that Ishita is…well, really interesting. Very intense.'

'She's…nice.' I flinch once the words are out, because of all the words that anybody could use to describe Ishu, *nice* is not one of them. Even Amma knows that. 'I mean, she *is* intense. But…I like that. And, you know, she gets me. And she's like… um…a good influence? With her intense need to study and everything.'

'You know I don't think you need to throw yourself into

your academics in the Dey style,' Amma says. 'I don't want her to convince you that that unhealthy attitude to academics is aspirational.'

'She won't,' I say. 'But…I…like her.' I don't know if I sound convincing. I must because Amma nods firmly.

'Well, good. I'm happy for you. You can tell Ishita that she's welcome at our place any time.'

'Oh, but she's not out to Aunty and Uncle,' I add quickly, as I begin to pour my cereal. 'So we should keep it on the down low, you know.'

'OK, got it,' Amma says. Just like that.

Sometimes, I feel astonished at how easy Amma and Abba have made things for me. How easily I can be myself with them. How easily they'll accept everything about me and their willingness to talk things out.

Today is one of those days for sure.

And for that reason, the guilt clenching my guts is just that much stronger.

Aisling and Dee don't bring up Ishu at all for the whole school day, but there's a kind of tension hanging over us. There has been since Ishu called me away at lunch yesterday. Like something unspoken in the shape of Ishu is standing between me and the two of them.

Still, Aisling goes on about how she failed her biology test like everything is normal. And Dee spends most of the day fawning over how Colm bought her tickets to her favourite band's concert for her birthday. She goes on and on about it, like Colm singlehandedly invented romance or something.

At the end of the day, as the three of us are gathering our books by our lockers, Ishu comes up to us tentatively. Aisling and Dee immediately stiffen, and silence washes over us. It's like just Ishu's presence is enough to make them both uncomfortable.

'Hey.' I can tell Ishu is trying to be pleasant, even through her clipped tone. 'Aisling, Deirdre…' She gives them both a nod of acknowledgment that's too serious to be considered friendly. Then, she turns to me and says, 'Ready, Humaira?'

'I'm going to need a couple more minutes,' I say. I brought my P.E. bag with a simple change of clothes – a dress and a pair of leggings. I even brought over my makeup bag, though I'm not sure exactly what the protocol is supposed to be here. All I know is that I definitely don't want to go to any fancy restaurant wearing my puke green school uniform.

'All right…' Ishu mumbles, still hovering by our lockers. She's dressed in faded blue jeans and a baby pink hoodie with a doodle of a cat on it. So I guess we're dressing down. 'I'll see you outside in ten?'

'Sounds good.'

With a curt nod, Ishu turns away, and disappears around

the corner of the corridor.

'You guys aren't really together,' Aisling says. It's a statement, not a question. 'I mean…you can't be.'

'Why would I say we were if we weren't?' I swing my P.E. bag out of my locker, avoiding eye contact.

'You're not even – I mean—'

'I like Ishita.' Dee's statement has both Aisling and me swinging around so fast that I'm pretty sure I get whiplash.

'You do?' Aisling makes it sound as if liking Ishita is as unthinkable as eternal life or visiting the sun.

'She's interesting!' Dee exclaims, like Ishu is something to marvel at. 'I've never really met someone like her before. I mean…I don't know her very well, but…' She shrugs her shoulders. 'She's my chemistry lab partner and she has such laser focus. It's amazing.'

'I didn't know you knew her at all,' I say. Ishu is not in any of my classes except biology. She takes some of the hardest classes you can take because I guess that's how she plans to enrol in the best university that'll take her. Plus, I know that she takes an extra subject outside of school as well. To make herself look even more impressive than she already is, I guess.

Dee shrugs again. 'You know, you should bring her to my birthday party on Saturday.'

'I will!' The words tumble out of me in a rush. I had been trying to figure out how I could suggest bringing Ishu without Aisling getting mad about it. Aisling still looks mad at the idea that Ishu might be coming, but since it's Dee's birthday and she made the invite unprompted, Aisling can't really say anything about it, can she?

Ishita is waiting by the gates of the school when I finally leave. I'm wearing a forest green dress that Aisling got for me for my last birthday. It has white flowers sketched all over it. I even managed to dab on some eyeliner. All of it is lost on Ishu though, because she barely glances at what I'm wearing.

'Come on, we'll take the Luas.' She turns and begins walking, her runners squeaking against the damp pavement. I have to jog to keep up with her.

We get the Luas into town together, an awkward silence hanging over us for the whole journey. I feel like I'm actually on a first date, rather than just a pretend one.

'Where are we going?' I ask when Ishu begins to lead me past streets I'm familiar with, and into alleys that I've never been in.

'Trust me, I know this really cool place that's halal,' she says. 'You'll love it.'

I wonder how she knows that I'll love it when we barely know each other. I guess just the place being halal is a good start.

We weave past a few more alleys, and I'm glad that we're close enough to the summer months that daylight lasts until eight o'clock. I definitely wouldn't want to be in these dodgy alleys after it's gone dark.

Finally, Ishu comes to a stop in front of a tiny restaurant, squeezed between a pub and a newsagent's. The name of it is written in fancy cursive writing at the top: Seven Wonders.

'This place is tiny,' I say.

'But nice,' Ishu counters. 'Come on. I made a booking, obviously.'

'Obviously.'

I take a quick picture for my Instagram story, even though it feels wrong. But we're here to document our 'date' more than anything else.

The place must be kind of a rare find. Maybe that's why it's called Seven Wonders, because it seems to be a wonder of its own. Only a dozen or so seats are squeezed into the tiny space, brimming with beautiful decorations. There are pictures of wonders of the world all over the walls: gushing waterfalls, lush rainforests and jungles, ancient buildings brimming with history. Each of the booths is parted from the others with a curtain of beads that clink together almost harmoniously. The music – Arabic from the sounds of it – is somehow both melodious and calming.

'How did you find this place?' I lean forwards to whisper to Ishu. I don't know why, but it seems wrong to do anything except whisper in this place.

She shrugs. 'I have my ways.'

'Table for two?' The waitress greets us with a smile. She's wearing a black vest and trousers that almost feel out of place here.

'Yes, we have a reservation. Dey.'

'Oh…this way.' Surprisingly, the waitress brings us away from the dozen tables stuffed into the room and to a set of stairs at the very edge. The staircase is almost completely hidden from view. Downstairs, the restaurant is even calmer and quieter. The waitress leads us to a booth towards the very back and hands us both menus as we slide into our seats.

'Wow,' I mumble, opening up my menu and taking in the choices. It's all Middle Eastern cuisine.

'I mean, there were a lot of Indian restaurants when I was looking for halal places, but…I figured we both have enough of that at home,' Ishu says. 'Not that you can really have enough of, like…really good biryani, but you know.'

Ishu is fumbling with her menu when I look up at her. She opens it and closes it, and her leg is firmly *tap tap tapping* away on the floor. I realise that she's actually a little bit nervous, and I'm not entirely sure why. Maybe because she was tasked with finding a place? Maybe she's not sure what I think about it?

All I know for sure is that in all the time I've known her, I've never seen Ishu nervous. It's strange to see. She usually carries herself with such unflinching confidence.

'I really like it,' I say. Ishu looks up to meet my gaze and the ghost of a smile appears on her lips.

'Well, don't say anything before you've had the food,' she says.

After we've ordered, I tell Ishu to sit down on my side of

the booth. Taking out my phone, I fix my hair in the camera.

'What?' I ask, when I notice her watching me with pursed lips.

'Nothing.' She shakes her head. 'It's just weird…pretending.'

'And we haven't even started yet.'

She takes a deep breath and says, 'It'll be worth it,' and it sounds as if she's trying to convince herself rather than me.

I settle into the crook of her arm and lift the camera above our heads. Ishu moves further away from me the closer I get to her.

I turn to her with a frown.

'What?'

'We look like we barely even like each other,' I say. 'Nobody's going to believe we're dating if you sit like that.'

'How do you want me to sit?' she asks, like she really imagines people in relationships have a gap the size of an ocean between them when they take a picture together.

'Well, for starters, you could actually sit next to me instead of having this gaping space between us.'

'This is barely any space!' Ishu's voice rises a pitch.

'Another whole person could fit in here. Maybe even two.'

She rolls her eyes and slides a little closer.

'You could also look a little less disgusted at the prospect of being in proximity to me,' I offer.

'I have resting bitch face, I can't help it.' She shrugs nonchalantly. I reach over and give her a light slap on her shoulder. It changes her expression from her usual dead and bored one to something a little more expressive – though it's not exactly happiness.

'I've seen you smile,' I say. 'I saw you smile a few minutes ago.'

She smiles like someone is pointing a gun to her head and making her.

'I guess I'll just tell people I'm dating a robot who hasn't learned human facial expressions yet?'

She groans and takes a deep breath. 'OK, OK. I'll act like I'm in love or whatever.' She rolls her eyes as if being in love is the most preposterous idea she's ever come across.

She does smile a little softer, and even snakes an arm around my shoulder.

Through gritted teeth she says, 'Take the picture now before my smile muscles collapse.'

'That's absolutely not a thing.' I roll my eyes, but lean closer. So close that I can smell the scent of her perfume – the earthy smell of jasmine mixed with the sweet scent of vanilla. I breathe it in for only a minute before clicking three consecutive pictures and pulling away. Putting as much distance between the two of us as I can.

Ishu smells as sweet as honey, and I have to remind myself that she's anything but.

She gives me a questioning look, the hint of that smile still on her lips.

'What?' I ask.

'Can I look at the pictures or are they for your eyes only?'

'You can—'

Before I can show them to her, the waitress comes in, balancing three plates precariously in her hands. As she sets them down, Ishu goes back to her side of the table. After taking a few more pictures – of the food, the booth, Ishu looking like she wants to be anywhere but here – we both dig in.

chapter twelve

ishu

I can't help but stare at Hani all through dinner. At first, it's because I'm afraid she's going to hate all the food we've ordered. She might be Muslim, but Bengali people are not the most open to other cuisines. And Middle Eastern food is really different from Bengali food. But after I've decided that Hani is in love with the food, I mostly watch her because she's the most expressive eater I've ever met. She makes a new facial expression after every bite, like each one is a new sensation.

'Have you never tasted food before?' I ask her as she's midway through her meal, still savoring each bite like it might be her last. She puts her fork down and looks at me with something like a pout. But a self-conscious one.

'I just like to appreciate my meals,' she says. 'I've never had Middle Eastern food before.'

'Seriously?' My voice goes a little high-pitched even though I don't intend it to. 'I mean…seriously?'

She sighs. 'My parents aren't really into eating out. They like ordering in pizza and fried chicken once in a blue moon.

They don't really have a wide palate or anything. And…Dee and Aisling don't really like…' – she pauses, looking down at her plate like she's considering her next words – '…ethnic food.'

I think about that for a moment, chewing a bite of my kabseh slowly. 'Is "ethnic" the word your friends use?'

Hani shoots me a glare. 'Does it matter?'

I shake my head. 'I don't understand why you're friends with Aisling and Deirdre.'

'They're good people.' Hani's voice is already defensive. 'They're my friends.'

'Friends who made fun of you because you're bisexual?'

'They didn't make fun of me.' There's a slight whine to her voice. 'It's…complicated. But now, everything will be OK. They just needed…time. And perspective.'

'OK.' I nod my head, mostly because I can tell Hani and I are about to veer off into another one of our arguments and I definitely don't want to make a scene here. 'Are you…going to apply to be prefect?' I try instead.

'Oh, um. I don't think so,' Hani says, taking another bite of her kofta. 'I don't think it's really for me.'

'You should apply,' I tell her.

She glances up to meet my gaze with her lips in a thin line. 'Yeah?'

'Yeah…I mean, it'll look weird if you don't.'

She blinks slowly. 'How will it look weird?'

'Like we're setting this up, you know. It'll look better if you want to be prefect and I want to be Head Girl. Like we're…supporting each other. Plus, everyone loves you and if you apply to be prefect they'll want to support you and by extension you can also ask them to support me.'

'Yeah.' She nods. 'I guess you're right. I hadn't really thought of it like that. Aisling and Dee suggested that I apply to be the international prefect.'

'Yeah?' I have to restrain myself from rolling my eyes. Of course Aisling and Dee would think a person of colour is only capable of being prefect for other people of colour…nothing else. They probably don't even care that Hani was born here and probably doesn't know a lot about the things that immigrant kids might have questions about. 'I think you could be prefect of anything you want to be.' I slip out the prefect application I picked up from the office earlier and slide it across the table towards her. 'I got one for you, and a Head Girl application for myself.'

Hani considers the application for a long moment before quickly slipping it into her bag.

'I'll think about it,' she says.

After we've eaten, and ordered baklava and coffee for dessert, I slide over to Hani's side again so we can decide which pictures to put on Instagram and with what captions. This is going to be our declaration to the school: Hani and Ishu are a couple. So it has to be good.

We actually do sort of look like a couple in the photos. We both look happy, and we're sitting close enough to be a couple, but…

'We need to be more obvious,' Hani says, as she clicks through the pictures. 'We just look like good friends.'

'Well, that's a step above enemies, at least,' I mumble.

Hani turns to me with a smile. 'You think we're enemies?'

'No…' I trail off, avoiding her gaze. 'I just mean…we're not exactly friends, so—'

'So we must be enemies?' She actually looks more amused than annoyed. Like she's taking the piss out of me.

I give her shoulder a bump so she leans to the edge of our seat. 'Shut up. Can we just take a picture?'

'I don't know. Can you look like you aren't my enemy?' she asks, positioning her camera up again.

'Shut up, Hani.' I roll my eyes, but I can't help the smile that slips on. Hani huddles so close to me that I can hear her breathing, and strands of her long, black hair brush against my face.

'Hani.' I push some of the hair out of my face, trying not to choke on the strands.

'Sorry.' She brushes it back to one side, away from me, sending a whiff of her shampoo my way. I try to ignore the strong coconut smell. So Bengali.

She looks back at me and bites her lip.

'What?'

'Can I, um, hold your hand?' she says. 'For the picture,' she rushes to add. Like I would have imagined it was for any other reason.

I reach up my hand and link our fingers together. 'There.'

She shoots me a smile and takes the picture, ensuring our linked hands are front and centre.

'Much better!' She taps filters on to the picture. 'OK… caption time.' She looks up at me expectantly, like captions are my specialty or something.

'Uh…with bae?'

She tilts her head to the side, taking me in like this is the first time she's seen me. 'Are you sure you're seventeen?'

'I'm not,' I say. 'I don't turn seventeen until August, actually.'

'How are you younger than me, and think using the word 'bae' is still appropriate?' She shakes her head and taps her phone a few more times. Then, she edges closer to me on the seat – almost uncomfortably close – and shows me the picture. 'See?'

We do look like a couple in this picture. Hani has even added a couple of hearts all around the photo just to be safe. It's cheesy, but it gets the message across. The caption just has lyrics from a song I don't know but that sound corny enough to work, and multiple kissy faces.

'Are you sure people will know?' I ask. 'I mean—'

'They'll know,' Hani assures me. 'Trust me.'

I know that I had already told Hani we would be paying for our own meals, but all things considered it seems a little unfair to make her pay when she's the one handling all the Instagram stuff. I mean, it's not like I could considering I have three followers, and one of them is Hani.

When we get the bill, I'm quick to hand over my debit

card. Hani settles me with a glare, though I can tell that it's harmless. It has more humour in it than anything else.

It's raining outside by the time we leave the restaurant and, though it's still supposed to be daylight, the awful weather has led to the sky appearing gloomy and dark.

'Maybe…we should get more coffee?' I suggest, looking at the pouring rain from the little porch outside the restaurant.

'This doesn't look like rain that's going to stop any time soon.' Hani sighs, slipping an umbrella out from her bag. It's so flimsy-looking that I'd be surprised if she even manages to get it open.

I'm about to tell her as much, when a bigger, sturdier umbrella appears overhead, as if ordained by God.

And when I turn around, I find myself face-to-face with my sister.

chapter thirteen

'NIK?' THE SURPRISE IN ISHU'S VOICE MAKES ME LOOK behind me. She's staring at a couple – a girl who looks strikingly similar to Ishu, and a boy who is a few shades darker than all of us and is looking a little out of place. His eyes flicker from Ishu to the girl beside him, like he's not really sure what's going on.

'Hey, Ishu, funny running into you here. Who's your friend?' The girl's voice is cheery in a way that feels insincere.

'Um. This is Humaira. A girl from my school. What are you doing here?' Ishu's voice is determined, but she's shifting from one foot to the other, and not holding this girl's – Nik's – gaze.

'Hi!' I abandon my efforts to open my umbrella – it was useless anyway – and stick my hand out. 'You can call me Hani. That's my dak nam.'

'I'm Nikhita – or Nik. I'm Ishu's sister.' She takes my hand and gives it a firm shake.

'Right.' When I take her in properly, she looks distinctly familiar. Not just because of the similarities with Ishu – the big eyes and sharp jaw – but because I've seen her around school and at Bengali dawats. She was a few years above us and must have graduated at least two years ago.

'This is Rakesh.' Nik points to the man beside her, who holds up a hand in acknowledgement. 'He's my fiancé.'

'Wow! Congratulations!' I exclaim. I can now see the gleaming engagement ring on her finger. I don't know how I missed it before. I bump Ishu on the shoulder. 'Why didn't you tell me your sister was getting married?'

Ishu just produces a guttural sound that doesn't sound fully human, and crosses her arms over her chest.

'You know, I think we were in the booth right next to yours in there. The food was really good, right?' Nik is wearing a smile and sounds pleasant, but there's an undertone to her words that I can't quite comprehend.

'I really liked it, yeah,' I offer, even though Ishu is currently glaring daggers at her sister.

'We should go,' Ishu says, and before I can say any more, she grabs my hand and leads me right out into the pouring rain.

Both of us are soaked within the space of about five minutes. And not soaked like our clothes are wet. Soaked like I can feel water inside my socks and my hands are already going numb from the freezing rainwater.

'What the hell, Ishu?' I have to shout to be heard over the rain against the pavement. Ishu just waves her hand over her head to acknowledge she's heard me and keeps walking.

'There's a café we can duck into here, and then I'll explain.'

'You better have a good explanation,' I mumble, more to myself then Ishu since she probably can't hear me.

The café is buzzing with people. Probably people who also ducked in to avoid the onslaught of rain. Still, Ishu and I manage to find a free table at the corner, facing the street.

Ishu, at least, has the decency to buy us both hot chocolates. As soon as they arrive, I wrap my hands around the mug, revelling in the comfort of its heat.

'OK, don't have a fucking orgasm from that hot chocolate.'

I shoot her the worst glare I can muster and she actually looks down at the table and mumbles, 'I'm sorry.'

'Can you explain why we had to flee from your sister and her fiancé?'

Ishu takes a long sip of her hot chocolate before setting it down on the table between us and clearing her throat. 'Nik said she was in the booth next to us.'

'So?'

'So…' Ishu's voice is thick with frustration. 'That means she heard…something. She knows something. And she's going to use it against me.'

I have to think back to our time at the restaurant. It's not as if we were talking about our deceptive plans constantly. Or talking about being in a relationship much at all, really. And why would her sister use it against her?

I shake my head. 'I don't understand. You think she knows about our plans? You think she knows you're queer? Why would she use it against you?'

'You don't have siblings, do you?' Ishu looks at me like I can't possibly understand the struggle of having siblings.

'I have two brothers. That's one more sibling than you.' My voice is more defensive than I intend it to be. 'I think…' I add as an afterthought.

She tilts her head to the side to consider me. 'And your two brothers have never…held something against you? Tried to one-up you? Bullied you?'

I shrug. 'They're quite a lot older than me. They're married and living abroad and—'

'That explains it.' Ishu cuts me off with a roll of her eyes. 'Nik is only a few years older than me. Unfortunately, we've spent our entire lives together and it hasn't exactly warmed us to each other.'

'So…you think she's going to blackmail you about whatever she found out from being in the booth next to us?' I ask.

'That's what I'm afraid of.' She sighs. 'My sister and I…are not friends. She's actually kind of the reason why I'm doing this.'

'You're pretending to date me because of your sister?' I have to ask the question slowly, because I'm not sure if I'm getting it right. What do I have to do with Nik?

'No…I'm pretending to date you because I want to be Head Girl because of my sister,' she says. 'My sister is like…perfect. She has been perfect in my parents' eyes for my entire life. I've been living in her shadow.' It's difficult to imagine Ishita living in the shadow of anyone. She is the most determined person I have ever met. She oozes self-assurance in a way that I'm not sure anyone else in the whole world does. Maybe Beyoncé, but that's it. Though I guess her sister didn't exactly seem insecure either.

'Well, now my sister's fucked up and it's my turn to step out of the shadows and be exactly what my parents want me to be,' Ishu says.

'You don't think that's…screwed up itself?' I ask. 'I mean… she's your sister. Shouldn't you be trying to help her if she's in trouble?'

'She's not in trouble.' Ishu shrugs. 'She just…finally made some mistakes.' Then, Ishu grins a wicked smile that both terrifies me and – if I'm being perfectly honest – makes me feel a weird tug right in my belly. I just shake my head and take a deep gulp of my hot chocolate. The rain seems to be dying down outside and I want to get home before it gets properly dark. I definitely don't need to get any more involved in whatever drama Ishu has going on.

chapter fourteen

~ishu

I'M NOT SURPRISED TO FIND NIK AT THE DOORSTEP OF the house when I get back from my 'date' with Hani.

'Have you really been waiting here in the rain?' I ask, trying to push past her to open the door. But she doesn't let me through. She stands firm.

'Ammu and Abbu are inside,' she says. 'So I don't want to go in yet.'

'Yes, well. This is where I live, so…' I make another attempt to get past her but I guess Nik is stronger than me, because she pushes me to the side and further away from the door.

'I just want to talk,' she says.

'I haven't spoken to Ammu and Abbu yet, if that's what you want to ask me about,' I say. 'And I don't know if I will and I don't know that if I do, it'll make any difference. And—'

'I spoke to them,' Nik interrupts. 'Yesterday. The four of us had dinner together.'

'The four—'

'Yeah, four. They met Rakesh.' From the way she says it, I

know it couldn't have gone well.

I still have to ask. 'And…?'

'Nothing I say is going to sway them towards my decision,' she says. 'Rakesh and I are going back to London tomorrow morning. I just wanted to see you before I left.'

'You already saw me.' I point out, though I don't really want to draw attention to our brief meeting outside the restaurant.

'Are you really seeing that girl?' Nik asks. 'Like…you're dating her? Like…you're gay?'

'I don't know what you're talking about.' I can't keep the waver out of my voice. And I can't help the fact that my heart is beating a mile a minute. It's so loud that I'm sure Nik must be able to hear it. This is the worst thing she could have found out about me. With this, she can make Ammu and Abbu hate me.

'OK.' Nik actually steps aside, like she's decided to let me through. That doesn't make me feel any less nervous. 'Just… she seems really nice and…if Ammu and Abbu ever find out and give you trouble, you just call me. OK?'

'What?' When I meet her gaze, Nik actually seems genuine. Like she's offering me a helping hand instead of using this information to help herself out.

Nik shrugs. 'We're not kids competing against each other any more, Ishu,' she says, like she's become all grown up in the few days since she got here. Like she's a completely different person to the sister I've known for most of my life. 'I know it's important for you to impress them, but when – if – things go south, you can come to me. I just want you to know that. OK?'

'Things aren't going to go south. Because…I have no idea what you're talking about.'

Nik nods slowly, though her expression says that she doesn't quite believe me. 'OK, whatever you say. I just…I want you to remember what I said.' She holds my gaze for a long moment before turning around and stepping into the rain.

Hani's Instagram post is a hit. By the time I wake up the next morning, it has over three hundred likes, and I'm not even sure who all the likes are from. There are people from our school, people from surrounding schools, and people that I don't recognise at all.

She even has a story up of our 'date.' Pictures of the restaurant that I don't even remember her taking. Pictures of all the food. There's even a picture of me where I'm looking off into the distance contemplatively while sticking a forkful of rice into my mouth.

Hani has even put up all of the photos into our 'guide,' under a heading that reads *Hani and Ishu's First Real Date*, and I have to wonder about the irony of using the word *real*. Each of the photos has a little caption underneath it, like *Seven Wonders restaurant! Our food – it was delicious!*

Our plan is working. It will probably succeed with Hani's help.

But for some reason, that thought doesn't fill me with the happiness that it should. Instead, I just feel a strange emptiness as I lie in bed, looking at the pictures. We could pass for a real couple. We look happy. We look like we could be in love. But the whole thing is staged. I don't know why that sends a jolt of hurt through me.

I wonder for a moment if Nik is already back home in London with her fiancé. Or maybe she's just getting on her plane now.

I don't even know where she's living. I don't even know her fiancé's last name, or what he's like. I don't know when they're getting married, or where, or if I'll even be invited to their wedding.

None of that should matter, because I'm on my way to winning this popularity contest. To becoming Head Girl. To becoming the golden girl for my parents, and to achieving my dreams.

My phone pings with a text. It's a message from Hani.

Filled in my prefect application – our plan is a go!

chapter fifteen

PEOPLE AT SCHOOL ARE WEIRD ABOUT ME AND ISHU. I guess, technically, we're the only 'out' couple here, though I'm sure there are at least a few closeted ones.

I can hear people whispering as I walk into school, and they shoot me looks as I walk towards my locker. I wonder if our plan is doomed by the fact that we're in a queer relationship. We are, after all, in an all-girls' Catholic school. Despite the fact that we got marriage equality a few years ago, there's something uncomfortable about being queer here. The same way there's something uncomfortable about being Muslim here.

But when I check my Instagram later that day, there are comments from girls at school sending heart eye emojis and telling us what a cute couple we are. I can't help the smile on my lips as I scroll through the comments.

Ishu and I do look like a cute couple in the picture. She somehow managed to set aside her resting bitch face for one smile where she looks genuinely happy. And so do I. If

I didn't know any better, I think I would full-on believe we were a real couple from this picture.

During lunchtime, Amanda Byrne comes over to our table.

'I didn't know you were dating Ishita!' She's smiling really wide, like she really loves talking about my dating life. 'You guys are the cutest couple!'

'Thanks.' I've never been told I'm part of a cute couple before, so I'm not sure if 'thank you' is the appropriate reply. But it's the only one I have. Amanda looks pleased, anyway, as she moves on to her group of friends at the table across from us.

'Bethany Walsh actually asked me how the two of us started dating today,' Ishu informs me by my locker at the end of the day. 'Like…she actually wanted to have a conversation with me about it.'

'And…are you pleased by that or annoyed?' I ask, because Ishu's expression and voice aren't giving anything away.

She heaves a deep sigh, and leans against the stack of lockers next to mine. 'You know, it'll be hard to give up the reputation I've worked so hard to cultivate here, but…'

'I'm sure you can get it back once you're Head Girl,' I assure her.

'Oh, I'm planning to.' She grins.

'By the way, it's Dee's birthday on Saturday. She's having a party and she invited you.'

'Really?' Ishu stands up straight, her grin broadening.

'I didn't think you'd be excited about a party.' I raise an eyebrow at her.

'I'm not really,' she says in a voice that I don't quite believe. 'It just means…this is working.'

'There's still time for us to mess it up so let's not get cocky. The party is your time to shine. Schmooze some people and… act pleasant.'

'I can do that,' she says in the least convincing voice ever. Still, if she managed a full conversation with Bethany Walsh, one of the bubbliest girls in our year, maybe she can schmooze everyone at the party.

When I get home from school on Friday afternoon, Abba is in the sitting room wearing his best panjabi.

I peer in through the door. 'Are you going to the mosque again?'

Abba turns the volume down on the Bangladeshi news on the TV screen and turns to me with a small smile. 'Just to pray Maghrib later.'

It takes me a moment to digest that information. I can't remember the last time Abba went to the mosque specifically to pray Maghrib.

'Why?' The question tumbles out before I can stop it. Abba doesn't seem to mind though.

'I just think it's important to go to the mosque during these times. To show that I'm very much a part of the community.' I'm not sure if showing up to the mosque for one Maghrib prayer will show that, when otherwise Amma and Abba only frequent the mosque for Eid prayers twice a year – if even that.

'Can I come?' I only ever really get to go to the mosque for jummah prayer while school holidays are on.

Abba's face brightens at that. 'Sure!'

A few hours later, we're both climbing out of his car in the car park of the mosque.

The sun is low in the sky, and I'm a little taken by the way the mosque looks in the light of dusk. The minaret with the crescent moon is almost faded in the darkening sky, but there is something beautiful about the domed shapes that make up the building. All the Islamic motifs threaded through the architecture. A sense of peace takes hold of me at the sight.

'I'll meet you outside the gate after the prayers, OK?' Abba says as he locks the car door.

'Sure,' I say. I think that by 'after the prayers' he probably means after he's spent long enough shaking everyone's hands and networking.

We split up by the gates as Abba climbs up the front

steps and I duck to the side to climb up towards the women's section of the mosque. I slide off my shoes by the double doors leading into the balcony and slip inside.

The plush carpet under my bare feet feels comforting, familiar. It's as familiar to me as the wood-panelled floors of our house. This space feels like the most peaceful thing in the world to me. There is something inexplicably wonderful about coming into this mosque. About the fact that everyone here is joined by one thing: our faith. About the azan, and praying namaz in unison. All of us together in our prayer – but separate too.

I find a space to sit near the front of the balcony. If I peek down, I'll be able to make out the men below us. I can already hear some of their quiet murmurs, floating up. The men's section is usually busy during Maghrib time. The women's section…

I look around, and find about a dozen women scattered about the place. There's a woman in a burqah and niqab with her palms joined in front of her face. She's mumbling prayers into her hand and rocking back and forth.

On the other side of the balcony, two girls – who can't be much older than me – in jeans and t-shirts are trying to pull headscarves over their damp hair. They've obviously just done wudhu.

I feel my phone vibrate in my pocket. I hesitate for a moment before pulling it out. It could be something important.

There are a bunch of different messages on the group chat I have with Dee and Aisling. I muted them before coming here, but there's a video call request coming through. I reject it, and scroll through some of their messages.

Aisling: which dress for the party tomorrow??

Aisling: [picture 1]

Aisling: [picture 2]

Dee: hmm definitely the second one!

Aisling: Maira??

Dee: I have a couple of dress options too...

The discussion of different dresses and accessories seems to go on for almost a hundred messages.

The azan begins, so I make sure my phone is in silent mode and slide it back into my pocket.

I'm waiting outside in the chilly air for a whole twenty minutes before Abba finally comes traipsing out. He's deep in conversation with a man wearing a cream-coloured panjabi and a white-patterned tupi on his head. After a few moments, Abba shakes his hand and heads over towards me.

'Sorry I'm a little late,' he says, though he doesn't look sorry at all. In fact, he's wearing the brightest smile on his lips.

'Who was that?' I ask. If he's a Bengali Uncle, I've definitely never seen him before.

Abba leads us over to the car, still smiling. 'He might be my ticket to winning this election.'

'So…someone important?' I ask. 'Is he Bengali?'

'He's an Uncle. He's been here in Ireland for a long time… longer than a lot of people.'

'So, he has connections,' I say.

We pile into the car and Abba starts the ignition, pulling out of the mosque's car park. It's almost completely deserted. It's still a while until Isha prayer.

'If he puts in a good word for me, then I'm sure to have a lot of people in my corner,' Abba tells me. 'He's influential. That's why it's important to make the right connections, Hani. Remember that.' He says it as if I aspire to be a politician. Even Abba wasn't really interested in entering politics until recently – until he retired early from the company he'd been working at for pretty much his whole career.

'So, do you think he's going to help you?' I can't help but ask.

Abba 'hmms' contemplatively. 'I think he'll probably need a little bit more convincing. We'll have to talk a little bit more. He's a very devout person and has a lot of aspirations for Muslims in our community, so I have to convince him that I have our best interests at heart.'

I'm not sure how exactly Abba is going to convince him of that, but I have no doubt that I'll be seeing a lot more of this Uncle soon enough.

I only check my phone again when I'm crawling into bed later that night. Other than the dozens of messages in our group chat, I have a private message from Aisling.

Where have you been all day?

I sigh, not sure how to answer that. It should obviously be easiest to just tell her the truth, that I decided to tag along to the mosque with Abba – because I like going to the mosque whenever I can. But I'm not sure how Aisling will react to the truth.

I was helping my dad with election stuff.

The three dots to suggest that Aisling is typing appear immediately. As if she's been waiting by her phone for me to reply to her messages.

Aisling: All this time????

Me: Yep

Aisling: you're still coming to the party tomorrow, right?

Me: definitely

Aisling must be satisfied with that answer, because her messages stop there. No questions about Dad's elections. No questions about what exactly I was doing that took up all my time.

It's good, of course. I don't have any answers to those questions. But I can't shake the discomfort itching its way through me as I pull my duvet over my head.

On Saturday morning, Amma slips into my room with a jar of coconut oil. It's our weekly tradition.

First, she brushes my hair and applies oil to it. Then I do the same to her hair. All the while, we catch up on the week's goings-on.

Now, Amma sits behind me on the bed, brushing back my hair slowly and gently. I close my eyes, reveling in this. It's my favourite time of the whole week.

'How was your week?' Amma asks, like she does every week.

'It was…complicated?' I bite my lip, not sure how much I want to share.

'Yeah?' Amma asks. 'How was it complicated?'

'Ishu is complicated. I…met her sister. And Ishu was really weird about it.'

'Weird how?'

I chew on my lips, half regretting bringing this up when I don't know how to share it with Amma. I guess she must sense my reluctance, because she puts down the hairbrush and shifts so that she's sitting in front of me. Her eyebrows are furrowed as she takes me in.

'OK…what's wrong? What happened?'

I sigh. 'Well…Ishu and I went out the other day…'

'And?'

'It was good until we ran into her sister.'

'Nikhita.' I don't know how Amma dredges up the name from memory. 'Because Ishita is hiding your relationship from her family?'

'No…because….Ishu said that her sister would use that to blackmail her. It was the first thing she thought her sister would do. Doesn't that seem strange to you? They're family!'

Amma smiles. 'You know, when Polash and Akash were young, they used to do things like that all the time.' She says it as if she's remembering a fond memory. 'Akash would take something that belonged to Polash and unless Polash agreed to do everything Akash asked him to do, Akash wouldn't give it back.'

'That was a game,' I say. 'When they were kids.'

'It was.' Amma nods. 'But it's not like they don't get into major disagreements now. Didn't you have a huge fight with Akash last time you saw him? You called him a sexist prick, if I remember correctly.'

'Because he made a 'get back in the kitchen' joke. That's not even original, Amma.' Even though Akash is far older than me, he still tries to get me riled up with this stuff, and I always hate it. 'Anyway…it's different. Akash *is* a sexist prick,' I say matter-of-factly, and Amma's smile broadens. 'But he would never blackmail me about something like that.'

'Family is complicated, Hani. Everyone has a different relationship to their family.' She leans forwards and cups my cheek with her palm. Her hands are soft and warm, and I immediately feel better about everything. Amma has a way of doing that. I don't understand it, but I appreciate it.

'If you're going to be with Ishu, the most you can do is listen and support her to the best of your abilities,' she says.

I wonder for a moment what Amma would say if I told her the truth. How she would react. What she would think of me.

I nod my head. 'Yeah. I guess I was just surprised. Her sister was so nice.'

'People aren't always who they seem to be.'

Unfortunately, I know that all too well.

chapter sixteen

I HAVE NEVER BEEN INVITED TO A WHITE IRISH PARTY before. I've gone to Bengali dawats and Eid parties and Desi weddings, but those are all easy to dress for because you just wear a fancy salwar kameez. For dawats, the simpler ones. For weddings, the most expensive and sparkliest ones.

But you can't wear a salwar kameez to an Irish birthday party without sticking out like a sore thumb.

I don't know when this became my go-to, but I video call Hani almost without thought. She picks up on the second ring. She looks different. Stripped down. Not the just-woke-up tired of the morning we chatted, or angelic like the first day she called me. She just looks herself, with her hair tied up in a towel.

'Hey.' Hani smiles into the camera. 'I'm kind of getting ready?'

'Me too.' I sigh. 'I don't know what people wear to a birthday party.'

'Clothes,' Hani deadpans.

'I know.' I roll my eyes. 'A dress? Jeans? Is it casual? Semi-formal? Is it—'

'Definitely not semi-formal,' Hani says. 'Show me some options.'

'Now?'

'Yeah.' She points to the wardrobe behind me. 'Just open it up and show me what you have.'

'It's kind of messy,' I mumble, inching forwards. I haven't properly organised my wardrobe in a while. When I throw open the doors, Hani's eyebrows shoot up right into her hair.

'This is messy?' she asks.

'Well, yeah.' I observe my wardrobe. It's mismatched, because I've been putting everything in without paying attention to colour coordination or anything.

'OK. You're never looking in my wardrobe,' Hani mumbles. 'Let's see what you were thinking.'

I pull out my favourite flannel shirt. Hani immediately shoots it down saying, 'Not unless you want to be an absolute lesbian stereotype.'

'I'm not even a lesbian,' I say.

Hani just shrugs. 'That's why I said stereotype. Plus, considering my friends' reactions to me being bisexual, I think most people at this party will be the types to pigeonhole identities.' *Like they have been our entire lives,* I think but don't say aloud. Maybe Hani has chosen to forget about my first few weeks in the school when the two of us were forced together by her friends. I bet they feel satisfaction seeing us as a couple now. Like they always expected it. We are culturally similar and, therefore, must be meant for each other. Never mind the vast differences in our language or our religious beliefs. To most white people, just having brown skin is going to mean we're one and the same.

We go through a few more things that Hani says no to and end up settling on a simple black dress and – on my insistence – a pair of leggings.

'It's almost summer, you know,' Hani says. 'You can show a little skin.'

'Yeah, but I don't want to.'

Hani just shrugs and lets it go. I've realised that's one of the things I really like about her. She doesn't press me on things – except when we're in the middle of an argument, I guess.

'So…I'll see you at the party? When are you going to be there?' she asks.

'I don't know. When I'm ready, I guess.'

'Are you nervous? Because you seem nervous.'

'Is it that obvious?' It must be, from the sympathetic look she gives me.

'It's just a birthday party. And everyone will be so focused on their own stuff that they won't even pay you mind.' I know she means that to be reassuring but the idea that I'm going to all this effort for a party where people won't even pay me attention makes me feel worse.

'If I'm going to this party, I want people to notice me. We *are* there to get people to notice us. You want your friends to know that you aren't just pretending to be bisexual. I want people to see me as someone who can be their Head Girl.'

'Right.' Hani nods firmly. 'Then you should definitely leave those leggings at home…' She trails off with a raised eyebrow. For a moment, it seems as if Hani is actually flirting with me. The thought of it fills me with a fluttery feeling that I don't like one bit. A moment later, Hani shakes her head and says, 'Actually…that would only work if you were running for Head Girl at the boys' school. I'll see you in a few hours?'

'Wait—' I say, before she can click the 'end call' button.

'Yes?'

'Do you…think I can come over and get ready with you? And then…maybe we could go over together?' I ask. 'I just… don't want to show up there and then you're not there. Aisling and Deirdre aren't exactly my friends.'

'They'll be nice to you,' Hani says, though she doesn't quite seem to believe her own reassurances. The next moment, she nods her head and says, 'Yeah…come over.'

A half hour later, Hani and I are in her bedroom once more. Me, in my black dress and leggings. Hani, in a purple dress with long, lace sleeves.

She makes me sit down at her desk and pulls at my hair with a brush.

'You know, there's not much you can do with short hair,' I tell her, even as she seems adamant about making it do something.

'Is that why you always cut it so short?' she asks, a little too close to my ear. I edge away slightly, though it's difficult when she's essentially holding me hostage with a hairbrush.

'Kind of,' I say. 'I mean…our hair is a lot of upkeep, isn't it?'

'What do you mean?' she asks. I want to roll my eyes. This seems like the kind of naive conversation she would have with her white friends because she wants to keep up this pretense of being exactly the same as them. But Hani's hair is almost down to her waist and she has to tie it up into a thick plait to keep it manageable.

'You know what I mean,' I say, trying to bite back the sarcasm that comes to me way too naturally. 'You have such long, thick hair. It must take a lot of work to keep it that way.'

'Well…just brushing it and putting oil in it and special shampoos and conditioners…and sometimes I put mehndi in it…but…I think everybody does that?'

This time, I have to spin around in my chair to see if she really is that naive.

'Hani, you know Aisling and Deirdre are not doing that to their hair.' Aisling used to have chestnut brown hair once upon a time, and even then it was wispy. Now, she has bleached it a peroxide-blonde that makes her look even more obnoxious than before. It was never as thick as Hani's – not even close. Deirdre's hair, though untouched by bleach or dye, is shoulder length and fine. Irish hair just isn't the same as Bengali hair.

'Maybe there are some differences,' Hani says, like she's really not willing to concede defeat here. She spins me back and begins to tug at my hair once more with her brush.

'But trust me, their hair comes with a lot of work as well. We're not the only ones having to go through hair care.'

'I just hate all of it,' I mumble. 'Having to spend so much time brushing it every morning, after school, before bed. Tying it up, different hairstyles. Putting oil in it and all of that shampoo and conditioner.'

'Well…' Hani says. 'Short hair suits you.'

'You can hardly say short hair makes me look ugly,' I point out. She smiles and grabs a few clips from her desk. She begins to slide them into my hair so that it's a little less messy than usual. It actually looks kind of sophisticated by the time she's done.

'If your hair made you look ugly, I would say it,' Hani says once she's finished. 'I don't really have anything to lose by telling you things as they are. So…you should believe me when I say you look very pretty with short hair.'

I can't help that my cheeks warm at the unexpected compliment. I can't remember the last time someone called me pretty. Maybe no one ever has; maybe this is the first time someone has ever called me pretty.

All I can manage to do is avoid Hani's eyes and stutter out a thank you.

chapter seventeen

ISHU'S LEGS GO UP AND DOWN AND UP AND DOWN FOR the entire car journey to Dee's house. Dee only lives twenty-five minutes away, so it's not exactly unbearable. Actually, it's still kind of sweet to see Ishu nervous about something. With her hair and makeup done, and her black dress on, Ishu could almost pass for any cute girl nervous about her first party.

'Call me when the party is over?' Amma asks. 'Unless you're planning to sleep over?'

'We're not planning to sleep over, Aunty,' Ishu says before I can even open my mouth. 'We'll call you. Thank you for the lift.'

'Have fun – tell Deirdre happy birthday from me!' With that, Amma backs out of the driveway. We watch her car disappear down the road, before turning towards the house. Ishu looks a little green, like she might just throw up into the bushes.

'Just stick with me, yeah?' I give her fingers a little squeeze before knocking on the door.

It only takes a minute for Dee to swing the door open. She throws herself at me as soon as she does, squealing, 'Hey, you're here!'

'Happy birthday!' I mumble, while trying spit out tufts of her auburn hair. When she pulls away, she fixes me with a bright smile before turning to Ishu with a tighter one. She invited Ishu. I remember it clear as day. I didn't even ask her to.

'Hey, Ishita,' she says flatly.

'Hey, happy birthday.' Ishu tries a smile of her own, but it's too much teeth and not enough eyes.

'Is everyone already here?' I change the subject, slipping inside and waving Ishu in behind me. 'I don't hear a lot of noise.'

'Most of us, yeah,' Dee says. 'It's actually a little more low-key than originally planned.'

'And Aisling was OK with that?' Aisling has never been low-key about anything in her life. She tried to hire a limo for her last birthday party and only decided not to because another girl in our class did it first and Aisling didn't want to be a follower.

'It is *my* birthday.' Dee smiles.

'You look really nice,' I say. She does. She has her hair all done up, and her dress is sparkling and pink like a princess's. That's kind of Dee's brand though. With her round face and sparkling eyes, she could pass for any Disney princess – especially Ariel with her auburn hair.

'Thank you!' Dee's grin widens. 'You look nice too. And you as well, Ishita.'

Ishu actually smiles for real this time. 'Thanks…Hani

helped me get ready.'

'Hani?'

'Oh, that's just my nickname,' I say.

'Oh, like a pet name?' Dee asks.

'Not exactly…' I trail off. I'm not sure how to explain the concept of Bengali dak nams and bhalo nams to people. 'It's just a nickname Bengali people have for me.'

'But your nickname is Maira.' Dee frowns, like the concept of two nicknames is a bit difficult for her to grasp.

'We should go in,' I say to change the topic. Thankfully, Dee's face brightens at that.

'Yes, into the sitting room, come on!' Even from the hall, we can hear the sound of rumblings coming from the sitting room.

'I was expecting more noise,' Ishu whispers. 'Should I take off my shoes?'

'White people don't really do that,' I say. 'I think Dee is probably keeping her big party for her eighteenth birthday, not her seventeenth.'

'That makes sense, I guess,' Ishu says.

Dee turns into the sitting room, without paying attention to whether we're following behind or not. Ishu stops by the door, her face a pallor that I haven't seen on her before.

'It's just a party, Ishu.'

'I know.' She takes a deep breath, and gives me a pained smile. 'Should we…?'

And we do.

The sitting room is full up with people. The couches and

armchairs have people draped all over them. Sitting, crouching, leaning. There are even a few people on the floor, which is basically blasphemous for white people as far as I know. There's music thumping along in the background, but it's too low to overpower the chatter – you can only really hear the bass.

'Hey, guys!' Aisling waves over from where she is on the couch, basically at the centre of everyone's attention. 'Good thing you're here. Now we can finally start the party.'

'You could have started without us. Aren't there more people coming?' I ask.

'A few, but we wouldn't do anything without you, Maira.' Aisling says in the sweetest voice possible. That's how I know that she has something planned. Probably something to do with Ishu. They've never got along, after all.

Aisling nods to a few people beside her to move along and make a space for us. She pats the empty spot next to her. It's really a tiny couch meant for two people, but somehow Ishu and I manage to squeeze in beside her. I sit in the middle. I don't think putting Aisling and Ishu side by side is a good idea.

'We were going to play Kings,' Dee says, bringing out a couple of bottles that I'm sure I've seen locked in a cupboard above their sink before. I doubt Dee's parents know that she's decided to sneak their drinks into the party, and I'm sure they won't appreciate it when they inevitably find out. This plan has Aisling written all over it.

'What's Kings?' I ask.

'It's a drinking game.' Aisling grins. 'The rules are a little complicated but you'll pick up on it.'

'Why can't we play a fun game? Like Never Have I Ever?' asks one of the other girls, rolling her eyes at the idea of playing Kings.

'Because Never Have I Ever is boring and cliché,' says Aisling. Her tone is harsher than it needs to be but nobody bats an eyelash at it.

Dee passes around shots to everyone as Aisling divides us into two teams. The three of us and Dee are all on the same team.

Ishu nudges me with her shoulder as Aisling is explaining the rules.

'Um, do you want me to tell them that you don't drink?' she whispers, leaning into me and sending a shiver down my spine.

I shake my head. I definitely don't want Ishu to have to deal with that. I hardly want to deal with it myself. But my options are pretty limited here. I'm obviously not going to drink for the sake of this game, but I also don't want to announce myself as the odd one out in the middle of this party.

I chew on my lips, weighing my options. If Dee or Aisling notice my discomfort, they don't say anything. I don't know how they don't notice, or how they don't realise that this is not an appropriate game to ask me to play. They know – they have known for a long time – that I don't drink. When they slink off somewhere under the blanket of the evening darkness and the seclusion of an open field to sneak a drink, I don't join them. Or on the rare occasion that I do, it's just to have a chat. What did they think all of that was?

'OK, everybody clear?' Aisling asks when she has finished explaining the rules. Most people in the room look like they have absolutely no idea what they're supposed to be doing. Aisling looks like she doesn't care. 'You'll get the hang of it as we go along.'

'Aisling,' I say. 'I think you'll need someone else for this team.' I'm hoping she and Dee will just find another way to divide the teams instead of drawing attention to me, but Aisling whips her head around and looks at me with narrowed eyes.

'Why?' I can't tell if she's being deliberately obtuse or if she really doesn't know. Maybe she's already been drinking, though it doesn't seem like it from the clarity in her gaze and voice.

'Because…I can't play,' I try again.

'You have to play,' Dee chirps. 'It's my birthday. You can't not play the game I want to play on my birthday!'

Now everybody has turned to look at the couch where the three of us are sitting. Exactly what I was trying to avoid.

I can feel Ishu tense beside me, and I just hope that she won't say anything. Ishu will only make things a thousand times worse.

'You know that I can't.' My voice is low and I hate the way it sounds. Defeated. Sad. Sorry, almost.

'Why not?' Aisling pushes. I don't know if she's just an excellent actor or if she really doesn't know.

'I'm Muslim…I don't drink,' I say finally. There's silence for a moment, as if this is the first time everyone in the room has realised that I'm Muslim.

'Yeah, but you're not that kind of a Muslim,' Dee says after a beat of silence. 'You don't even wear like the…' She makes a circular motion around her head. To indicate a hijab, I guess.

'Well. I don't know what kind of a Muslim I am, but I don't drink,' I say, trying to swallow down the lump in my throat. 'Sorry…'

Aisling smiles, and even though it's friendly, there's some cruelty hidden behind it. 'That's OK. We'll find someone else for our team…Hannah? Can you swap seats with Maira?'

Changing seats with Hannah feels like something shameful. Like it's supposed to be a punishment for not participating in the game. Everybody watches as we change seats, the silence in the room palpable. The whole time, I'm biting back tears.

Hannah was at the very edge of the room, and as everybody gathers to play the game, it feels like I'm even more left out. Like they've all entered into a circle, and I'm the only one on the outside looking in.

Everybody forgets about me the minute I change seats. Everybody…except Ishu.

She offers me a smile. Not the forced, awkward kind she offers people when she's trying her hardest to be pleasant.

A real, genuine smile.

It's the only thing that gets me through the next hour.

chapter eighteen

By the time the game is over, everybody but me is a little tipsy. More and more people filter in as we play Aisling's ridiculous game. The music grows louder. The party grows bigger and wilder. All the while Hani sits on the edge of everything, looking absolutely miserable but trying her hardest to hide it.

Everybody breaks up into different rooms almost as soon as we finish. Deirdre calls Domino's to order pizza, and Aisling turns up the music in the sitting room so loud that you can barely hear yourself think, driving out half the people in the room.

I weave through them, grab hold of Hani and slip out with the crowd until we find a secluded corner in the hallway. The music is still so loud we have to stand a little too close to hear each other.

'Are you OK?'

Hani shrugs. 'Of course, why wouldn't I be?' She gives me that smile, which is ridiculously fake.

'You know Aisling and Deirdre planned that, right?' Hani flinches and backs away, like hearing the truth is physically hurting her.

She shakes her head. 'Why would they do that? They're my friends.'

'Because they're assholes?' I try.

Hani just shakes her head again. I don't know who she's trying to fool because we both know whatever happened earlier on is not how friends treat each other.

'We should get back to the party,' she says. 'You're not going to be Head Girl by standing around here talking to me.'

The last thing I want to do is go back inside and talk to people, or be in close proximity to Aisling. But Hani is right. I didn't come here to try to get her to believe that she deserves better than her asshole friends. I came here to try and convince people that I should be Head Girl. To network. To make friends.

This is Hani's problem, not mine.

I still feel a pang of guilt in my gut when I nod my head. 'Yeah, you're right…we should go and…talk to people.'

'Come on.' We veer away from the sitting room, where Aisling has cleared away the tables and pushed the couches to the walls to create a makeshift dance floor. In the kitchen, people are drinking and eating snacks. They're waiting on the pizza, I guess. My stomach rumbles at the thought. I haven't eaten anything since breakfast. I'm starving.

'Hey, guys!' Hani waves to a group of girls in one corner of the kitchen. I recognise them as people from our year: Gemma Young, Aoife Fallon, and Meg Hogan. They turn to us with static smiles.

'Hey, Hani,' they mumble in uncomfortable unison. Hani either doesn't notice or doesn't want to notice their discomfort.

'Enjoying the party?' Hani smiles.

'Sure. That game of Kings was really fun.' Gemma's tone is pointed. Hani tucks a strand of hair back, but doesn't let Gemma faze her.

'It looked like a lot of fun, yeah,' she says. 'Still early days though.' She shakes her head, and turns to me. 'You guys know Ishita, right?'

'Yeah.' Aoife gives me a smile that doesn't quite reach her eyes. 'Hey, Ishita.'

'Hi!' My voice comes out unnaturally high. Hani even cracks a smile at how strange it sounds. 'Ummm...I'm excited for the, uh, pizza.'

The three of them fix us with another smile. They're huddled so close together and haven't opened themselves up to allow us into their circle. I don't know if they will.

'Do you need a special kind of pizza, Maira?' Gemma asks. Her voice is dripping a kind of pity that's tinted with cruelty. I want to steer Hani away from them. Away from this party. This is why I don't come to these things.

Hani doesn't budge from her position. She raises an eyebrow and says, 'Don't you need a special kind of pizza, Gemma? You're a vegetarian. And Meg, you can't even eat pizza, can you? Did you mention that to Dee?'

Meg, who has been quiet all this time, looks a little frightened at having been dragged in. Her eyes widen and she shakes her head.

'I ate before coming here,' her mousy voice declares.

'Well, I can find something gluten free for you anyway. I can ask Dee. I don't mind; she won't either.' Hani gives them a smile and says, 'I'll be back,' before taking my hand and leading me away from them.

'That was pretty skilful,' I whisper to her as we weave past more people. 'But you know, you don't—'

I cut myself off when I suddenly find myself blasted with the cool outside air. It's almost summer but the weather obviously hasn't picked up on that, because it's still cold enough for you to need a coat. I don't have one, but Hani doesn't care as she marches us both into the dark back garden, towards a bench pushed against the fence.

She takes a seat, and I sit down beside her. The only thing illuminating this place is a sliver of light pouring in from the kitchen.

Hani lets out a deep sigh, and I know immediately that this night hasn't been easy for her. Maybe it's been even more difficult for her than it has been for me.

'I'm sorry,' she says. 'This isn't working.'

'Are you breaking up with me?' I joke. But Hani turns to give me a look that suggests that maybe she *is* breaking up with me.

'You wanted me to pretend to date you because it would

get everybody to like you, but…I obviously can't do it. Aisling doesn't like you and she's made sure everybody knows.'

'So that's why everybody is acting the way they are? Because of me?' I don't know why I didn't think of this before. This party is the way it is because I'm here. If I wasn't, Hani would probably be out there laughing with her friends. Dancing with her friends. Eating with her friends. Having the time of her life. Because of me, she's sitting here looking miserable.

'Because of Aisling. I don't think this is going to work,' Hani says. 'I'm sorry I couldn't help you.'

'You can,' I say. 'I mean…more people already know who I am because of you. I'm sure some of them will vote for me.'

Hani turns to me with a small smile. I feel a flutter in my chest at the sight of it. After looking so sad the whole night, it's nice to see her smile again. I'd almost forgotten how her smile illuminates her whole face.

'I never took you for an optimist,' she says.

'I'm definitely not an optimist,' I scoff. 'I'm…an opportunist. And without you, I'm definitely not going to be Head Girl. With you, I at least have a chance. Plus, don't you need me too? Or are you going to start holding auditions for a fake girlfriend that your friends don't hate?'

Hani shakes her head again and for a moment I'm afraid she really is going to call the whole thing off. Then she says, 'Yeah. Maybe…maybe this still has a shot. I don't know.'

It's not exactly a vote of confidence, but I guess it's the best I can hope for during this disastrous party.

chapter nineteen

WE DON'T LAST AT THE PARTY FOR A PARTICULARLY long time. Trying to ignore everyone's snide remarks and side eye is pretty difficult when it's all you're dealing with. And Dee and Aisling don't even acknowledge me the rest of the night – like I haven't been their best friend for years.

The cake hasn't even been brought out by the time Ishu and I take our leave, quietly sidling out of the front door, leaving the loud thumping of the music behind us.

Nobody seems to notice us leaving. Nobody seems to care.

Least of all Aisling and Dee.

'I should call Amma.' I slip the phone out of my pocket. Before I can give my thumb print Ishu places her hand on mine, closing it over the phone.

'It's a nice night, you know,' she says. 'Maybe we can walk… my house isn't too far from here.'

'But—'

'You can stay over, if you want.' Ishu shrugs, like she doesn't care either way – which is not exactly the best way to be invited to spend the night at someone's. Still…I can tell Ishu really does want me to stay over from the way she slumps her shoulders and looks away, like she doesn't want to look too eager about it.

'Sure,' I say. 'That would be OK, I guess.' It's nice to actually be invited somewhere after tonight's disaster.

Ishu smiles, and my breath hitches at the sight of it. She smiles so rarely that each one – the genuine ones that light up her entire being – feels like a gift. Like something private she has only reserved for me.

'Come on then, follow me.' She turns and begins to lead the way. We're both in heels, wearing flimsy dresses. Even though the night is surprisingly nice now – clear and cool – we're not exactly dressed for a walk.

When we're far enough away that we can't hear the party any more, and instead we're surrounded by the sounds of the nighttime – silence broken by the soft whooshing of the wind and the sound of leaves rustling – Ishu finally speaks.

'Can I ask you a question?'

'I…guess.' I'm a little afraid to hear her question, especially since she's looking ahead instead of meeting my gaze.

'Why…do you never curse?' I don't know what kind of question I expected, but it definitely wasn't this. I can't help the giggle that escapes my lips. Ishu looks at me with a raised eyebrow and an amused glint in her eyes.

'It's a serious question,' she insists. 'I've been curious.'

'Well…because…I'm Muslim,' I explain once my giggles have died down.

'What?' Ishu actually looks a little taken aback. Considering everything that happened at the party just a few hours ago, I don't think she should be.

'Yeah…' I say slowly. 'It's just something that's important for me. Like going to the mosque for jummah during school holidays and reading the Qur'an every weekend.'

'I'm assuming your friends don't know this stuff about you.' Ishu says it less like a question, more like a fact.

A feeling of shame blooms somewhere deep inside my chest but I try to push it down.

'No…they don't need to know.' I shrug.

'Why?' She sounds genuinely curious. She even steps closer so our fingers are almost brushing against each other as we talk. Like she doesn't want to miss a word that I say.

'Well…I don't…want to be too much, you know?'

Ishu blinks at me slowly. 'I can't ever imagine you being… too much.'

I chuckle. 'I mean, like…I don't want to be too…Muslim. I don't know where the line is that you cross over to be too much. Once you cross it people start acting like you're different and weird, and then you're the outsider.'

'Like what happened today?' Ishu asks. There's a tinge of sympathy in her voice that fills me with discomfort. I rub my elbows with my hands, even though it's not really that cold any more.

'Yeah, I guess.'

'You know, you should be able to be yourself with your

friends. If being Muslim is important to you…you should be able to share that with them,' Ishu says.

'It's not that easy.' I shake my head. Ishu doesn't get it. Ishu is the type of person who doesn't care what other people think of her. That's why we're here, pretending to date each other. Because Ishu needs to pretend she cares what other people think of her. But she's never had to stretch herself, change herself, bend herself, to fit in where she doesn't belong.

'Do you believe in God?' I ask instead. An easier thing to discuss than this somehow.

'God, no.' Ishu scoffs.

I have to laugh. 'You see the irony in that, right?'

Ishu looks at me with that smile again. 'You do?'

'Obviously.'

'I don't really get it,' she says. 'The whole believing-in-God thing…my parents have never been big believers. I think my nana, nani, dada, dadi…they all used to be big believers. We would always celebrate the big holidays with pooja when I was younger. Since we came here, though…' Ishu shrugs.

'It's not for everyone,' I say.

'You can talk to me about it if you want…' Ishu trails off, like she's not really sure about making me this offer. 'I mean…' She glances at me quickly. 'Since you can't talk to your friends about it…yet.'

The idea of talking to anyone who isn't Muslim about religion feels strange, but Ishu's offer still sends a bloom of warmth through me.

'Thanks, I guess.'

I have never been to Ishu's house before. It's a narrow terrace house that feels sparse. The walls are a dull beige colour, and there are very few things inside, other than the absolutely necessary furniture.

'This is…nice.' I walk around the place, peeking around the corners. I expect to see Aunty and Uncle pop out at any moment, but they're nowhere to be seen. Inside the house is even quieter than the outside.

'Ammu and Abbu aren't home,' Ishu says, watching me with amusement flickering in her eyes. I feel a flush working up my body at the way she's watching me. 'They're at their own party.'

'Oh…there's a dawat?'

'Yeah…it's an Indian party, actually. Not a Bengali one. They don't go to those as often but…' Ishu shrugs. 'Come on, my room's this way.'

Ishu leads me upstairs to her bedroom, and I'm not surprised to see that it is the image of perfection. There isn't a single thing out of place. No clothes on the bed or the floor. No books that aren't on the shelves. Her bed is perfectly made.

'Wow,' is all I can say as I take it in. 'I knew you were a perfectionist but this is…'

'I'm not a perfectionist,' Ishu says defensively. She looks around the room like she's seeing it for the first time. 'I just… like things…organised.'

'Right.' I smile, stepping forwards and flopping down on her bed with a thud. I actually see Ishu wince at that, and it makes me smile even wider. It's actually kind of adorable how much of a sucker for perfection Ishu is. How meticulous she is. I mean, adorable when I'm not actually dating her, or her actual friend, I guess. I can imagine it gets tiring fast.

She sits down gently on the bed beside me. So gently that the bed barely shifts or makes any noise.

'So…can I ask you a question?' I say, staring up at her.

She glances back – having to crane her neck slightly. It's funny, because the way she's sitting, in the corner of her bed, makes her look out of place. In her own room and her own bed. It's the place where she should fit in the most.

'You already asked me about the God thing,' Ishu points out.

'OK…can I ask you another question?'

'I guess.' She shrugs.

'Why do you want to be Head Girl so bad?' It's the question that's been bothering me ever since this whole thing started. It's not like Head Girl is a coveted position, really. Sure, it's impressive to be chosen as the top among the entire year. It also comes with a lot of responsibilities – like having to sort out the debs, the class photos, the graduation ceremony, the class hoodies. All of that can't be considered fun, especially for Ishu.

Ishu sighs. This time the bed does move. I guess that's how deep her sigh is. She lies down right beside me, her black hair fanning out around her head.

'My sister wasn't Head Girl,' she says after a moment. 'And…I want my parents to see that I'm not my sister. That I'm…focused on the goal.'

'What's the goal?'

Ishu turns so that we're face-to-face. 'To go to the best university I can get into. To become a doctor. To make everything…worth it.'

'Everything?'

Ishu closes her eyes and takes a deep breath. 'My parents immigrated here with nothing…they have this tiny shop now. When we first came here, my dad used to drive a taxi and we used to live in a tiny one-room apartment. They missed my nana, nani, dada, and dadi's funerals. They did all of it so that we could be…you know, the best versions of ourselves. So we could have the best life. The lives that they had to sacrifice… we can have that. I don't want my parents to think that they did it all for nothing.'

'They wouldn't think that,' I say. I can't imagine Amma and Abba ever thinking that I'm not worth all of their sacrifices just because my life hasn't turned out exactly as they pictured it. Especially since Amma already told me that they had to shift their perspective ever since I came out as bisexual.

'I just…don't want to disappoint them,' Ishu says. She gives one firm nod of her head like that settles that, before yawning so loud that it shatters her veneer of perfection. 'Oops.' She covers her mouth and glances over in my direction. I can only grin. I wonder who the people are that Ishu lets herself just be around. Her sister? Her parents? Does she have any friends outside of school? I feel like I can't ask her any of that though.

'I guess we should get to sleep, huh?'

'I can get you pyjamas.' Ishu leaps off the bed and towards her wardrobe, digging around until she withdraws two pairs of PJs. Both of them look to be in such pristine condition that I'm a little afraid of putting them on and getting them all messed up.

Still, we both get changed, and – after one quick text to Amma – I crawl into one side of Ishu's bed. Ishu, though, just kind of looks at me while rubbing her elbows.

'What?'

'I can sleep on the floor?' she offers, like a total weirdo.

'You know we're Bengali, right?' I ask. 'I've slept in a single bed with three other people that I hardly know.'

Ishu cracks a small smile. For a moment, it seems as if she wants to say more. Instead, she crawls into bed beside me, pushing herself so far towards the edge there might as well be an ocean between us.

'Good night, Hani.' She sighs against her pillow.

'Good night, Ishu.'

I'M BASICALLY WOKEN UP BY CHOKING ON HANI'S HAIR. As good as her shampoo smells, nobody needs that much hair in their mouth first thing in the morning. Coughing slightly – and trying not to wake Hani – I shift away from her.

My phone reads 5:56 a.m.: four minutes until my alarm is supposed to go off. I turn it off for the day and move to the edge of the bed once more. The bed frame creaks with every movement, and I keep glancing back to see if Hani stirs. But she's still sleeping like a log. I guess she's a pretty heavy sleeper.

She's sleeping almost in the middle of the bed, as if this room and bed belong to her. What an odd position to sleep in, but whatever I guess.

I squeeze my eyes shut and will myself to go back to sleep. After all, we were out late enough yesterday. My routine has been thrown off. I should be able to sleep for longer. But no matter how long I close my eyes for, sleep doesn't come. I'm wide awake.

So I decide to get up, slip into the bathroom, and get ready for the day ahead.

When I get back into my room twenty minutes later, Hani is already dressed. She's folding up the pyjamas I gave her for the night.

'Hey, good morning!' she says in the kind of cheerful voice nobody should use in the morning. Or ever, really.

'Morning…' I mumble. 'You were like dead to the world when I woke up a few minutes ago.'

Hani catches my eye and shrugs. 'Guess I came alive to the world? I should go…do you know if there's a bus that goes from yours to mine?'

'My parents can drop you off. You should stay for breakfast, at least,' I say. If Hani leaves without eating something, that'll be a huge offense. Hani should know that.

'I should really go.' She insists, not looking me in the eye. 'I mean, I wasn't home last night and I don't want to go home super late this morning, you know.'

'It's literally six thirty in the morning?'

Hani heaves a sigh. 'Yeah, but…' She shrugs, like it is what it is.

'You know most buses haven't even started running yet. It's Sunday…what's up with you?' There's a weird restlessness to Hani this morning that I don't think I've ever noticed with her before.

She tucks a strand of hair behind her ear and finally meets my gaze.

'It's just…I missed the night prayer yesterday. And if I go home now, I can pray the dawn prayer before time's up.'

'Oh.' I have never heard Hani talk about prayer or praying before – not that I'm friends with her or anything. Still, I didn't even know she was someone who prayed consistently. I doubt she shares that with her friends, considering her hesitancy in telling even me. 'You can't pray here? I mean, we don't have a prayer rug, but…'

'Yeah, I could.' Hani nods. A bloom of pink tints her cheek like she's embarrassed at having to ask. At having to occupy space to do this thing that makes her different from me.

'Well…you know what?' I ask, slowly edging away towards my bedroom door. 'I'm going to go downstairs and make us breakfast and…you come down whenever you're ready. You can take anything from my wardrobe and use the bathroom. Or you can…not do any of those things. Your choice.' I shrug. 'I'll see you in a bit, yeah?' I don't wait for her to speak before shutting the door behind me.

Hani comes downstairs fifteen minutes later, with embarrassment still written all over her face. I just shoot her a smile and ask her to take a seat.

'Your parents are still away?' she asks, looking around like

Ammu and Abbu are just going to pop out from under the dinner table.

'No…they're probably still asleep.' I shrug. 'I usually wake up early on the weekends to…study.'

'Oh.' Hani regards me with some interest, before digging into her breakfast of porota and omelette. It's the most I could do in just a few minutes.

'You know you could have just fed me cereal,' Hani comments, happily eating away. 'I wouldn't have minded. You didn't have to go to all the trouble of making this.'

I shrug. 'No big deal. Ammu and Abbu would have been annoyed if I just gave you cereal. You're a guest.'

'Right.' She nods. There's a minute of near silence, where it's just the sound of the two of us chewing. Then, Hani pauses and looks me in the eye.

'You know, this is strange.'

'…Sorry? I'm not a great cook.'

'No.' She chuckles. 'Being in your house and eating… porota and…praying in your bedroom. It's strange. It's…nice.'

So, she did end up praying in my room. That makes me feel warm for some reason, but I try to ignore it.

'Yeah, I guess,' I say. I'm not sure if I would call it nice, but it definitely is strange. If only because I would have never imagined this in a million years.

'Thank you.' She stares down at her plate. 'I can't really be like this with my friends.'

I want to ask her again, *why*. Why is she friends with

people who don't let her be who she is? Who make her feel uncomfortable and embarrassed of who she is? But I figure we've shared enough for the time being. Multiple deep conversations. A bed. Breakfast. That's more than enough for an entire lifetime.

'Don't mention it.' I shrug, getting back to my breakfast.

Ammu and Abbu still aren't awake by the time we're finished eating, but Hani pulls up the bus timetable on her phone.

'If you wait for a little while, they can give you a lift,' I say.

Hani shakes her head. 'I don't want to bother them; it's the weekend.'

I see Hani to the door, and she hovers there for a moment. It's like neither of us really knows how to say goodbye.

'Well…thanks,' Hani mumbles finally, not quite meeting my gaze. 'I'll see you at school on Monday, I guess.'

After Hani leaves, I come upstairs to find my room exactly how I like it. The pyjamas I lent her have been put away, and the bed is perfectly made. The thing is, even though everything is exactly how it normally is, something feels distinctly different about my bedroom. Like something of Hani is lingering here that I can't get out of my mind. I can almost smell her shampoo and her perfume. I don't know if it's because she's been in my room or because she's on my mind.

I shake my head and take out my school books.

Time to get back to normal.

chapter twenty-one

I PROBABLY SHOULDN'T ACCEPT AN APOLOGY – OR anything – from my friends. I still keep checking my phone, expecting them to explain what happened the night before. Why they suddenly turned against me.

It feels like a punishment for associating with Ishu when I know that Aisling doesn't like her. But…Aisling wouldn't really do that, would she?

Getting everyone to vote Ishu Head Girl is the least I can do for her. Yesterday, she was the only person who acted like my friend. And this morning…

I shake my head, trying to get her out of my mind.

The thing is, I'm finding it increasingly difficult to not think about her. I don't think anybody has made me feel the way Ishu has in a long time. Safe. Protected. Appreciated. Like myself.

But I'm not supposed to feel like that around her. We're just pretending, and maybe she's too good at that and I just haven't realised.

So, instead of focusing on Ishu, my friends' betrayals, and all of my spiralling thoughts, I sit down with my Qur'an. The one thing that actually helps me centre myself.

'Bismillahir Rahmanir Raheem.' I begin.

The buzzing of my phone distracts me from the Qur'an after more than an hour has passed. As soon as I pick up the phone, all of the peace and calmness I had been feeling immediately dissipates.

Can we meet up? Dundrum?

The text is from Aisling in our three-way group chat. It doesn't spell good news.

Sure, when?

The dots indicating Aisling is typing appear almost instantly. A moment later her message appears:

30 mins?

Dee's reply comes in immediately: **perfect, see you then**

I can hardly leave them hanging. So I type back as well: **see you.**

I take one last longing look at my Qur'an. I was in the midst of reading surah kaf. I place the ribbon on the page to mark my place before shutting the book with a thud.

Mumbling an Ameen under my breath, I unwrap my

headscarf and throw on a pair of jeans and a plain white t-shirt. My hair is kind of a mess – hijab head – and I have no makeup on. But it'll have to do if I want to be on time.

When I get to our usual meeting place at Dundrum – the fountain at the front of the shopping centre – Aisling and Dee are already there.

They're huddled together, deep in conversation. The sight of them makes my stomach drop and for some reason, all I want is Ishu by my side.

'Hey, guys!' I paste the brightest smile I can manage on my lips as I approach them. 'What's up?'

'Hey, Maira!' Dee's voice is too chipper. Somehow, she's wearing a full face of makeup. So is Aisling, actually. And they're both dressed nicely. I wonder for a moment if they came here together – if they had been planning this. 'You left the party pretty early yesterday.'

'Yeah…' I say, unsure of how to follow it up. The thing is, I've never quite been good at confrontations. And I definitely don't want to confront Dee and Aisling. Especially not like this: two against one with everyone at Dundrum around us. It's too public. Too humiliating. So should I just ignore everything that happened at the party? Pretend that they had no part in it at all? That they didn't make me feel horrible?

'Come, sit.' Aisling pats the empty space beside her, and I gingerly prop myself up beside her.

'So…why did you leave so early?' Dee presses, leaning forwards as if to hear better.

I shrug. 'I was just…it was crowded and loud?'

It's obviously not the answer they were looking for because Aisling presses her lips into a thin line.

'Look…I know you have a new girlfriend now or whatever,' Aisling says. 'But that's not a good reason to abandon your friends. We have boyfriends and we make time for you. We would never abandon you like that on your birthday.'

I bite my lip to stop myself from replying how I really want to: with the truth about how they treated me. But I don't. Instead, I just nod my head and say, 'Yeah, I'm sorry. Ishu – Ishita…isn't really a party person.' The words out of my lips make my stomach clench.

Aisling rolls her eyes. 'Why does that not surprise me?'

Dee sighs. 'What do you even like about Ishita? Like… you two seem pretty different from each other. You know you don't have to be with her just because you guys are both from Bangladesh.'

I shake my head. 'Ishita isn't even from Bangladesh. She's Indian. And…she's…nice and smart and…she…makes me feel good.'

'Ew, like in a sexual way?' Aisling scrunches up her nose.

'Are you even allowed to do that with her?' Dee asks. 'I mean, because you're Muslim and all?'

I feel a blush of both embarrassment and rage crawl up my skin.

'No, not in a sexual way.' I snap.' She's just…' I sigh. 'If you guys actually gave her a chance, you would like her.

I'm sure of it,' I say even though I'm definitely not sure of it. Actually, I'm kind of sure of the exact opposite. Though maybe with some training I can get Ishu to be the kind of person that Aisling and Dee will like.

'I don't know…' Aisling shakes her head like she wants to give up even before she's given Ishu a chance.

'Come on.' I plead. 'I've given Barry and Colm chances… I even spent that entire date with Fionn, though I didn't like him at all. You can give my girlfriend a chance. I really like her.' And as I say it, I realise that it's at least a little bit true.

Dee and Aisling exchange a hesitant glance between them. After all the events of yesterday, I don't expect them to concede. But then, Aisling shrugs her shoulders and says, 'How about we go on a triple date next Saturday?'

I can't help the grin that appears on my lips. 'I'll check with Ishita, but that should be perfect. Thank you, guys!' As I throw my arms around the two of them, I've almost – almost – forgotten about everything that happened at the party.

chapter twenty-two

~ishu

'A TRIPLE DATE WITH AISLING AND DEE?'

'…and their boyfriends,' Hani adds.

'Oh, right. That helps. Because I love hanging out with the boyfriends of people I don't like.'

Hani smiles, and tosses her hair out of her eyes in a way that makes my stomach drop. It's been almost an entire week since we last properly hung out with each other, though she always smiles at me at school, and she's begun texting me random stuff. Every time my phone rings these days I get goosebumps and I fucking hate it.

Having a crush – and I've decided that is unfortunately what I'm afflicted with – is the worst thing that's ever happened to me.

'You know you're not going to be Head Girl unless you put in some effort. Aisling and Dee have a lot of power,' she says. 'As you saw at the party…you want other people to vote for you, you need to get them to like you.'

'Might as well give up now,' I mumble under my breath,

but obviously Hani hears me because the mic on my phone is exceptionally good for some reason.

'Look, I can come help you out,' she says. 'I know Aisling and Dee like the back of my hand.'

'And how well exactly do you know the back of your hand?'

'Come on,' Hani says. 'You want this, right? You said you wanted to be Head Girl. I'm just trying to help you out.'

'Fine.' I agree begrudgingly. 'You can come help me out. You know the way to my place, right?'

'Like…now?' The shock on Hani's face is actually kind of adorable. I look away from the screen and roll my eyes. I definitely do not want to sound too eager. I can imagine Hani is one of those people who are all good with you until they know you have a crush on them. And if she doesn't reciprocate it – and she definitely doesn't – then she's going to look at you like you're a kicked puppy. I do not want anyone to look at me like that, least of all Hani. So I have to kill this ridiculous crush while it's still young.

'Saturday is just a couple of days away,' I point out. 'So when else?'

'OK…' Hani stands up, and the light from the sun hits her in such a way that once again she's transformed into an angel. I groan inwardly. It's like the universe is conspiring against me. 'Um, I'll have to get changed and stuff first and then—'

'What you're wearing is fine,' I say. Though it's more for my benefit than for hers. 'I'll see you soon.'

'Ammu!' I call down to her. She's only just come back from the shop, and Abbu is still there. 'Hani is coming over, OK?'

'Again?' Ammu asks. 'Why's she at our house every day now?'

I roll my eyes. 'Ammu, she does not come to our house every day. She hasn't been to our house since, like, last week… can she have dinner here?'

'OK, sure,' Ammu says, though she doesn't sound particularly happy about it.

When Hani rings the bell though, Ammu doesn't even give me a chance to rush downstairs before she flings the door open. By the time I get downstairs, Ammu and Hani are already in the middle of a language-confused conversation.

'Tell your Ammu and Abbu that next week there's a dawat at our house,' Ammu is saying to her, even though I know for a fact that she was on the phone to Aunty just yesterday so they already know. Hani's eyebrows are furrowed like she's concentrating really hard on trying to understand what Ammu is saying.

'OK, I'll tell them,' she finally says after a moment. 'Hey.' The look of concentration on her face disappears as soon as she catches sight of me, and a smile stretches out on her lips. It sends a jolt of electricity through me that I ignore.

'Ammu…can we go upstairs? Are you done inviting her to dawats?'

Ammu rolls her eyes. 'You took so long to come downstairs, am I supposed to ignore the guest?'

'No, Ammu.' I sigh. 'Sorry…we're going upstairs, OK?' I almost want to add something about how Hani isn't a guest – not really. She doesn't quite feel like it. She fits into our house like she's part of the family. She knows all of the cues, and how everything operates here. Sometimes I think better than even I do.

Now, I motion for her to follow me and the two of us leave Ammu downstairs to head up to my bedroom.

'Does your mam not remember inviting my mam to the dawat next week? I heard them on the phone the other day?'

'Ammu is just not very good with young people. You should be glad she didn't start asking about your results and your future.'

'Thanks for saving me from that.' Hani flops down on to the bed once more. Like this is something she has done a thousand times. Like we're friends, and she's already used to all this.

I sit down beside her, pulling my legs on to the bed and crossing them over each other.

'So. Tell me all of these things I need to know about your best friends.'

'You don't have to say best friends like that.' Hani looks a bit put off.

'Like what?'

'Like the concept of best friends isn't real.'

I shrug. 'That's not why I said it like that. I said it like that because they're awful friends.'

'They offered to hear you out and give you a chance,' Hani

says. Her obliviousness to her best friends' assholery creates a throb of anger inside me, and I have to push it down. 'Because they know I like you and you're my girlfriend.'

'They know you like me?' I don't know why my stomach drops at that sentence.

'I mean, you know. Because we're pretending.' There's a blush on Hani's cheeks and I have to look away.

'Right. I guess you've got pretty good at that…' I shake my head, because I definitely can't be doing this, or feeling this. I have a goal here and I have to focus. We both do. 'So, tell me. What do I need to do, who do I need to be, for them to be on board with me being Head Girl?'

'Well…' Hani tosses her head up and strokes her chin like she's having to really think about all of this. 'Dee really likes… fashion.'

I don't know what I expected Hani to say but it wasn't that. I raise an eyebrow.

'So I need to be more fashionable?'

She smiles and elbows me. It shouldn't make butterflies flutter in my stomach but it does. If I could tell my brain to shut up and stop functioning right now, I would. Though are crushes even the territory of the brain?

'No, you don't need to be more fashionable. I like the way you dress.'

'In t-shirts and jeans,' I say hesitantly. Maybe she hasn't really seen my clothes properly.

'Yeah.' Hani shrugs. 'There's a kind of casual, I-don't-give-

a-crap attitude to it. People gravitate towards that, you know.'
She nods, like this is a fact of life.

'Right. This is why I can't get people to stop gravitating towards me.'

Her smile broadens, like I've said something really amusing. 'I'm just telling you their likes and dislikes so we can figure out how you can bond with them.'

I groan and lie back in bed. The idea of bonding with Aisling and Deirdre, of all people, truly disgusts me. I can't say that to Hani, though she already knows to some extent. She definitely knows. I still can't say it, can I?

'Go on then,' I grumble, staring up at the ceiling. The bed squeaks, and I can feel Hani shifting around, until she's right beside me, with her legs pulled up to her chest.

'So…Dee loves fashion, and she wants to be a hairdresser. She's really into like…doing hair and makeup and stuff. She's obsessed with the Kardashians…'

I didn't think anybody in real life was obsessed with the Kardashians, but if it's going to be anybody, it's definitely going to be Deirdre.

'And Aisling—'

'Let me guess.' I interrupt. 'She wants to be a makeup artist and she watches *Love Island* religiously.'

When I look up at Hani, she's rolling her eyes. 'Well, who doesn't watch *Love Island* religiously?' she mumbles under her breath, before quickly adding, 'You're being very dismissive and judgmental, you know. I'm trying to keep our deal intact.'

'Right. Our deal.' I sit up and take a deep breath. 'So... Aisling...'

'She loves...royals.'

'What?'

'She just loves...monarchies and royals. Like she talked about the royal wedding for, like, months, sometimes she still does. And she had theories about Prince Harry's baby before journalists even started reporting on it. She's obsessed. You can't get her to shut up about it.'

'Has anybody told Aisling that she's Irish?' Somehow her interests are worse than I could have imagined them to be. Way, way worse.

Hani elbows me again. 'Just because she's Irish doesn't mean she can't be obsessed with the monarchy.'

'Yeah, but the British monarchy? The people who colonised Ireland and basically all of the world? Seven hundred years of oppression? The famine?'

'You definitely shouldn't say any of that to Aisling,' Hani says.

'Can I at least talk about the racist British media attacking Meghan Markle?' I ask.

'I would keep it to lighthearted topics only,' Hani advises. 'I don't want you to get into a fight.'

'Good call, I guess,' I mumble. I can imagine getting into an argument with Aisling far too easily. Actually, it's going to be a real struggle to not get into an argument with her. 'Anything else?'

'Well...Aisling and Dee are both obsessed with *Riverdale*,'

Hani says slowly. 'I guess they both have huge crushes on KJ Apa and…Cole Sprouse.' She shrugs, like she doesn't get the appeal.

'And who do you have a crush on?' I ask. She turns her head towards me a little too fast, a blush rising up her cheek.

'Um, n-no one,' she says too quickly.

I narrow my eyes. 'Isn't that the show where everybody is apparently ridiculously attractive? You don't have a crush on anyone from there?'

Hani lets out a nervous laugh. 'Oh, um…well. I haven't actually watched it. I watched one episode and that was it.' She shrugs. 'Have you watched it? Because that could be the easiest topic, you know. There's no chance of veering off into talking about how much you hate the British monarchy.'

'I'm sure I could find a way,' I say.

Hani smiles fondly, holding my gaze a little longer than necessary. 'I'm sure you could…'

'I haven't watched it, though.' I break off our eye contact and shake my head. 'I don't know if I can sit through that. There's just too many white people.'

Hani laughs. 'Well, I'll watch it with you if you want. We… can decide who our crushes are amongst all the apparently attractive people?'

Unfortunately, I already know who mine is. But all I do is shrug and say, 'Sure. Why not?'

chapter twenty-three

SATURDAY CREEPS UP FASTER THAN EXPECTED. EVEN with me telling Ishu about all of the things that Aisling and Dee love, and all of the topics that she should definitely 100 percent avoid, I'm not convinced that she's prepared for this 'triple date.' To help her prepare, I even typed up all of my suggestions into our Google Doc, so Ishu can use it like a cheat sheet. But things are bad enough with just Aisling, Dee, and the two of us. With their boyfriends involved too, I can only imagine how things will turn out.

I text Ishu bright and early on Saturday morning.

Hani: Aisling hates rice

Ishu: ...in what situation would that come up??

Hani: if we're picking a restaurant to go to??

Ishu: right, because I only love 'rice' restaurants

Hani: you're bengali!!!

Ishu: don't stereotype us

Ishu: does she like potatoes, or are her tastes also monarchical

Hani: you should just agree to whatever she suggests, that's the best way to play it...

Ishu: yeah, I got that about a hundred texts ago

I'm about to type back when my phone lights up with a call instead. I'm still in bed, so I sit up straight and pat down my hair to make sure that it's not too messed up.

'You know that we've been talking about this nonstop for days now, right?' is the first thing Ishu asks. She is, obviously, already dressed and ready for the day ahead. She's sitting at her desk, and I can see her biology and chemistry books peeking out on the corner of the phone screen. Who studies biology and chemistry first thing on a Saturday morning? 'I can handle this – you need to stop freaking out.'

Ishu actually looks pretty calm for someone who has to spend the day sucking up to people she obviously detests.

'I just don't want us to mess this up,' I say. 'They're the key to you becoming Head Girl. Everybody listens to Aisling... she would be Head Girl, you know. If her grades weren't so awful.'

'Right.' Ishu sighs. 'Well, I've been brushing up on my knowledge of royals. Did you know that the royal family member with the highest net worth is Princess Charlotte? Five billion dollars.'

'Are you planning on kidnapping her?' I ask.

Ishu heaves a sigh. 'Five billion dollars wouldn't even be enough for reparations considering all the colonization and war and genocide. And the fact that most of us are still suffering from the results of colonisation and—' Ishu shuts up when she sees my sharp gaze. 'I've…also been working on keeping my mouth shut.' She doesn't look happy about it. And obviously she hasn't worked that hard on it.

'Do you want me to meet you in town or do you want me to pick you up?' I ask, changing the subject.

'By 'pick me up,' you mean getting the bus to my house so we can get the Luas into town together?' There's a hint of a smile on her lips. 'Isn't that a little bit of a roundabout trip for you?'

I shrug. 'I don't mind. This is important.' I'm also deathly afraid of her being stuck with Aisling, Dee, Barry, and Colm without me. I'm even afraid of her being with them when I'm there. I can't even imagine how things would go if I leave her alone with them.

'Then…sure. Five o'clock?'

I nod. 'See you then. Don't study too much.'

Not that that's possible for Ishu.

Ishu's dad opens the door when I ring the doorbell. His face breaks out into a smile at the sight of me.

'Kemon acho, Babu?' he asks. 'Porer shapta amader bashai tomra ashcho, na?'

'Good, Uncle. Yeah…we'll be here next week.' I shuffle inside, wondering why Bengali parents are so bad at making conversation.

'Tomar school kemon cholche?' he asks, as I will Ishu to come downstairs and rescue me from this conversation.

'Pretty good,' I say.

'Exam to er porer bochor taina?' he asks. 'Ishu to shara din raat khali pore. Tar iccha shey Cambridge theke graduate korbe. Daktari porbe.'

Ishu never mentioned that particular goal to me, but it sounds like her. The way Ishu studies, her absolute determination to be Head Girl, I guess this is where it's all leading up to. I don't know why I feel my stomach clench at the thought. Maybe because I can't imagine myself going anywhere other than universities in Dublin, like DCU, UCD, or Trinity. And I haven't even figured out what I want to do.

Ishu and I are just now becoming friends…kind of. The thought of her moving to a whole other country to obsess over her studies is the kind of thing I don't want to think about. The kind of thing that shouldn't make me feel like somebody has pulled the rug out from under me. But it does.

I try to shake it off and smile at Uncle. 'I'm sure she'll get in…she's like the smartest person in our entire school.'

Uncle smiles proudly at that. Thankfully, before he can start interrogating me about where I rank in terms of my results, we hear Ishu's quick steps on the stairs.

'OK…pore dekha hobe.' Uncle waves his hand and

disappears into the kitchen, just as Ishu appears in my line of sight.

She's wearing a dress. No leggings. I don't know if it's that she's trying to look more malleable for Aisling and Dee or what. All I know is that she looks amazing. She even has her hair neatly parted to one side and clipped away from her face.

'Hey…' She pulls down at the bottom of her dress – it almost comes up to her knees, but not quite – clearly not feeling particularly comfortable in that getup.

'You look nice.' I offer, even though it's kind of an understatement. She looks amazing. She also looks not quite like herself. The easy confidence that Ishu normally exudes seems to have disappeared. And I don't know if it's because of the dress, the situation, or because of our current relationship… whatever that is.

'This is my sister's dress,' Ishu explains, taking a seat at the bottom of the stairs and pulling on her shoes: heels that will actually make her slightly taller than me for once. 'It's…itchy.'

I laugh. 'Well, it suits you. But…you don't look comfortable. Maybe you should change into something more…comfortable?'

Ishu raises an eyebrow in my direction. 'If there was ever a time to wear something uncomfortable, it's in this very uncomfortable situation I'm getting myself into.' She pulls the straps of her shoes on, before turning to me with a frown. 'You don't think I look like a clown, do you?'

'What? No!' I don't even know where she'd get that idea.

'Just…you know how Aisling and Deirdre can be. I don't

want them to…make fun of me for…trying too hard,' she says. 'This is a dress from House of Fraser.'

'Wow…'

'I mean, I'm pretty sure my sister got it during sales… she's very thrifty,' Ishu says. I definitely can't imagine House of Fraser being a regular shopping spot for them. Not just because it's a posh shop, but because it doesn't really seem like their thing anyway. Ishu is so down-to-earth. House of Fraser is not.

'I feel kind of underdressed compared to you, you know.' I comment. I'm wearing a pair of black jeans and a red polka dot blouse. I guess I should have dressed up a bit more, considering this is supposed to be a date.

Ishu looks at me with scrutinizing eyes for a minute. I shift around, balancing my weight on one leg, then the other.

'You always look good,' she says finally. 'You don't have to worry.' I know I shouldn't take it to mean much, but I still feel heat rise up my cheeks. I want to say that she does too, but I don't want to piggyback on her compliment.

'Should we get going?' I say instead, reaching out my hand. She takes it, pulling herself up off the last step.

Taking a deep breath, Ishu says, 'I guess so.'

Since it's May, the weather has started looking up. It's actually warm, and the sun has decided to come out for a few days. We meet Aisling, Dee, Colm, and Barry at St. Stephen's Green, which is full to bursting with people. People who are lying on their backs and sunbathing, people who have picnics laid down on the grass. And people who have sneaked cans into the park and are trying to subtly drink without any gardaí seeing them.

'Took you guys long enough,' Aisling says, as Ishu and I walk up to them. She's wearing sunglasses and sitting with her legs crossed. Barry has his head on her lap, his eyes closed. Colm and Dee are nowhere to be seen.

'Dee and Colm aren't even here yet.' I sit down, crossing my legs. Ishu stands for an awkward moment, before slipping down right next to me.

'They are, they've just nipped down to the shop,' Aisling says. 'We've been here for ages and ages. The park's going to close soon, you know.'

'Well, I thought we were supposed to be going for dinner, not just hanging out in a park.'

'Well, plans change when the weather changes,' Aisling says. 'Hey, Ishita. You look very summery, unlike Maira here.'

Ishu shrugs and shifts close to me. Like I'm some kind of a safety blanket for her discomfort. 'You look nice too,' she adds after a beat of silence. 'I like your sunglasses.'

'Thanks.' Aisling grins. 'This is Barry, by the way.'

Barry just raises a hand to acknowledge us. He doesn't even

open his eyes or look at us. It's very rude, actually. But what else is new?

'So, we were thinking we would go to Captain America's,' Aisling says. 'It's just down the corner and we can get the student dis—'

'That's not halal, though.' Ishu interrupts.

'Maira doesn't mind. She'll just eat vegetarian like she always does.' Aisling shrugs. 'Right, Maira?'

'Yeah.' I nod. 'It's not a big deal.'

'Captain America's has like one vegetarian option,' Ishu says. She digs into her bag and pulls out her phone. She taps twice before spinning the screen around towards Aisling. 'This is a list of halal restaurants I found…some of them are pretty close. Most of them, actually. And—'

'Why do you have that list?' I peer over her shoulder and take a peek. It's a long list.

'Because…I needed to know where we can go that you would like.' Ishu shrugs like it isn't a big deal. Still, it feels like a huge deal. I knew that she had specifically looked for a halal restaurant for our 'first date,' but I didn't realise she had made a whole list and saved it on to her phone. Like there would be a time when she would be out and about with me again. As friends?

I try not to think about it because it's making me feel something that I don't want to feel.

'I've never heard of any of these places. Are they even any good?' Aisling barely glances at the phone. 'Will we like the food? Maira isn't the only person here, you know.'

'I'm sure you can venture a little out of your comfort zone of low-price greasy pizza,' Ishu says. She's smiling – she's got much better at that – but her voice contains so much venom that it's pretty much just passive aggression. Or really just pure aggression. I'm not sure if I'm touched by Ishu's support of me or annoyed at how much she's pushing this.

Thankfully, before any of us can say anything else, Dee and Colm appear.

'Hey, you guys made it.' Dee grins. 'So, are we off to get food? I'm starved.'

'We were thinking Captain America's,' Aisling says, like the previous conversation never happened.

Something dangerous flashes in Ishu's eyes. I reach over and place my hand over her clenched fingers, afraid that she's going to say – or worse, do – something that's going to jeopardise everything. Ishu's face softens at the touch – whether this is because she's deeply confused about it or what, I'm not sure. Because the whole thing is sending goosebumps along my body in a way that I definitely do not enjoy. Or, don't want to enjoy.

'You guys go ahead. Ishita and I will join you in a bit,' I say.

Aisling and Barry are already standing up. Barry looks at us over his sunglasses like he's only just noticed our presence.

Aisling dusts off her dress and says, 'OK, but hurry. We're hungry.'

As soon as they're out of sight, I pull my hand away

and settle Ishu with the best glare I can work up under the circumstances. 'What are you doing?'

'Um, making sure you can actually eat at the place we're going to?'

'Well. While I appreciate your concern, it's not going to get you any Head Girl voters.'

'Right.' Ishu blinks like she had forgotten about the Head Girl thing – the entire reason she's here and we're doing this. 'I just thought…' She shakes her head.

'Just remember everything I told you. Remember *Riverdale*.' I look her right in the eye as if I can transfer all of my knowledge and love of Aisling and Dee through eye contact. If only.

'*Riverdale*,' Ishu whispers. 'KJ Apa and Cole Sprout.'

'Sprouse. Cole Sprouse.'

'Cole Sprouse.' Ishu smiles. 'I got it. By the end of the night, I'll be Aisling and Deirdre's new best friend.'

chapter twenty-four

ishu

IT'S SAFE TO SAY THAT BY THE END OF THE NIGHT, I DO not become best friends with Deirdre or Aisling. But I also don't become mortal enemies with them.

In fact, I spend our date laughing at all of their bad jokes and pretending that all of the basic white boys they find attractive are actually attractive. I even pretend that dating Barry and Colm – like making the decision to date them – makes any kind of sense.

We decide to part ways at the Luas stop. Hani declares she's going to drop me home like we're some antiquated heterosexual couple and not two queer teens who don't even have access to a car. Aisling and Dee are catching a bus home, and Barry and Colm are getting two separate buses.

Aisling actually flashes me a smile as we say goodbye – and it's not the kind of smile that suggests she wants to destroy me.

'You know, you should come hang out with us during lunchtime at school,' she says.

Hani nudges my shoulder with hers like I've just received

an invitation to visit the Queen at Buckingham Palace, and Dee nods her head up and down a little too fast, like a bobblehead.

'Sure, that might be nice,' I say, with a smile of my own.

'Great, see you later!' With that, Aisling, Dee, Colm, and Barry turn and begin to make their way home.

'She likes you!' Hani exclaims, turning to me with delight etched into every inch of her face.

'I guess I should have tried to date her, not you.' I smile.

Hani slaps me lightly on the wrist. 'Shut up. Like you could have achieved any of that without my help.'

We pile on to the Luas and, surprisingly, manage to find seats together. Hani is still smiling so brightly that I'm surprised her cheeks don't collapse from the effort.

'A lunch invite doesn't mean we're friends,' I point out. 'Or that she's going to support me as Head Girl.'

'It's a step in the right direction!' Hani nudges me again with her shoulder. 'Don't be such a pessimist, Ishu.'

I sigh and glance out the window. The warm, sunny day has descended into a cool evening. Considering the gathering clouds, it might not be the nicest night. For some reason, the thought of our plan working fills me with a dread I can't quite explain.

'Ishu.' Hani's voice draws me out of the stream of thought I had lost myself inside.

'Yeah?'

'Our plan is working. You should be happy.'

When I turn, Hani is analyzing me a little too closely. Our

faces are inches apart and I can make out the exact shade of warm brown that her eyes are – far lighter than mine. I can make out every imperfection on her skin – there are too few – and the tiny mole she has just by her right ear.

'Ishu?' I jump back, almost hitting the window of the Luas with the back of my head.

'Fuck, sorry.' I rub at the back of my head, trying to bite down whatever the hell is going on with me. Except I can't. I don't know how to tell Hani that the best part of this whole evening was in the park when she took my hand in hers, and now, when she's sitting so close that I'm pretty sure her scent has spread to me through osmosis.

'Hey...' Hani places a hand on my shoulder. 'I'm sorry. I know this whole thing is important to you, and this isn't a guarantee or whatever. But lunchtimes with Aisling and Dee mean that everyone will think you're part our group. That already ups your cool factor by like...' She places her hand above her head to indicate how cool I apparently will be soon.

I have to smile at her concern. And her enthusiasm. Hani obviously doesn't – and can't – know that the thing weighing on me heavily at this point in time is not my social status or being Head Girl. But my increasing crush on her. Not helped by anything she's doing.

'I know,' I say finally. 'Thank you...for everything you've already done. I'm sure at least a few more people won't hate me after seeing me at lunch with you guys.'

Hani looks at me with her eyebrows furrowed. 'You know

that people at school don't hate you, right?'

'They don't?'

'No…they're…intimidated by you. You can be intimidating. I was intimidated by you.'

'You were?' I find that a little difficult to believe.

Hani rolls her eyes. 'Stop repeating everything I say. Yes, I was intimidated by you. A little. I mean…' She looks away from me now, staring at the empty space in front of us, and takes a deep breath. 'You're like…super smart. The smartest person in our entire year. Not just in results. You also just know… so much. About so many things. And you always speak your mind and you can stand up to anybody. You're basically like… invincible.'

'So…everybody at schools thinks I'm Superman?'

Hani turns back to me with another smile that lights up her whole face.

'No.' She chuckles. 'They think you're a lot of things they're scared to be…so it's easier to just not interact with you.'

'So…that's why you've steered clear of me all these years.'

'You were the one who didn't want to be friends with me when you first started at our school!' I know she's not really accusing me because she chuckles as she says it. I guess she's not wrong.

'You know why. They were trying to pigeonhole us – the two Bengali girls should be friends. Then we could just be the two Bengali girls and nothing more.'

'So, now that we are friends, are we pigeonholed?'

'Are we friends?' I ask, instead of answering her question.

'I sure hope so.' She laughs nervously. 'Do you…not want us to be?'

'I thought…' I say slowly. 'We were girlfriends?'

A flash of surprise registers in Hani's expression. Just surprise – not disgust or amusement.

We hold each other's gaze for a moment longer than necessary. I will her to say something – *yes, we are a couple.* Or laugh – *no, how could you ever think that?* I will her to do something. Lean in? Lean back? Anything.

It's just then that the automated Luas announcement clicks on, and it's as if it breaks our trance. Our strange moment when we were almost…something. And I'm not sure what that something was.

'Milltown,' says the electronic voice. '*Báile an Mhuilinn.*'

'Shit. That's us.' I jump out of my seat, and I'm halfway out the door when I notice that Hani isn't following behind. 'Hani?'

She doesn't get up. Doesn't even meet my eyes. 'I'm just going to go to the next stop and get my bus.'

'Oh…OK.' There's so much more I want to say, but there's a beep, indicating the doors are about to close, and I step outside. It's only as the Luas starts up once more and begins moving that I catch Hani's eyes through the window.

I have no idea what she's thinking.

hani

WHEN I STEP OUTSIDE THE LUAS FIVE MINUTES LATER, it's raining. And not the usual Irish drizzle that barely gets your hair wet – it's a downpour.

I guess that's what I get for skipping out on my promise to walk Ishu home. That's the thought swimming around in my head as I leg it all the way to the bus stop. Not that it makes any kind of a difference because a) the other thoughts, the ones I'm not doing such a great job of suppressing, are still trying to push their way to the surface, and b) it's raining so hard that just taking the few minutes to run gets me absolutely soaked.

What is it about Ishu that being with her always leads to me getting drenched?

I shake my head, slip on to the bus and settle down in my seat. When I glance at my phone, I find three missed calls from Ishu. And six messages in my group chat with Dee and Aisling. I slide my finger over both the notifications so that they disappear. I turn on Spotify, hit shuffle, and turn the music up the loudest it will go.

I drown out the world – and, most importantly, my thoughts – and just stare out the window, focusing on the rain against the glass, the hazy cars passing, and the music.

Aisling: actually had a lot of fun tonight

    Dee: Ishita is really different from how she usually is in school!

    Aisling: she's kind of fun?

    Dee: right??

    Aisling: maybe we can do something together tomorrow??

    Dee: yeah I'd be up for that

    Aisling: movie at mine??

    Dee: Maira????

    Aisling: hellooooo?

I wake up to all of these messages in my inbox and heave a sigh. The last thing I want to do is spend the day watching a movie with Dee, Aisling and Ishu. I'm pretty sure Ishu doesn't want to do that either. So I send them back a quick reply:

Hey, sorry…was asleep. No can do on the movie today, sorry. Maybe next weekend?

There's another message from Ishu. All it says is, **are we good?** and I'm not sure how to respond to that. Because I don't know if we are good, but I don't want her to know that. So I just send a thumbs up emoji and hope she leaves me alone.

What I want to do more than anything is talk to someone about what happened yesterday, because I still can't wrap my head around it.

The way Ishu was looking at me…the question she asked…

I lie back in bed and stare up at the beige ceiling, wishing that feelings and relationships made any kind of sense. But of course they don't. That would be too easy.

Under normal circumstances, this is the kind of thing that Amma would be able to help me with. She always gives the best advice about everything. It's like she's already experienced everything I've experienced, so I can avoid making the exact same mistakes as her with her stellar advice. But I'm pretty sure Amma has never fake dated a girl and then discovered that actually, she might be developing real feelings for her. And – because the whole thing is a big fat lie – I can't tell Amma about it anyway. She'll tell me to come clean to everyone about everything. We can't do that. Not now that my friends actually like Ishu, and might be getting on board with who I am. And Ishu is on track to become Head Girl.

Still, there's comfort in just knowing that Amma is there if I need her. Yes, she'll make me come clean, but she'll probably at least let me cry on her shoulder first.

So, after grabbing breakfast, I peek into Amma's room. She's at her desk, typing away on her laptop.

'Amma? You busy?'

She looks up and flashes me a smile. 'Not really. What's up? Did you eat breakfast?'

'Yeah, I just ate,' I say. 'Where's Abba?'

'He has some meetings today,' she says. 'Won't be home all day.'

'He's been really busy lately, huh?'

She just shrugs, like she's used to it. Ever since he started running in the county council elections, it's been pretty difficult to get ahold of him. The only time I see him is when I'm helping him out with something, because he's always in different meetings. Even when he is home, he's hard to talk to because he's answering emails or on the phone. I don't know how Amma deals with it, when it even annoys me sometimes.

'Do you want to watch a movie together today?' I ask. 'You can pick the movie...I won't even complain if it's a Bollywood one.'

Amma studies me for a moment. 'Everything OK? How was your date last night?'

'It was fine. It was...nice,' I say. 'It started raining at the end of the night and I got soaked and now I feel a little sickly, so...I just want to watch a movie with my Amma now.'

She doesn't look convinced. Still, she nods. 'OK...but it will definitely be a Bollywood movie. What's new on Netflix?'

'I can check!' I'm already pulling out my phone.

'I can make lunch...your favourite: akhni.' She closes her laptop and stands up, ready to go to the kitchen.

'Amma, if you start making akhni, how will we watch the movie?'

'After the akhni,' she says, like it's obvious. 'It won't take a long time.'

'Akhni takes a long time,' I insist. 'How about we just order biryani from Suraj Uncle's restaurant?'

'It's not the same as akhni,' Amma says. Akhni is Sylheti biryani, which is why everyone in my family thinks it's the superior form of biryani.

'I know, but it's biryani, and you won't have to spend the day in the kitchen,' I say. 'We can have akhni another time. For my birthday, or something.'

Amma hates getting takeout when she can cook a better meal for cheaper at home, but she concedes.

An hour later, it's just Amma and me, our plates full of really good biryani – which is not as great as akhni – and Sonam Kapoor and Fawad Khan in *Khoobsurat*. For a little while, at least, I manage to pretend that my problems don't exist.

chapter twenty-six

~ishu

HANI DOESN'T ANSWER MY PHONE CALLS OR REPLY TO any of my messages Saturday night and just sends me a thumbs up emoji on Sunday morning. I'm pretty sure I've royally screwed everything up with my ridiculous feelings. Now Hani doesn't even want to talk to me. This was one of the things I predicted would happen if I confessed any of my feelings, except it's worse because I haven't even confessed anything – not really. I've just scared her off.

I try to ignore the gnawing feeling of hurt and betrayal in my stomach, but I barely get any sleep on Saturday night. Hani didn't even message to let me know that she got home OK. I keep opening our guide, because it feels like a history of us. Hani always updates it with all of the pictures she takes, and until yesterday she was filling up the latest pages with information I should know about Aisling and Deirdre. But since our triple date Hani hasn't added anything. That makes me feel even worse.

I throw myself into my studies on Sunday since I spent Saturday dawdling around, doing basically nothing productive.

Because I'm sure that Aisling and Deirdre will not be my friend if Hani isn't even talking to me.

I have to keep control of what I can control: my results and my future. Whether that contains becoming Head Girl or not. We have another biology test on Monday and I'm determined to get as close to a perfect result as I can get.

'Hey.' Aisling slides right next to me in biology class. 'Did you have a good weekend?' She smiles at me like we're friends, which obviously means that Hani hasn't told her friends about whatever is going with her and me. There are a few people who glance over their shoulders at the two of us – trying to be discreet but failing horribly at it.

'Yeah, it was good. Quiet Sunday.' I shrug.

Hani strolls in and gives us both a wave before taking her place in the seat in front of us. At least she's not straight out ignoring me, I guess.

'Did you study for the test?' Aisling asks, taking her biology book and copies out of her backpack.

'I did, yeah,' I say.

'I bet you're going to get another A.' She grins.

I shrug. 'Here's hoping.'

Ms Taylor interrupts our conversation just then by entering

the classroom. A quick hush falls over everyone as she click-clacks her way to the front of the room.

'OK, today's the big test. Your summer exams are coming up so this is good practice,' she says. As if she doesn't give us a test every week. 'I hope everyone studied.' She barely gives people time to register her words before passing the tests back row by row.

Hani whispers a 'good luck' to both of us as she passes the bundle of tests down.

I write my name at the top of the test paper and open it up. It's a long test – it's supposed to last for the entire class. It has most of the things that we've studied this whole year. Still, it's not difficult. The last thing I studied yesterday – ecology – is the first thing on the exam. And it's just definitions, which is easy. It's just having to memorise a bunch of stuff.

I'm scribbling down what a biosphere is when I feel a slight nudge on my ribs. I look up, but everybody's head is bent down over their own test. Even Aisling – who is the only person who could have nudged me – is staring down at her test with furrowed eyebrows. Maybe it was a mistake?

I'm about to go back to my test when Aisling slides a note across the narrow space between us.

Let me take a peek?

I can only stare at the words for a moment. I should have known this was why Aisling decided to sit right next to me in class today. Why she has been so friendly. Maybe why she agreed to hang out with me on Saturday, and probably why she invited me to sit with them at lunch.

If I let her take a look at my test, if I let her cheat, does that mean I'm good in her books? Does that mean we're friends? Or friendly enough for her to tell people that they should vote for me for Head Girl? Even if she doesn't, isn't the association already going to be much more than I'd ever get without her? People have already started treating me differently, just because I'm 'dating' Hani. Who knows how things will change if I'm dating Hani and I'm friends with Aisling and Deirdre?

It's not like letting her cheat on the test actually has any effect on me. She's the one looking, and she's the one who's going to struggle when it comes to her Leaving Cert. Really, she's just hurting herself, and I'm just doing what needs to be done in order to make sure the school has the best Head Girl.

Before I can think about it for too long, I lean back in my seat and push my test paper a little closer to Aisling. So it's easy enough for her to make out what I've written. All she has to do is look over. I finish the test definitions like that, and ignore the look of satisfaction and delight on Aisling's face.

'How'd you do?' Hani asks when she comes over to collect our test papers at the end of class. She barely glances at me.

'Pretty good, I think.' Aisling slings an arm over my shoulder as she says this. Like we've been best friends our whole lives. 'I actually studied this weekend, so…I think I'll do pretty good.'

Hani looks slightly confused, but she just nods her head. 'Ishita?'

I shrug. 'Yeah…OK. Probably. You?'

'Yeah. OK, probably.' She grabs our test papers and passes them to Ms Taylor.

Later that day, when I join the three of them for lunch in our base classroom, Hani is sitting facing the wall, with Deirdre beside her and Aisling opposite her. Conveniently, this is the only position where it's impossible for me to sit beside her. If the others think this is strange, they don't mention it. They just look happy to see me. I've never seen my classmates happy to see me before. A strange feeling surges through my chest at their expressions. I'm not sure if I like it or hate it.

'We should totally do something again this weekend,' Aisling says as we tuck into our lunch. 'Like…we could go to a movie. What's on the cinema?'

'Um…' Deirdre pulls out her phone and tinkers around on it for a moment. 'Well…there's like a bunch of superhero movies, obviously. There's a new Pixar but it looks kind of bad. There's another Disney remake and…basically nothing interesting.'

'So…not the cinema,' Aisling says. 'Suggestions, Ishita? What do you like doing in your free time?'

'Um…studying?' I say.

Aisling and Deirdre burst into a fit of giggles like I've told a joke. Even Hani's lips twitch like she's trying very hard not to smile.

'OK, we're definitely not doing that,' Aisling says.

'Maybe Humaira has some suggestions?' I shoot her a look, and she finally looks up to meet my eyes. I still can't read her expression. Usually, Hani is like an open book. Anger, frustration, happiness…all of that is written on her face clear as day. Now, though, it's like she's closed up the book for me, and I don't know how to get her to open up once more.

'I don't know,' Hani says. 'Maybe we should just play it by ear.'

'Well, I think Colm and Barry have that football match Saturday morning? Maybe we could go support them and then hang out together?' Deirdre suggests.

'That sounds perfect,' Aisling says. 'We can go to Eddie Rocket's and get milkshakes.' Another place that has barely any vegetarian options. I don't say that out loud this time. I've learned from my mistakes. And I don't want to jeopardise everything now. Still, I try to catch Hani's eyes, but she's not looking at me. She's looking everywhere but at me.

'Hey, Hani…do you think we can talk outside the classroom for a second?' Hani's eyes snap to me and a frown appears on her lips. Before she can reply though, Aisling cuts in.

'Sorry, you're not allowed to do that.' She slings an arm around me once more and it takes a lot to not try and claw her hands off of me. The way she touches me feels too familiar, too comfortable. Way more comfortable than I want her to be.

'We're not?' I ask, trying to wiggle out of her grasp without making it seem like I am.

'No…because it would be pretty unfair of you guys to go off somewhere and start shifting or whatever, when we can't do it.'

Hani does catch my eye at that. I'm happy to say that she looks as confused as I feel.

'Um, you could shift Deirdre anywhere you wanted,' I say. 'I mean, I wouldn't stop you.'

'No…' Aisling rolls her eyes and finally lets me go. 'I mean, because we're in an all-girls school, and Barry and Colm are like super far away. It's not really fair. It's like…heterophobia.'

'Well, we weren't going to—'

'Heterophobia doesn't exist, Aisling.' Hani snaps before I can finish my sentence. 'That's a ridiculous word.'

'If homophobia exists—'

'Yes, because…' Hani trails off, before shaking her head and standing up abruptly. Her chair scrapes loudly when she does. She doesn't really look at any of us. 'I have to go. I… didn't do my Irish homework, so…I have to go.' With that, she grabs her bag and rushes out of class.

'What's up with her?' Deirdre asks. 'She's been in a bad mood all day.'

Aisling asks. 'I'm sure she'll come around.'

'I should talk to her,' I say, getting up too. 'I'll…make sure she's OK…and help her with her Irish homework.'

'Is this you guys' way of—'

'No.' I cut Aisling off before she can say anything else homophobic. I shoot her a small smile. 'See you guys later.' I give them both a little wave before slipping out of the classroom.

hani

'*CONAS ATÁ DO CHUID OBAIR BHAILE AG DUL?*' ISHU WALKS UP
to me with a hesitance that is definitely not on brand for her.

I sigh. 'What are you doing here?'

'Helping you with your *obair bhaile*, obviously,' she says,
sitting down beside me on the ground. It's going to get her
skirt dirty, but she doesn't seem to mind. 'Aren't you cold?'

'A little,' I say.

'I would give you my jacket if I hadn't left it in my locker,'
Ishu says. 'That would be like…the thing to do, right?'

This is exactly the reason why I didn't want to talk to Ishu.
Because she says stuff like this and sends my heart into a tizzy.
Makes me think that there could be something going on here,
reminds me that we maybe could have been something, but
we obviously aren't. And really, it's my fault. I came up with
this whole fake dating gimmick to start with.

I just sigh and scoot away from her. I dig into my bag and
look for my Irish book, but of course I've left it in my locker.
I don't even think I have Irish after lunch, but since it's the

excuse that I used, I'll have to stick to it. So I just take out a copy and my *foclóir*. Opening up my *foclóir*, I begin to sift through it, like there's a particular word I need to find.

'Your Irish homework is…?'

'Writing,' I say. 'About…stuff. A *timpiste*. So I need to find some words. To do that. Let me focus, please.' I don't glance at her, but I can feel her looking at me for far too long.

'Should we talk about Saturday?' Ishu finally asks. 'Like… we don't have to, but I don't like you being mad at me.'

I put down my *foclóir* and glare at Ishu. 'I'm not mad at you.'

'That's convincing.' She deadpans.

'Don't be cute!'

'I'm not being cute!' Ishu exclaims. 'I'm just…I'm sorry,' she says. That word still sounds strange coming out of her lips. 'I'm sorry if I said something that made you uncomfortable. I just…I was just joking on Saturday and…' She takes a deep breath. 'I'm sorry.'

'I just don't like when people joke about stuff like that,' I say. 'Because…the whole thing with Aisling and Dee and…I don't know.' I shake my head. 'I want us to be friends. And I know that we're doing this dating thing, but…we can't…I don't want us to make it into a joke, even if it's not real.'

'I won't,' Ishu says quickly. 'I didn't…I wasn't trying to…' She seems at a loss for words. Flustered. There's even a slight flush rising up her cheeks. If only Ishu wasn't joking about being girlfriends. If only this weren't a fake relationship. Then things would be a lot easier.

'Are we friends?' I interrupt her stutters.

'Yes.' Her voice is more confident than it has been this whole conversation. 'Even if it pigeonholes us or whatever, we're friends.'

I nod. 'Good. And we're…pretending to be girlfriends.'

'Yeah…' Ishu says. 'And we love heterophobia.'

I have to laugh at that. 'Aisling is so ridiculous sometimes.'

'She is,' Ishu smiles. 'She's…' Ishu hesitates, like she's having to really choose her words here. Like she's not sure how to say the next words she has to say. 'What do you like about Aisling?'

That's definitely not the question I expect.

'I don't know. She's…a good friend,' I say.

'In what way?'

'Um…she's fun. I always have fun when I'm with her,' I say. 'I mean…you can see why I'm friends with her. You've hung out with her. With them both. You like them, right?'

She nods slowly. 'Yeah. They're both…interesting.'

'Aisling definitely likes you,' I assure her. 'Like…she thinks you're cool.'

'She told you that?'

'No, but I can tell,' I say. 'She sat next to you in biology. On purpose. She could have sat next to me, or on the other side of the table like she usually does.'

Ishu nods again. 'Yeah, you're right. I guess our plan really is working, huh?'

I smile. There's not a whole lot of time until we vote for Head Girl. I just have to find a way to keep my feelings at bay and get through these next few weeks.

'We obviously came up with a really good plan.'

I make the decision to try and lay low for a little while. After all, the summer exams are only weeks away and I definitely haven't been focusing on my studies. If I can steer clear of Ishu and me spending time together alone, I should be all set. Hanging out with Aisling and Dee is fine because they always take over the conversation anyway.

I can do this.

At least that's what I tell myself. I've convinced myself of it.

The next morning, Ishu greets me at my locker like that's something we do.

'Morning,' she says.

'Morning…' I'm definitely not a morning person, but I'm even worse when I'm ambushed like this by a girl I was dreaming about just a few hours ago. 'What are you doing here?'

'Well…applications for prefect and Head Girl are closing today,' she says. 'You applied for prefect, right?'

'Yeah…obviously. I told you that I did, didn't I?'

'Well…that means the teachers are going to start considering us soon. We're going to have our interviews and then the votes.' Ishu's eyes are getting wider and wider with every word that she speaks. 'And then—'

'Ishu…stop freaking out.'

'I just think we need to make more of an effort, you know?' she says.

'An effort to…?' Instead of answering my question, Ishu leans forwards and takes my hand in hers.

'To look like the couple we're supposed to be?' she says. 'I mean, other than some Instagram photos it's not like we're going to win cutest couple in our yearbook or anything.'

'OK, we don't vote on that crap,' I say, pulling my hand away from hers and pretending that I have to eagerly search for a book in my locker. I mean, I do have to search for books in my locker but suddenly I can't even remember what subjects I have this morning.

'Did you just curse?' Ishu sounds amused.

'Crap is not a curse word,' I say. 'Other words that are synonyms of crap might be. But crap…isn't.'

'OK, OK,' Ishu says. 'Look…I know it might not be comfortable but it's kind of what we both signed up for. Holding my hand isn't that bad, right?' She looks at me with the kind of smile that definitely looks strange on Ishu's usually grumpy face.

I sigh. 'No…holding your hand isn't…that bad,' I concede. If I was being honest, I would say that holding her hand was probably the nicest thing I have done in a really, really long time. But I guess I've not done the honesty thing for a while now, either. 'We don't have to do any weird couple-y things, right? Like…canoodle?'

'What the hell does canoodle mean?' Ishu asks.

'I don't know, like…the stuff you see couples doing.' I feel my cheeks warm because suddenly us being a couple is all I can see.

'Just holding hands. Hanging out?' she asks. 'Is that OK?'

'Yeah,' I say. I know Ishu is only asking because of what happened on the Luas the other day. I guess I appreciate her checking my boundaries.

'So…are you finished with your books?' she asks, extending her hand like she's been waiting for me. 'I'll walk you to your first class?'

I have to smile, because things like this do not seem like Ishu things at all. I guess she's pretty dedicated to being Head Girl. And this is definitely a great way to show everyone that she is a likeable, charismatic person. Who knows the right people.

So I shut my locker door and slip my hand into hers. Her hand is soft and warm, and somehow the exact shade of brown as mine. And also somehow the exact shape and size to fit into mine perfectly.

'So…did you do anything fun after class yesterday?' she asks. I know she's trying to make small talk but it just feels awkward. Everything about this feels awkward and weird and unnatural.

'Just…studied,' I say. 'We have exams coming up so…I need to brush up on stuff. I'm really bad at maths.'

'Oh,' she turns to me with a frown. 'You know I'm really good at maths? I could help you study?'

'That's…OK,' I say in the nicest way I can. 'I'm not great at studying with other people.'

'Right,' she says. 'That's fair.'

'Well…' I point to the double doors of the art classroom. 'This is me.'

'OK…I'll see you at lunch?' Ishu asks.

'Yeah.'

She shoots me a smile and turns away. Towards whatever class she has, I guess. The strange thing is, despite how weird and awkward and unnatural Ishu walking me to class felt, I still feel a strange emptiness at her being gone.

As much as I don't want to have any feelings for Ishu, I can't help that I keep opening up our guide. It almost feels like second nature.

I haven't added anything to it since that day on the Luas – neither has Ishu. Still, I can't help but scroll through it every once in a while – always wondering about what it would be like if all of this were real and not pretend.

It's as I'm looking at the guide wistfully on Thursday night that I notice a new user appear at the top of the screen. Unlike Ishu's circular blue *I*, this circle has an orange *N* inside it.

I blink my eyes, wondering if I've imagined it, because the next moment it's disappeared. But my heart is hammering in my chest. I couldn't have imagined it.

Slowly, I click the blue share button at the top of my screen, half afraid of knowing the truth. And what I read makes my breath hitch in my throat: *Shared with: Ishita Dey and Nikhita Dey.*

chapter twenty-eight

BY THE TIME THE WEEKEND ROLLS AROUND, HANI AND I are still as awkward as ever. The easy comfort that we once felt with each other seems to have been stripped away. In fact, for most of the week Hani spent as little time with me as possible. Sure, she let me walk her to her classes like we're a real-life couple, but for the entire week we barely texted or talked at all. Like we're not even friends.

'So, will we see you at the football match tomorrow?' Aisling asks at the end of Friday. 'Ten o'clock at St. Andrews, and lunch afterwards?'

Hani catches my eyes at the invitation, and I'm not sure what exactly she's thinking. She's been a closed book all week.

'You know, I probably won't make it,' I finally say. 'Exams are coming up and…I have some family plans?'

'Oh.' Aisling doesn't exactly sound disappointed, but she doesn't look happy either. Who would have thought Aisling of all people would want to spend her weekend hanging out with me?

'Well, we'll miss you,' Dee says. 'But it'll be like old times, with the three of us, right?' Dee's smile flickers between Aisling and Hani.

'Actually, I won't be able to make it either.' Hani doesn't look at any of us as she says this. Instead, she focuses on her locker, fiddling with the books inside. 'I'm busy this weekend.'

'Are you guys ditching us to hang out together?' Aisling does look a bit annoyed now, though she chuckles like it's supposed to be a big joke.

'Definitely not.' Hani finally turns to her with a reassuring smile. 'We wouldn't do that to you guys.'

'Are you really busy this weekend?' I ask Hani as the two of us head out of school. Hani is walking towards the bus stop as usual, and I'm off to the Luas.

'Did you really forget?' Hani asks.

'Did...we have plans this weekend?' I distinctly remember Aisling and Dee trying to make plans with us, but as far as I know we didn't settle on anything other than the football game.

'Your parents invited us to a dawat?' Hani turns to me with a raised eyebrow. It finally dawns on me – the dawat that Ammu and Abbu had reminded Hani of every time they ran into her. Turns out, they should have been reminding me.

'Shit.'

Hani chuckles, though her heart doesn't seem quite in it. We reach the fork in the road, where Hani turns left and I turn right. She hesitates for a moment. That moment is all it takes for my heart to start hammering in my chest.

'You remember...the rules from the guide, right?'

I don't know what I was expecting her to say, but it was definitely not *that*.

'Yeah?'

She chews on her lips before shaking her head. 'I'll see you tomorrow.' She doesn't look me in the eye as she says this. Before I know it, she's turning around and heading to the bus stop.

I heave a sigh, watching her retreating form for a minute, wondering why she would bring up our rules. Tomorrow will be the first time the two of us are going to be together without Aisling and Deirdre in a long time. Maybe, we can fix whatever is broken between us. Maybe there's still time for us to figure things out.

Ammu is in the kitchen from five o'clock on Saturday morning. Even though I'm in my bedroom with my door closed, I can hear the sound of clinking pots and pans as she cooks, and the hoover as she cleans. At one point I venture downstairs, peeking into the kitchen to see her bent over the stove.

'Do you need help, Ammu?' I offer. Abbu is working at the shop until just an hour before the guests are supposed to arrive, so it's just been Ammu all on her own, working away.

'Shouldn't you be studying for your summer exams?' Ammu doesn't even look up from stirring her pot of biryani.

'Yeah, but you're all on your—'

'Go, study,' Ammu says. 'I'm fine.'

Heaving a sigh, I slip back upstairs, trying to ignore my stomach rumbling at the smell of the delicious food. Ammu always goes all out when we have a dawat. She makes so many dishes that there's hardly space for them on our dining table. She invites so many people that they can barely squeeze into our narrow three-bedroom house.

I try to go back to my studying but it's difficult to focus when all I can think about is how Hani is going to be here in just a few hours.

Before I know it, it's almost time for the guests to arrive. I change into a pink and white salwar kameez that's pretty plain except for the floral patterns on its edges. It's the urna of the salwar kameez that really makes it. It's a mesh urna with garlands of pink and white flower patterns from one end to the other. I drape the urna on my front first. When I look in the mirror, it doesn't look right, so I wrap it around the back of my neck instead. The patterns on the urna get hidden that way, so I settle for placing it across my shoulder instead.

Still, something feels off. I brush my hair back and pin up the sides of it so it doesn't get into my eyes. I even apply a little eyeliner – making my usually huge eyes a little smaller – and some pink lipstick to go with my salwar kameez. Ammu peeks into my room while I'm putting on my makeup.

'I didn't know you wore makeup.' She takes me in slowly, a small frown on her lips. 'I didn't even know you owned makeup.'

'I own makeup,' I say. 'I wore it to that wedding we went to.'

'That was a year ago,' Ammu says.

'Yeah, well.' I shrug. 'This is the biggest dawat we're having this year. I wanted to look nice.' I'm regretting brushing my hair out of my face, because I'm afraid Ammu can see the flush on my cheeks. Then the bell rings, and she forgets all about me.

'Come downstairs and greet the guests.' She calls as she hurries down the stairs.

'OK, Ammu.' I take one final look at myself in the mirror. Deciding it's the best it's going to get, I slip downstairs.

chapter twenty-nine

Going to Ishu's house for a dawat is the last thing I want to do. But I can't really skip out on it. For one, it would be pretty rude. But more than that, if I tell Amma I don't want to go, she'll know something is wrong and press me for more information. And of course I can't tell her that I've developed real feelings for the girl I'm supposed to be fake dating, or that I think she's broken my trust.

For the past few days, I haven't gone on to our guide at all, though there have been times when I've thought about deleting it altogether. But what good would it do if Ishu's sister has already seen everything? What I don't understand is why. Ishu seemed so sure that day at the café that if her sister knew anything she would use it against her. So why would Ishu share this with her?

As Abba, Amma, and I wait outside Ishu's front door, I notice that Abba is shifting his weight from one foot to the other. His nervous gaze doesn't settle on one thing for too long. He's wearing a panjabi again today – one that is pure white with gold accents around the collar and cuffs. He's even wearing the tupi he brought to the mosque the other day.

I frown. I'm about to ask Abba exactly what's going on but then the door swings open. Dinesh Uncle stands on the other side, wearing a brilliant blue shirt and an even more brilliant smile.

'Welcome, welcome! Come in!' He waves the three of us inside, and immediately I can hear the buzz of Bengali chatter and smell the aroma of Bengali food. The former a curse, the latter a gift.

'Sajib!' A man approaches us from the sitting room. It takes me a moment to recognise him – after all, I only saw him briefly and from a distance at the mosque. But there's no mistaking his white-flecked beard and white tupi.

'Assalam Alaikum.' Abba reaches forwards to take his hand in his own. Then he turns towards us, an oddly cheerful smile pasted on his lips. 'This is my wife, Aditi.' Amma gives salam. 'And my daughter, Humaira, though we call her Hani.' Abba smiles at the man. 'This is Salim.'

Salim Uncle considers me for a moment. It's honestly a little creepy, like he's staring into my soul with his dark brown eyes.

Finally, he says, 'Humaira is a beautiful name.'

'Thank—'

'Did you know it was the nickname the Prophet Muhammad gave to his wife, Aisha?'

I exchange a glance with Amma who – thankfully – looks as freaked out as I feel.

'I didn't,' I say. Before he can say any more, Amma shoots him a polite smile and excuses us, pulling me away towards the kitchen where most of the women are seated.

'He was intense,' Amma whispers to me. I can only nod in agreement, because I've already spotted Ishu standing by herself in one corner of the room. And it's a little hard to look away from her. She's wearing this salwar kameez that is white, fading into a soft pink. The colours seem to soften her. All of her hard edges seem to have disappeared and there's some vulnerability to her standing to one side of the room, twisting the edges of her urna around her fingers.

'Hey.' I step towards her almost instinctively – though I had planned to do my best to avoid her today. Ishu turns to me so fast that her urna floats off her shoulder. She manages to grab it at the last second, haphazardly draping it around her shoulder once more.

'I…like your salwar kameez.'

Ishu looks down at the bottom of her kameez, like she has forgotten what she's wearing. She tugs at the rose-gold hem. 'Thanks…I like yours too.'

She looks up and finally catches my eye. I can't help the smile that appears on my lips. She returns it. Then we descend into a silence that seems only for the two of us, a quiet pocket within the usual bustling noise of a Bengali dawat.

'It's a little—' I begin, at the same time that Ishu mumbles, 'How was—' We both cut ourselves short, catching each other's eyes again. I feel a familiar knot in my stomach, and there's nothing uncomfortable about it. And I know that I have to ask Ishu about the guide. About her sister. No matter how much I don't want to.

Aparna Aunty calls Ishu away to help with setting the table, and pretty soon all the chatter is interrupted by Aparna Aunty calling us to dinner. She's laid the table with so many different types of food that there's no empty spaces on it at all. On one side, there's a pot of biryani – the aroma coming off of it absolutely divine. Surrounding the biryani is chicken korma, and lamb curry. On the other side of the table, there's white rice, surrounded by mixed vegetable curry and fish cutlet. In the middle of the table, there's a plate of shorisha ilish – this has always been Aparna Aunty's speciality. Amma can definitely make shorisha ilish, but not in the way that Aparna Aunty can. Even the look of the fish sitting in the golden mustard paste is heavenly.

The food tastes even better than it looks. Almost as soon as I'm finished eating, Ishu grabs my hand and pulls me up the stairs.

'I hate dawats,' she mumbles under her breath.

'Well, the food is always good,' I say. Ishu raises a questioning eyebrow but I don't think she should question how good her mam's shorisha ilish tastes.

She opens up the door to her bedroom, and almost as soon as the two of us are through it I hear the click of the lock behind us. It's not like we haven't been alone in her bedroom, or in my bedroom, before. But for some reason, now the thought of us here together in a *locked* room makes my heart beat a million times faster than usual.

'It's just so the kids can't come in,' Ishu explains.

'Yeah…that's what I figured,' I say. 'You're pretty obsessive over everything being organised.' I cast a sweeping look over her bedroom. It's pristine. 'How is this cleaner than the last time I was here? There aren't even any books on your desk.' If I didn't know this was Ishu's room, I'd be doubtful anyone lived in it.

'I wasn't going to let the guests see a messy bedroom.' Ishu's voice sounds a little insecure. Like she really thinks she's capable of having a messy bedroom.

'Because Uncles and Aunties love coming to scope out your bedroom?'

She shrugs and settles on to her bed. There's so much space beside her, but I hesitate before finally sitting myself down at the farthest end of the bed, as far away from Ishu as I can get without making it weird. Though from the way Ishu glances at me, I'm pretty sure things are already weird enough between us.

Time seems to slow down as the two of us sit there. It's deathly silent, though we can hear the hum of voices floating up from downstairs.

Finally, after what feels like hours, Ishu turns her whole body towards me, a frown etched into her face.

'So, are we going to talk about what's bothering you?' she asks.

My heart stops, and I glance up. I can only meet her gaze for a moment before looking down once more, at the bright blue of her duvet cover. She's given me the opening to ask about her sister and the guide, but the words feel clogged in my throat. 'Nothing…nothing's bothering me.'

Ishu heaves a sigh and the bed creaks with the weight of it. 'This should have been one of the rules in our guide, right? What to do if our fake dating leads to…awkwardness?'

I glance up once more to see Ishu looking up at her ceiling like something up there will have the answer to her question. Does she really not know?

'Something…happened.' The words slip out of me. For a moment, I'm not sure I'm the one who's said them. But then Ishu looks at me with curiosity written on her face and I know that I have. 'Your sister…'

Curiosity turns into confusion on Ishu's face, and she scoots forwards. 'My *sister*? Did she…*do* something?'

'I thought you knew,' I say, but the more I speak the more sure I am that Ishu didn't break any of the rules. Ishu didn't tell her sister. She didn't share our guide with her. 'I was looking at our Google Doc a few days ago, and…your sister was on it. She…has access to it.'

Ishu blinks slowly, like she's having a hard time processing this information. 'You didn't share it with her?'

'I couldn't even if I wanted to.'

'You think *I* sent it to her? On purpose?'

'It's the only explanation,' I say, even though now it sounds ridiculous. Of course, Ishu wouldn't send her sister this on purpose. Not after *literally* running away from Nik after our first date. Not after what she told me about her relationship with Nik.

'Why would *I* send it to her?' Ishu asks.

'I guess…you wouldn't,' I say. 'I just assumed…but…after everything that happened at Seven Wonders, I should have known…'

Ishu bites her lip. 'What if I sent it to her by accident?' Pausing, she looks up to meet my eyes. 'She didn't say anything about it to me, so…she must not have told anyone yet.'

It's the 'yet' that makes me afraid. I can't imagine what would happen if people found out that all of this has been an act. Aisling and Dee would never let me live it down – they would never ever believe that I'm really bisexual. They'll be convinced that I did this whole thing as a stunt for attention.

'So, you think she's going to tell someone?' I ask. 'Because if people find out…'

'I know.' Ishu's voice is little more than a whisper. 'She could…tell my parents.'

Silence sits between us again. But this time there's nothing awkward about it; it's heavy with the knowledge that someone knows our secret. That with just one click, someone can undo everything that we've been working towards.

Ishu's face is contorted into an expression that I've never really seen on her before. I edge towards her until we're basically face-to-face. 'It's going to be OK. Your sister…she won't tell anyone.' I try to say it with conviction that I definitely don't feel.

Ishu meets my gaze, and her expression softens. For the first time today, I notice that she's wearing makeup. There's a hint of eyeliner around her eyes, and a tint of pink on her lips. I don't think I've ever seen Ishu wearing makeup before. The familiar knot tugs at my belly, and I feel warmth creep up my neck.

'You don't know Nik,' Ishu says. 'And…you don't know what our relationship is like.'

'Maybe we can talk to her and…explain the situation…'

Ishu is smiling now, as if I've said something really funny.

'What?'

'It's just…nice that you think Nik will listen to reason,' she says. 'And…I guess it's nice that I'm not dealing with this on my own.'

'We can figure out a solution together,' I say, trying to ignore the fact that Ishu's words are making me warm all over again. And that I'm distinctly aware of the fact that we've gone from sitting at opposite ends of the bed to being dangerously close to each other. But I don't know how to put space between us again without going back to our awkwardness from before. Without making Ishu aware of how being close to her makes me feel things that I definitely do not want – or need – to be feeling.

'Maybe,' Ishu surprises me by saying. It seems she surprises herself, because she blinks slowly like she's not sure she's said those words herself. 'I mean, since it's not just going to be me dealing with it…maybe together we *can* find a solution.'

Ishu's eyes are peering into mine, and somehow I've never noticed just how warm they are. The light of the sun pouring in through her window illuminates a hint of golden brown in them. Suddenly, all I can think of is the lack of space between us. The fact that if I inched my hands forwards, I would reach her fingers. If I leaned my face forwards, I would find hers. I guess Ishu must have been thinking the exact same thing, because she *does* inch her hand forwards. Instead of my fingers, she finds a strand of hair and curls it around her fingers. Her touch sends a shiver down my spine. Before I know it, my body is leaning forwards of its own accord. The bed creaks beneath me. I close my eyes, and—

'Ishu!' Aparna Aunty's voice screeches from downstairs. Ishu bounces back from me. I nearly fall off the bed in my rush to get away from her, even though the bedroom door is locked and Aunty's voice is ridiculously far away: 'Niche eshe mishti khao.'

Ishu rolls her eyes at me. 'OK, Ammu. We're coming.'

Whatever was happening between us, whatever emboldened us to make something happen between us, is broken by Aparna Aunty's intrusion. I still can't get my heart back to a regular pace. And I can't look Ishu in the eye.

She shoots me a smile before getting off the bed. I don't know what it means. 'We should go downstairs. You like mishti, right?' She swings the door open and looks back at me.

'I only like some mishti.' I get up and follow her down the stairs. I'm not sure if we've made things between us better or infinitely worse.

chapter thirty

~ishu

After the dawat is finished, and everyone has gone home, our house suddenly feels too empty. After being filled with Bengali chatter for the whole day, the silence seems to press into us.

I change out of my salwar kameez and strip my face of makeup. All the while, I can't stop thinking about Hani. And I can't stop thinking about Nik. Two people I definitely don't want to be thinking about.

I crawl into bed and pull out my phone, scrolling to my text thread with Nik. The last messages we sent each other were that day she came home to surprise us. It feels like an eternity ago, though it's only been a few weeks.

Hey Nik...

That's all I type out before pausing. Because how do I ask my sister if she accidentally discovered the truth about my fake relationship? And how do I ask her what exactly she's planning to do with that truth? Thinking about all of the possibilities, all of the ways that Nik can use this to get back into Abbu and Ammu's good graces, makes me feel queasy.

Erasing my message, I click into my Instagram DM thread with Hani instead. I'm still trying wrap my mind around exactly what had happened in my bedroom earlier today. There was one inexplicable moment where I was sure that Hani and I were on the exact same page. That we wanted the same thing. But the moment was fleeting – it passed as quickly as it came. Maybe it was just a moment of weakness, spurred by the fact that someone knows our secret. That all of our plans might come undone if Nik decides to do something about our guide.

Should we talk about what happened today?

The unsent message glares up at me, and I erase it almost immediately. If Hani got a message like this, she would probably run for the hills. If there's one thing I've learned about her, it's that Hani's not the kind of person who confronts things head on. Even coming to me about Nik seemed like it was killing her.

I click away from my message thread and end up on my Instagram timeline instead. The first photo that pops up is from the dawat today. It's Hani's, and it's of the two of us sitting side by side. There are plastic white bowls of mishti balanced in our hands. We're both half-smiling, Hani's looking down and I'm staring straight into the camera. The awkwardness between us is almost palpable – just from looking at that picture.

I lie back in bed, and close my eyes. Maybe Hani uploading the picture is her roundabout way of saying something. Or maybe it isn't – but it makes me happy all the same.

I had hoped that sleep would give me some clarity about both the Nik and Hani situations, but my thoughts are still a jumble when I wake up on Sunday morning. I spend the day helping Ammu clean the house up, my thoughts whirring around my head all the while.

As I clean, I think about how to bring up the subject of *us* with Hani. About whether I should bring it up at all. After all, the last time I tried, Hani shut me out. What if I'm simply building everything up inside my head? What if Hani doesn't feel anything for me at all? What if I blow up our tentative friendship over nothing?

I kind of wish I had someone to talk to about this. Hani, at least, has her friends, though I doubt she would ever ask them for advice about *me*. The only person I've ever had is…Nik.

You can come to me. I just want you to know that. OK?

That's what Nik said the last time we saw each other. She seemed so sincere. I can almost picture her face now – the sympathy written all over it. I wanted to believe her – I *want* to believe her. But Nik and I have *never* been sisters like that. Not even before our academic competition began.

And now…Nik is the one who holds all the cards. Heaving a sigh, I go back to my cleaning, putting Nik out of my mind. My sister is definitely not someone I can trust. She's not someone I can go to. Not even if she pretends that she is.

chapter thirty-one

IT'S A LITTLE DIFFICULT TO GET ISHU OUT OF MY HEAD over the weekend. I'm still trying to figure out exactly what it means that she leaned forwards – that I leaned forwards. I want to believe that it meant something, but what if it was just both of us being overwhelmed by the idea of someone else having access to our guide? By the idea that our secret might not stay a secret for much longer?

More than anything, I wish I could speak to Amma about everything. She would know exactly what we should do about Nik. Exactly what I should say to Ishu. I even have a fleeting thought that if our secret is about to come out, why *not* just come clean to Amma?

But I know that I can't do that. It would be betraying Ishu. And I'm just not ready for anyone to know yet. But I do wish I had someone who would tell me what I should do.

When Abba mentions his plans of canvassing during lunch on Sunday, I almost leap out of my chair with excitement.

'Can I help?'

Abba and Amma exchange a glance. I'm not sure what it means but I don't think it's anything positive.

'Are you OK, Hani?' Amma asks. 'You've been acting…a little odd for the past few days.'

'I'm fine.' My voice comes out squeaky, suggesting that I'm not fine at all. I clear my throat and give Amma and Abba the biggest smile I can muster. 'It's just…the summer exams are almost here and…that's…stressful.'

'And…you're in a new relationship.'

I can almost feel my smile falter at that, but I try to keep it up. 'Yeah…and that.' The thought of Ishu tugs at my stomach but I try to shake that odd feeling off of me. 'But…I want to help canvass!' I turn to Abba. Getting out of the house and helping Abba with the election is exactly the thing I need to do. 'I already know all your policies. Who better to help you?'

Abba doesn't quite look convinced. 'I don't know, Hani. I don't know how comfortable I feel with you going door-to-door—'

'I've done it before,' I remind him. 'How many times have I gone door-to-door for the MS read-a-thon or the annual walk-a-thon?'

A smile flickers on Abba's lips and I know that I've convinced him. 'That was in this neighbourhood.'

'So…I'll canvass right here, close to home!' I gulp down the last of my sandwich and stand up. 'I'll be the best canvasser, Abba, I promise.'

Abba heaves a sigh. 'OK…but this is a big responsibility,

and you need your friends to help you.'

All the enthusiasm I was feeling simmers out. 'Why do I need them?'

'You're not doing this on your own, Hani. Your friends can help. They came with you to my speech at the mosque, right? It won't take long.'

'And afterwards, you guys can get pizza and watch a movie or something,' Amma chimes in. 'Or I can even make them dinner.' She beams, like making dinner for my friends is her favourite thing to do. Every time Aisling and Dee come over, Amma has to make 'white people food.' Not even 'white people spicy' food as she would for other non-Bengalis, just white people food, because Aisling and Dee won't eat any Bengali food – though they've never even *tried* it.

'Yeah, I'll text them,' I say, though it's really the last thing I want to do. At the mosque, they didn't even want to stay until the end of Abba's speech – they got fed up almost as soon as they got there. I'm not sure they'll be much help here either, but at least they wouldn't be able to accuse me of ditching them to hang out with Ishu for the weekend.

I throw on a pair of jeans and a campaign t-shirt that Abba had made ages ago. It's bright blue and says *VOTE KHAN*

#1! across the chest. The doorbell rings almost as soon as I'm dressed. It buzzes once, then twice, then one loud long buzz that lasts until I fling the door open. I try hard not to frown at Aisling and Dee standing in front of me, their arms crossed over their chests and looking like this is the last place they want to be.

In fact, they look like they're about to go to a party instead of out campaigning for Abba's election. They both have on full faces of makeup. Dee is wearing a crop top and a skirt that barely covers her thighs, while Aisling is wearing a black dress that reaches just above her knees.

'Hi…' I don't mean the greeting to sound like a question, but it does. Because I have a lot of questions as I take the two of them in. I hold out the t-shirts that Abba has stashed in our store room. 'These are my dad's campaign t-shirts.'

Dee and Aisling exchange a glance. It makes discomfort settle in my stomach, but I try to shrug that feeling off of me.

'Cool, thanks.' Aisling reaches out and grabs both the t-shirts, cradling them in her hands awkwardly. Neither of them make any indication of wanting to come inside the house to get changed. They just…kind of stand there, looking odd and out of place outside my front door.

I glance back at Amma in the kitchen. I can hear the water running in the sink where she's doing the dishes. 'Amma, we're going,' I call back in Sylheti. 'Allahafez.'

She glances back and gives us a quick wave as I step outside to join Dee and Aisling.

'So…' I dig through my bag to get hold of the bundle of leaflets that I grabbed from Abba earlier. 'This has everything that we need to know about my dad's campaign.' I hold out one leaflet each to the two of them. But they both look at them as if I'm offering them something disgusting instead of a piece of paper.

'Look…' Aisling says slowly. My stomach drops. I feel like I already know exactly what she's going to say. But there's no way – *no way* – she's going to try to talk me out of campaigning for Abba today, right? Not when I specifically asked them to come over for this. 'We really want to go canvassing, or whatever.'

'Really!' Dee's eyes brighten like she's trying to convince me that campaigning for local elections has been her lifelong dream – but it's not as convincing as she seems to hope.

'But…Colm and Barry asked us last minute to go into town and hang out. We couldn't say *no*. We're supposed to be celebrating their victory from yesterday,' Aisling finishes.

'Which you missed, by the way,' Dee adds matter-of-factly.

I try to tamp down the anger bubbling up inside me. 'Well, fine. You guys go and celebrate with Barry and Colm. I promised my dad that I would—'

'We know you lied to us.' Aisling cuts me off.

My breath hitches in my throat. Is this the moment of truth? Do Aisling and Dee know that Ishu and I have been faking it this whole time?

'I saw your Instagram picture,' Aisling continues when I

don't reply. 'Of you and Ishita.'

It takes me a moment to realise what exactly Aisling is talking about. Last night, after coming home and trying – and failing – to get Ishu out of my head, I ended up uploading the sole picture of the two of us together from the dawat last night. I meant it as a way to tell Ishu that we're OK, no matter what happened – or didn't happen – between us. So that she can see I'm still on board with our plans to make her Head Girl.

'You said you had a "family thing".' Dee actually sounds genuinely offended as she puts air quotes around 'family thing.'

'It *was* a family thing,' I insist. 'Or…at least a Bengali thing.' It's difficult to separate the two – I'm not sure if a separation even exists. 'Look…I was obligated to go.'

'Right.' Aisling rolls her eyes, crossing her arms over her chest. 'I'm sure you were obligated to hang out with your girlfriend at a 'Bengali' thing.'

'Don't say it like that.' My voice rises an octave and I have to remind myself that I'm not supposed to get angry. That I shouldn't get angry.

'I just…don't like the person you're becoming.' Aisling's voice softens as she says this. 'The kind of person who ditches her friends to hang out with her girlfriend.' Beside her, Dee just nods her head solemnly. I wonder how much time they spent discussing this before they came here – if this was always the plan, whether I had decided to call them over or not.

'That's not what happened,' I say. 'You don't get it. Going to our Bengali parties…that's something Ishu and I both *have* to do. We were just there…together. We didn't plan it.'

Aisling drops her arms by her sides and steps closer to me. 'Dee and I invite you to everything.' There's a pleading tone to her voice. 'Why do we get excluded from things you and Ishita get to do together?'

'Because…' I scrunch my eyebrows together, trying to figure out how to explain it. 'It's…different. Our Bengali parties are our chance to be around our community. Other people can't be a part of it. It's…intimate.'

Aisling and Dee don't look convinced by my words when I look up to meet their gazes, and I do feel a little bad. I guess from where they're standing, it does seem like I ditched the two of them with a lie to hang out with my girlfriend.

I cast one last look at the leaflets in my hands. I'm sure 'celebrating' with Barry and Colm won't be terrible. And Abba will understand if we don't manage to canvass just today, right? If we leave it for another day? He *did* have qualms about me going in the first place.

I heave a sigh, glancing down at myself. I definitely can't go into town wearing my campaign t-shirt.

'Here.' Dee digs into her bag and tosses me a black jumper. It's a little too tight, and I definitely don't look ready for a night in town. But it'll have to do.

As we head towards the bus stop, I can't help the gnawing dread in my stomach.

chapter thirty-two

~ishu

I STAY PREOCCUPIED WITH HANI AND NIK AND HOW TO deal with everything until I get to school on Monday. Beside the office, there's a list of names tacked up and I know exactly what *that* is about. It's only a few weeks until the exams and the end of our school term. I knew that the Head Girl candidates would be announced sooner or later. I guess I thought it would be later.

With everything else going on – the fake dating guide in Nik's hand and this ridiculous crush on Hani – I had almost forgotten about Head Girl. But now a strange dread gnaws at me as I slowly make my way towards the list. What if I've been too preoccupied with all of this stuff? I had been so worried about not making Head Girl because I need everyone's vote to make it happen, but to get there, I need to first of all *make the cut* and be chosen as a viable candidate by the teachers.

Taking a deep breath, I start to scan the list. The first couple of names are for the candidates chosen for prefect who need to interview with the teachers. Hani's name sits in the middle:

Humaira Khan, International Prefect: Wednesday 3 p.m. in the library.

I'm not surprised to see Hani there. Everybody loves her, after all. And it's not like there's stiff competition for prefect applications when there are more than a dozen positions available.

The Head Girl candidates are listed at the very bottom, and I have to take another deep breath before I can look:

Head Girl interviews will take place on Tuesday in the principal's office at the following times:

Alexandra Tuttle: 9 a.m.

Siobhán Hennessey: 9:30 a.m.

Maya Kelly: 10 a.m.

Ishita Dey: 10:30 a.m.

I barely get the chance to breathe a sigh of relief before I spot Hani coming around the corner, concern written all over her face.

'Hey…' she says hesitantly, and I'm not sure if this is because of this weekend or the list that's hanging in front of us.

'I'm on the list. I have my interview tomorrow.' The words out of my lips feel like relief, but there's a sense of dread there too. Because this is just the start. Nik was on this list too during her fifth year, but even with her charming smile and winning personality she couldn't convince people at this school to choose her as the Head Girl. I don't have Nik's personality – what hope do I have to win what she didn't?

Hani's face brightens, the smile that's become so familiar to me on her lips now. 'That's amazing, congratulations!' Then, lowering her voice she asks, 'So…why do you look disappointed? This is what you wanted, right?'

'I mean…' I take a deep breath, stepping away from the office and towards the browbeaten bench opposite it. We sit down side by side and I'm a little too aware of the fact that we're so close I can smell the coconut scent of her shampoo. 'These are the parts I can't control.' My voice is barely a whisper, but Hani must hear them because her smile disappears.

'They'll vote for you.'

'And you know that because…'

'Because…our plan worked,' Hani says matter-of-factly. 'It worked…kind of better than we could have ever imagined, hasn't it? Aisling and Dee are on your side now. There's no way you're going to lose this.'

Somehow, Hani sounds completely convinced of this fact. I can't help the smile that breaks out on my face from her strangely confident gaze.

'You've just jinxed it, you know.'

Hani just rolls her eyes, but she's smiling. 'I made the prefect shortlist, you know.'

'Yeah, obviously you did. Congratulations.'

'So…Aisling and Dee were saying we should celebrate after school? You're going to come, right?' There's a hint of a plea in her voice and I heave a sigh.

'Maybe we should…talk about…' I hesitate and Hani gazes down at the hem of her skirt, her fingers wrapping around the ends. '…the guide?'

Hani looks up to meet my eyes again. I know there are other things we have to talk about too, but this seems more pressing. 'I mean…if something happens with that, all our hard work will be blown, right?'

'Right.' Hani nods. 'So, you need to talk to your sister.'

And that's what I was afraid of her saying, because I don't know how a conversation with my sister about this would go.

'What if that makes it worse?' I ask. 'I mean…right now, she hasn't said anything or done anything, but…if I bring it up, maybe that'll make her do something.'

'We can't just wait around and hope for the best,' Hani says. 'And we can't exactly take it back.'

'We could delete the whole thing!' I say, even though the idea of deleting it makes me feel a little hollow inside. The fake dating guide might be filled with evidence of our lie, but it also feels like a history of us.

Hani shakes her head slowly. 'We could delete it…but Nik already knows. She could have saved the whole thing if she really wanted to use it against us.'

I slump back in the uncomfortable bench, feeling the wood of it digging into my skin. It was donated by the graduating class of sixth years a while back. It even has a gold plaque in the middle announcing it. I don't know why they couldn't have donated something with a cushion.

'Ishu…' Hani sighs. 'I know you don't want to talk to her—'

'It's the last thing I want to do.' It's been weeks since Nik and I have come into contact – I've barely even thought about her since that day outside our house. And maybe that should make me feel bad, but I'm not the one who threw everything away for the sake of a guy. Though, when I see the way Hani is looking at me, I think maybe I can understand Nik's motivations at least a little.

'…but I can help. We can come up with a script or something. And, you know, I can be there when you guys talk. I can—'

'I'll talk to her,' I blurt out. 'Today…or…tomorrow, maybe. I don't know. It was my fault she found out…I'll deal with it.'

Hani meets my gaze with a smile and I realise that there's so little distance between us again. Even with the humdrum of students around us, it feels like it's just Hani and me here. Just the two of us separate from the rest of the world somehow.

The bell rings out, shrill and sharp, and Hani jumps up, brushing her long black locks of hair out of her eyes.

'We should get to class,' she says.

'Yeah.' I sigh.

Can we talk?

I send the text before I can think about it too much. As soon as I send it, I toss my phone on to my bed and open up my maths books. I'm going to test myself on some theorems and try to forget about tomorrow morning.

But before I can even glance at a single theorem, my phone buzzes with a call. My heart leaps into my throat. When I glance at the screen, it's Nik's name that flashes on it. I slide to the right to accept the call.

'Hey.'

'You wanted to talk?' Nik's voice is hesitant. In the background, I can hear the hum of music, and the cheers of people.

'Are you out?'

'Not really,' Nik says.

'How can you 'not really' be out? Either you're out or you're not.'

'Well…' Nik heaves a sigh. 'I'm…at a party, it's at my place, so I'm in, but…'

'You shouldn't have called me from a party. I'll—'

'No!' Nik exclaims before I can hang up. 'I want to talk. The party isn't important. Are you OK? Did…something happen?'

'I don't know…' I say slowly. '*Did* something happen?'

Silence hangs between us for a moment. Or as silent as it can be when I can hear the low hum of music coming from her end.

'So, I guess you're going to be super cryptic,' Nik says finally.

'Well…maybe I wouldn't have to be cryptic if *you* could

just be fucking straightforward about things.'

Nik breathes a heavy sigh. 'I really don't know what you're talking about, Ishu. Is this about Ammu and Abbu? The girl you're seeing? School? You know I'm here for you. I told you that I—'

'You have something of mine.' I cut her off. The words are all rushing out of me suddenly, like if I don't get them out of me immediately I'm going to explode. 'I sent it to you by accident and I don't know what you're planning on doing with it, but I just need you to know that I'm not the only one who'll be hurt if you tell people about it. Hani, she's…my friend, and she'll also—'

'Ishu.' There's a strange waver in Nik's voice. If I didn't know any better, I would think she was on the verge of tears, but she's the *last* person who should be upset here. I'm not the one holding information hostage over *her*.

'I saw the document, yeah. Your…guide to fake dating or whatever it is,' she says. 'I didn't even read it all the way through. I figured, yeah, you sent it to me by accident. And I don't know what it means or why you'd pretend to be in a fake relationship with Hani, but…I meant what I said last time we saw each other. We're not kids any more. I'm not trying to hold things over you, to win over Ammu and Abbu by screwing you over. Ishu…you can always come to me. About anything. OK?'

I don't know why there's suddenly a lump in my throat, but I gulp it down. 'OK.'

'OK…' There's another pause filled with silence, but

it doesn't feel as uncomfortable any more. 'So…is there something you want to talk about?' she asks.

'Um, yeah, actually. I was wondering…why didn't you become Head Girl in your final year of secondary school?'

Nik lets out a chuckle. I guess this wasn't the question she was expecting. 'Ishu…you never change, do you?'

'It's a valid question. I have the interview tomorrow so…'

'You'll be fine,' Nik says. 'You'll be great. Just…remember that Head Girls are there in a leadership capacity. Try to show that you're good at working with people. You're not just your results – you're a person with likes and dislikes and positive qualities.'

'So…what kind of questions will they ask?' I say.

'Probably stuff about how you'd solve certain problems, you know? How you'd handle debs stuff? Conflicts between students…things like that. Be confident and be assertive. Which are basically your two best qualities. So…you'll be great.'

'OK, thanks,' I say. Confident and assertive. I can definitely do that.

'Is that all?' Nik's voice suggests that she thinks it isn't. 'Or…did you call to talk about something else? Something about—'

'Nope, nothing else.' I cut her off. Before she can bring Hani up. I definitely don't want to hash out the fake dating guide and my feelings with Nik. 'Thanks for answering my questions. Enjoy your party. Bye!'

'Wait, Ish—' Before she can say anything else, I tap the button to end the call. I breathe a sigh of relief as I shift back to my desk.

I don't think Nik's going to tell anyone.

I send the text off to Hani. From her fast reply, I know that she's been waiting by her phone, worrying.

Are you sure?

Am I sure? Nik sounded so sincere, like she really believed what she was saying. Sure, my sister and I don't have the best track record in the world, but maybe things have changed in the past few years. Nik is definitely far from the ambition-driven person she was in secondary school.

So, I text Hani back with the best I've got:

I want to believe her.

chapter thirty-three

~ishu

THERE'S A KNOCK ON MY BEDROOM DOOR THE NEXT
morning as I'm changing into my uniform. There are only two
people it could be – Ammu or Abbu. But it's still strange for
them to knock on my bedroom door this early in the morning.

I pull on my jumper and swing the door open to Abbu's
grim face. His eyes are slightly bloodshot, like he hasn't slept
in a while, and his usually clean-shaven face has bits of stubble
all over it. I wonder if it's to do with the Nik situation – or if
it's something else entirely.

'Morning, Abbu.' I try not to let confusion seep into my
voice, even though that's really all I'm feeling.

His lips stretch out into something that only slightly
resembles a smile – it's more of a grimace. 'They're choosing
the prefects and Head Girl in school soon.' It's not a question.
I wonder how he found out, when I haven't told him anything.

'Yep…' I trail off, going back and forth in my head about
whether to tell him about the interview or not. On the one
hand, I've already lost enough sleep about it because I'm a

nervous wreck. I don't know if I can deal with Ammu and Abbu putting pressure on me about it right now as well.

'This time last year, Nikhita was preparing too.' His face softens at Nik's name, and I try not to let it bother me. 'She made me do mock interviews with her.' There's fondness and regret mixed together in his voice. 'And she was so disappointed when she didn't get it. Didn't even want to talk to us about it.'

'She's very ambitious,' I offer.

'Was.' Abbu's face darkens. 'I know you're on the right track, Ishu.' He places a hand on my shoulder and peers into my face, cracking a smile. As if this is the highest compliment he can give me. It kind of is, from Abbu.

'Thanks, Abbu,' I say. 'I'm keeping my head down and staying focused.'

'You'll tell us what happens with the Head Girl thing?' There's hope in his voice, and I don't want to give him more hope and then crush it. So I just nod my head.

When I become Head Girl, I tell myself. *I'll let them know then.*

On the bus to school, I put in my headphones and hit shuffle on my Spotify. I want to avoid thinking about the upcoming interview, and somehow find myself on my Instagram page. It's pretty bare – I'm hardly ever on it. But I've been tagged in so many pictures since I started hanging out with Hani. I scroll through the pictures of us on our first date, where we look happy, if a little uncomfortable with each other. Then there are pictures of all of us during our triple date at Captain America's. I have such a forced smile on my lips that I have to stifle a giggle as I scroll past the photos.

I shake my head and click out of my picture tags. I definitely can't let myself get distracted this morning, even though I've spent equal amounts of time thinking about Hani as I have about this interview.

I'm about to close out of my Instagram when I see a picture of my sister on my feed. I quickly scroll back up to it. The picture is of her and Rakesh, dressed up. She's in a bright red dress that makes her brown skin glow; he's in a suit and tie. They're both grinning with their arms wrapped around each other like this is the best day of their lives.

The caption reads:

thank you so much for the engagement party @ gemmabakesscones, couldn't have asked for a better night or a better bunch of friends to celebrate with. Lucky to be marrying the man of my dreams!

The picture is from last night and was only uploaded this morning. The more I look at, the more I feel a lump rising in my throat, and a prickling behind my eyes. Did Ammu and Abbu know about this? Were they invited? Or have we got to a point where we don't even bother inviting each other to big life events like this?

Is Nik really going to get married without Ammu and Abbu? Without me?

This must have been why Abbu was reassuring me that I was on the right track. Ammu and Abbu have given up on

Nik. The thought of it unsettles me. Fills me with a kind of dread I've never felt before. Sure, I knew that they were angry at her. I knew that she was frustrated with them. I know what Abbu and Ammu are like.

But I didn't think they were really going to go this far. How could they miss their eldest daughter's wedding?

By the time Principal Gallagher calls me into her office for the interview, I'm a mess of emotions. My nervousness about the interview and becoming Head Girl has somehow combined with the sudden dread of Nik getting married without the rest of us. I try to take a deep breath and forget about the latter as I step inside the principal's office and take in her plush maroon carpet and cream walls covered with all kinds of academic certificates. I can't let my emotions sabotage my chances at Head Girl, even if it suddenly doesn't feel that important any more.

'Ishita.' Principal Gallagher gives me a tight smile as I sit down. Ms Proudman, the guidance counselor, is supposed to be in here with us too, but there isn't a chair for her. Instead, there are two chairs placed on either side of me, like they're expecting more people to interview with me.

'Good morning, Ms Gallagher,' I say hesitantly, trying to

maintain my friendliness and politeness. 'Um, are we expecting more people?'

Principal Gallagher maintains a tight smile as she takes me in. 'Actually, we are…postponing the interview this morning.'

'Oh…then why—'

Before I can ask the question on my lips, the door to the office bursts open and Ammu and Abbu pour in.

'Is everything OK?' Ammu asks, at the same time that Abbu demands, 'What happened?' in a gruff voice.

'Mr and Mrs Dey, please take a seat.' Principal Gallagher fixes them with that same tight smile and points to the two chairs on either side of me. I feel a sense of dread rising up within me. Something is wrong. Something must be gravely wrong for my parents to have been called in. There's something sinister behind Principal Gallagher's smile.

My parents sit down, Ammu on my left and Abbu on my right. But there's no comfort in having them here. Actually, it feels kind of suffocating, and for some reason all I can think about is Nik and how quick they were to cast her out when she wasn't exactly who they wanted her to be.

'One of our students has brought a serious matter before me, involving Ishita,' Ms Gallagher says, looking from Ammu to Abbu but not glancing at me at all. She reaches under her desk and pulls out two sets of papers and sets them down side by side. The top of both say: *Fifth Year Biology, Ms Taylor.*

The names at the top of the tests have been covered up

with sticky notes, but I recognise my own messy handwriting on one, and Aisling's loopy writing on the other.

'The student told Ms Taylor, Ishita's biology teacher, that she suspected Ishita had cheated off of her test. She didn't want to say anything at the time because she was afraid of what Ishita might do, but…well, the evidence is right here.'

I can only blink at the tests in front of me, as the realisation slowly dawns on me. How could I have been so ignorant? How could I have let Aisling manipulate me like this?

'I didn't cheat,' I say, finally looking up and right at Ms Gallagher. 'I wouldn't do that. Aisling is the one who cheated. She was looking at my test and copying off of it. You can look at my other results; I always get similar marks, because I study. Not because I cheat.'

'Well.' Ms Gallagher sighs, like I've not consistently been the top student in all of my classes ever since I started school here. 'You have had excellent results in all of your classes in the past, but we'll have to open an investigation. We're going to be conducting interviews with some of your peers—'

'That's bullshit!' I stand so quickly that my chair almost topples over. 'I have *never* cheated. I've never needed to. I *study*—'

'Ishita Dey, that's enough.' Ms Gallagher's voice doesn't rise. She just eyes me with an almost bored expression on her face. 'We have to investigate this matter, as it's been brought to our attention. That's just the normal procedure when—'

'Is Aisling being investigated too?'

'The student who brought this case to our attention hasn't—'

'You just have to look at her other results to know that this is unusual for her. That she's the one who—'

'—been accused by anyone of cheating. For the time being, I'm afraid we can't consider you for the position of Head Girl, as I'm sure you understand, Mr and Mrs Dey.' Ms Gallagher looks at Ammu and Abbu like I'm not even there. Like they're the ones who have spent five years working their asses off.

'This is fucking bullshit.' I clench my hands into fists. It's all I can do to not reach over and break something on Ms Gallagher's desk.

'Ishita, we can't tolerate outbursts like this in—'

'But you can tolerate false accusations and lies and—'

'Ishu.' I feel Ammu's hand around mine. 'Raga ragi kore kono lab nai, Ishu. Ekhon amra bashai choli.'

'Pore amra discuss korbo.' Abbu adds with a grim nod. 'Thank you, Principal Gallagher.'

Ms Gallagher gives Ammu and Abbu her tight smile and looks at me with pity written across her face.

The lump in my throat has returned, and it's swiftly rising up. But I can't say or do anything. It's not like my words matter at this point. It's not like everything I've been working for matters at this point.

Even though I still have an entire day of classes left, Ammu and Abbu tell me to grab my stuff so we can get home. It's break time so everybody is milling around, and I don't look like the odd one out – as long as I can keep my anger and tears at bay. When I get to my locker to pick up my bag and books, I catch sight of Hani. She's standing by her own locker with Aisling and Dee. Crowded together and whispering. She doesn't even see me watching them.

For a moment, I wonder if this has all been an act. Our fake dating, our friendship, all of those moments we've spent together where I was sure that we felt the exact same way about each other. I know the way she makes me feel is real. More real than I want it to be.

Can Hani be that good of an actor?

I shake the thought away, grab my bag, and leave the school.

With the way everything is going, now is not the time to mull over Hani and our relationship. My life is off-kilter and I have to get it back on track somehow. I have to prove that I haven't been cheating, that Aisling is lying.

'What happened?' Abbu asks as soon as our car is on the road home. He catches my eye in the mirror for a moment, and Ammu wrings her fingers together on her lap.

'I don't know.' I shake my head. 'Aisling…the girl who accused me of cheating. She's the one who cheated off of me, and now she's lying because she obviously has something against me.'

Ammu and Abbu share a brief glance.

'I know things have been weird because of your sister,' Ammu says slowly. I guess she's playing good cop. 'But no university is going to accept you if they think you've been cheating. Forget about Head Girl.'

'I haven't been cheating, Ammu,' I insist. 'I wouldn't do that. Have I ever given you reason to believe I would? I've been going to that school for years! I've never come home with less than an A because I work my ass off. You've seen me study hard day and night. Why would you believe the word of someone you don't even know over me?'

Ammu shakes her head. 'OK...so you say you didn't cheat...'

I have to stop myself from groaning.

'Then...we have to find a way to prove that.'

'If we can do it quickly, you could still become Head Girl,' Abbu says. 'And we'll have to keep this whole thing under wraps. No word of it to anyone until we can clear everything up.'

I heave a sigh and stare out the window, at the buildings passing by. 'Ammu, Abbu...did Nik invite you to her engagement party?'

They share another glance between them. 'She did. She called us a while ago,' Ammu says. 'The wedding, too. It's over the summer. July.'

'That's so soon.' I turn to them. 'Where is it? In London?'

'Yes, I think so,' Ammu says.

'We're going, right?' Ammu and Abbu don't say anything. Abbu keeps driving, staring at the road ahead, and Ammu clenches her fingers on her lap, staring out the window.

'I want to go,' I try again. Louder. 'She's my only sister. She's your oldest daughter.'

'We're not going.' Abbu's voice suggests that it's already a done deal. That we're not discussing this any further.

'Are you really going to cut her off because she's dropping out of university?' I ask. 'Because she's not doing what you want her to do?'

'We're not cutting her off,' Ammu says. 'We just don't support what she's doing and we have to show her that, so that she can go back to the right path.'

'So...if I told you that I actually have been cheating all this time, you would cut me off too?' I ask. 'Because I'm not going down the right path?'

'No, of course not,' Ammu says immediately. She turns to me with pleading eyes. 'Can we just...talk about this later? We have to figure out a solution to your problem here.'

I cross my arms and sit back in my seat, because I know the answer. If we can't find a solution to my problem, maybe I won't be a part of this family either.

chapter thirty-four

Can I come over?

The text from Ishu has been sitting on my phone for a couple of hours now, but I only see it when I take my phone out of my locker at the end of the day.

Now? I type back, and the three dots indicating that she's typing show up immediately. Like she's been waiting for me to text her back.

Yes, comes her reply.

I had made plans with Dee and Aisling but considering Ishu left school after her interview, without a word, I assume that this is important. And I'm not going to leave her hanging.

I'll be home in twenty, I quickly text Ishu, before stuffing the necessary books into my bag and turning to Aisling and Dee.

'Hey…something came up. I have to go home.'

'Everything OK?' Dee asks, as Aisling folds her arms over her chest.

'Is this about your girlfriend?' she surprises me by asking.

'What?'

'Look…' Aisling takes a deep breath and nervously tucks a strand of hair behind her ear. 'I didn't want to be like…weird about it or whatever, but…I kind of reported her to Principal Gallagher. Ishita.'

'You reported her? For what?' I suddenly feel like I've entered into a parallel universe. This whole conversation feels surreal. The way Aisling is acting – closed off and nervous – feels like she's a whole different person altogether.

'Well. She kind of cheated off me in our biology class, so…I don't know.' Aisling shrugs. 'I had to say something, didn't I? It's not exactly fair. Who knows who else she's cheating off of? It's probably how she's top of the class. I mean, it wouldn't exactly be difficult for her. She can probably get most answers off of her sister—'

'Ishu doesn't cheat,' I say.

Aisling finally meets my gaze, a frown tugging down her lips at the edges. 'Well, then explain why she was copying off my test.'

'If she was, why didn't you tell Ms Taylor when it happened?' I ask.

'Because she's your girlfriend?' Aisling says. 'Because…I thought she was my friend?' Aisling takes a step back and shakes her head. She glances at Dee, like she's searching for support. 'I…talked to her about it, obviously. Before I went to the principal but…she wasn't going to turn herself in. I'm sorry, Maira. She's not good for us.' Except she doesn't sound sorry at all.

'Why are you only telling me now?' I ask. 'Why have you spent all this time pretending to be her friend? Why—'

'I was just trying to spare you,' Aisling says, with pity in her eyes. 'I knew it would hurt you and I was hoping she would come clean about it herself. Look, are we really surprised?' She glances at Dee once more, who shakes her head like she was expecting this all along. 'Ishita has always been weird and abrasive and…whatever.'

'She was never going to be Head Girl,' Dee says. 'She was playing you this entire time, Maira. She was obviously taking advantage of the fact that people like you. And she picked the best time, when you're still figuring out your sexuality or whatever.'

'I'm not…' I begin, before stopping myself. It's pointless. My head is swimming with so much stuff that I don't know where to start. I can feel the pounding of a headache starting. 'I have to go, OK?'

'You believe me, right?' There's a desperation in Aisling's voice that I've never heard before.

'See you guys tomorrow.'

Ishu is sitting on the ground by the front door when I arrive. She has her head buried between her knees, and she doesn't look up until I'm right next to her.

'Hey…'

'Hey.' She glances up. Her eyes are puffy and red like she's been crying.

'Um…you know you could have gone inside?' I ask. 'My mam is in there. If you'd just rang the doorbell—'

'I wanted to wait for you.' She gives me a weak smile.

'OK…' I open up the door and tell Amma that Ishu's here. She gives us both a smile before passing me a questioning look. She must notice how upset Ishu looks, but she doesn't ask any questions. The two of us head up to my bedroom.

Ishu is already changed out of her school uniform, so as she makes herself comfortable on my bed, I nip to the bathroom and get changed out of the itchy skirt, see-through shirt, and heavy jumper.

'My sister is getting married,' Ishu says when I come back. It's the last thing I expect her to say. 'And we're not even going to the wedding. Because my parents suck.'

'That's not what I expected you to say.' I sit down on the bed beside her. She looks at me with those watery eyes and attempts a weak smile.

'Aisling told you,' she says. 'I'm sure you believe her. You've been friends with her far longer than you've been friends with me.'

'I'm just…' I heave a sigh, rubbing my temples. It's only Tuesday. Nobody needs this kind of a headache on a Tuesday. 'I'm confused, I guess. I don't know what or who to believe.'

Ishu turns to me fully. 'Look…Aisling cheated off my test. She's tried to do it before. I've never let her. I let her this time because…'

'Because you wanted to be Head Girl,' I finish off when she trails. 'You were that desperate?'

'No.' Ishu shakes her head. 'Yes…I don't know. Not like it matters anyway. Principal Gallagher believes Aisling. I'm pretty sure even my parents believe her. Who's going to believe me? Nobody even likes me.'

'You have been top of our class for like ever,' I says. 'How can anybody possibly think you've been cheating?'

Ishu looks at me with that watery smile again. I've never seen her cry, but now I can see the tears glistening in her eyes, threatening to fall. 'Don't you see? I've fallen right into their fucking trap, haven't I?'

'What do you mean?'

'I've never fit into whatever goddamn boxes they've wanted to fit me into. Of course I could never be Head Girl, and now they've gleefully taken me down a peg by accusing me of cheating. And of course who's going to believe the brown, immigrant girl when Aisling is the one making the accusation?'

'I don't think that's what's going on here Ishu. That's so… devious. Aisling isn't like that,' I say.

Ishu shakes her head, wiping her tears away with the ends of her sleeves. 'She hasn't been making you feel like shit for being bisexual all this time?'

'She hasn't.' I shake my head. 'She told me that you were

her friend. She said that she talked to you about the whole thing before going to Ms Gallagher, and—'

'You really believe her?' Ishu sniffles.

'I don't know,' I say. 'I'm not sure what I believe.'

'Do you remember how Aisling and Deirdre punished you for being with me, before they agreed to even consider me as a part of their group?' Ishu asks. The party seems so long ago now, even though it was only a couple of weeks back. I don't think I'll ever forget how everybody was focused on me as Aisling and Dee singled me out for not drinking. For daring to be so visibly different. But would they go this far?

'You know…' Ishu says slowly. 'If I'd never agreed to date you, I would not be in this mess right now. I wish I hadn't accepted your offer.'

'My offer?' I fix her with a glare. 'You agreed to do this because you wanted to be Head Girl. I didn't cajole you. I didn't force you. When I called, you said you didn't want to do it and I was OK with that. You can't blame me now.'

'Actually, I can.' Ishu comes to a stand, rubbing away the last of her tears. 'Because I know you're going to stand with Aisling. No matter what…' She trails off, taking a deep breath, like she can't bear to think about us and our relationship any longer. 'I don't think we are right for each other anyway,' she says instead. 'We're two very different people.'

I'm not sure if I believe that, but I nod anyway. 'I guess we are.'

I don't try to stop Ishu as she gathers her things and walks towards the door. She hesitates by the edge of the door, and I feel my heart pick up speed. Beating so fast that I'm afraid it's going to burst right out of my chest.

'I hope you know that you deserve better friends than Aisling and Deirdre,' Ishu says finally. 'Friends who you don't have to hide yourself from, and who don't try to get you to be someone you're not.' With that, she slips out of the door.

I wait until I hear the click of the front door before I let my tears out.

chapter thirty-five

I feel like a fool for going to Hani's house, for thinking that she would actually stand with me. Hani is a lot of wonderful things, but she definitely isn't the type of person who can stand up to people. For as long as I've known her, I've seen her endure horrible things that her friends have said to her, or put her through.

Now, I guess I'm stuck in this mess all by myself, trying to figure out what comes next, with no one on my side.

I try to go to sleep when I'm home finally, but sleep doesn't come. I just toss and turn in bed, thinking of the fact that everything has gone wrong, in ways that I couldn't have imagined. Thinking about how I should have seen this all coming. How I should have never let my guard down, never let Hani in, never let myself…

I end up on my phone. First, on Hani's Instagram page, where she has far too many pictures of the two of us together. After I've stared at them all for so long that I've seared them into the back of my eyelids, I go on my sister's page, looking at her engagement photos once more. There were more than a dozen people at her engagement party, I can tell from looking at all of the different pictures. Most of them are friends – probably from university. But I also see Rakesh's family – his parents and siblings. It sends a jolt of pain through my chest. I should have been there. Ammu and Abbu should have been there.

Before I know it, I'm typing a message to Nik:

Saw your engagement party photos...congratulations.

Wish I could have been there.

To my surprise, the three dots indicating Nik is typing appear almost immediately.

I missed you and Ammu and Abbu.

I wish you could have been there too.

I chew on my lip as my fingers hover over the blank text box. What do I have to lose, I guess?

One of the girls in school accused me of cheating today...

I'm not allowed to run for Head Girl because of it.

And I don't think Hani and I are even friends any more.

I wait with bated breath for Nik to message back. The bottom of the messages say seen, but the dots to indicate she's typing don't show up. Five minutes pass. Then ten.

I take a deep breath and shake it off. I shouldn't have expected Nik to come to my rescue – not when everything else is going belly up. Sure, last time we spoke Nik said – insisted – that I could come to her about anything. But we've never had a relationship like that, so why would I even dream Nik would help me now?

I'm about to put the phone back on my nightstand to get back into bed for good when my phone buzzes with a phone call. From Nik.

I take a big gulp of air before answering.

'Hello?'

'Why didn't you tell me all of this was going on?' Nik's voice is high-pitched. There's the sound of clacking coming from the other side of the phone call. I wonder what she's doing for only a moment before she starts berating me again. 'Why didn't you tell me all of this was going on when you called me yesterday?'

I sigh. 'All of this stuff…just happened, really. It's been…a bad day.'

'The worst day, from the sounds of it,' Nik says. 'Are you… OK?'

'It's one o'clock in the morning and I'm wide awake, talking to you. What do you think?'

'Right…and it's a school night,' Nik adds. 'Look…I want to hear everything in excruciating detail. Maybe I can help?'

'OK—'

'But not now.' She cuts me off, her tone taking on some of the harshness that it usually has. 'I'm going to come over.'

'Nik…you live in another country,' I say. 'You can't just nip down.'

'Shut up. I've been looking up flights since you messaged me…I can get a flight out tomorrow morning—'

'Nik.'

'Ishu.'

'Nik.'

'Ishu.'

'Nik, how will you uprooting your life to come here help?'

'Because…it will,' she insists. 'Look…I know what Ammu and Abbu are like. And I know what that school is like. So…I'm coming. And it's not uprooting my life to take an hour's flight to the island next door, you eejit.'

I roll my eyes but can't help the smile that tugs at my lips. This is definitely more like the Nik I know. 'OK, I guess I can't stop you.'

'I'll see you tomorrow, Ishu. You'll be OK,' Nik says. 'You're…kind of the strongest person I know.'

'Can you say that again so I can record it?' I ask.

Nik laughs. 'Please. Get some sleep. Good night.'

I tuck the phone away and lie down on my bed, facing the ceiling with all of its chips and cracks. The smile on my lips widens. Yeah, everything is shit, but…at least this one thing is not as shit as it could be. At least Nik will be here soon. Maybe she can reconcile with Ammu or Abbu. Maybe she can help.

All I know is that it feels like I finally have someone on my side. Even if it's my annoying older sister.

When I pretend to be ill the next morning to get out of going to school and facing everybody's judgement, Ammu doesn't even blink. Like she was expecting exactly this.

'We're going to be at the shop all day, Ishu,' she says through a crack in my door. 'If you need anything, you call.'

'Got it.' I roll over in bed, trying not to think about the fact that Abbu and Ammu won't even bother taking a day off from work to make sure that I'm OK.

In all my years of school, I have never missed a single day. I have a strange feeling in the pit of my stomach about still being curled up in my bed midweek. It feels strange to be lying in bed when I could be studying. But what does it matter, anyway? It doesn't feel like any of it matters as I stare up at my ceiling.

My phone pings with a text and when I pick it up, there's a message from Nik:

Are Abbu and Ammu out? I'm coming...on the road.

I type back a quick text before going back to staring at my ceiling listlessly: **they're at the shop...will be gone all day probs.**

The next thing I know, the bell is ringing. I finally crawl out of bed, rubbing sleep out of my eyes and stretching laziness out of my body.

When I open the door, Nik looks me up and down with a frown. 'God, you look awful.'

'Thank you.' I roll my eyes. 'Exactly what I wanted to hear.' Nik follows me inside, putting down her backpack by the side of the door.

'You've just been home all day?' she asks. 'Just…lying in bed?'

I shrug. 'Yeah.'

'And Ammu and Abbu just left you?'

I shrug, and Nik heaves a sigh.

'Well, get dressed, all right?'

'What?' When I turn around, she's adjusting her shirt like she's getting ready to leave. 'I thought we were going to talk or something. Come up with a plan, or—'

Nik shoots me a glare. 'We can talk later. First, we have to fix everything. To do that you need to get dressed.'

'But—'

'No questions, Ishita. Get dressed – we're going.'

The last thing I want to do is let Nik drag me off somewhere, but she did fly all the way here to help me. So I can hardly turn her down. I slip into jeans and a t-shirt before stumbling down the stairs. I guess Nik isn't particularly happy with what I've done because she looks me up and down once more and sighs.

Digging into her bag, she pulls out a hair brush and smooths down my hair, parting it right in the middle and pulling out all the tangles. 'Better,' she says, though she's obviously not super satisfied.

Still, we head outside. She unlocks her car – 'Rental,' she says while guiding me in – and we head off.

hani

AMMA OBVIOUSLY KNOWS SOMETHING IS WRONG without me having to tell her. After Ishu is gone, and I've been holed up in my room for too long to explain away, she comes in, her feet shuffling against the plush carpet softly as she settles down on the bed beside me.

She brushes locks of hair out of my face and wipes a thumb over my cheeks to wipe away any remnants of dried tears. 'Did you and Ishu have a fight?' she asks.

I shake my head while sitting up. 'No...yes...kind of. I don't know.' I don't know if I can describe what we had as a fight. That doesn't feel like it's doing it any justice. 'It's... complicated.'

'I'm listening,' Ammu says.

Then, before I can really even think about it, everything is pouring out of me in great big waves. From Aisling and Dee's dismissal of my bisexuality all those weeks ago, to Ishu and I agreeing to start a fake relationship, all the way to our growing closeness, Aisling's accusation, and our fight. Ammu listens with rapt attention, her expression almost never changing. When I finally reach the end, Ammu nods her head sagely like she understands exactly what I'm going through.

'Why didn't you tell me any of this before?' she asks after a brief pause.

I can only shrug. Maybe if I had told her from the beginning, I wouldn't be stuck in this mess. Maybe she would have helped me make better choices to begin with.

'I don't think you've exactly been fair to Ishu here,' Amma says finally. 'Do you?'

'I don't know...' I trail off. 'I mean...Aisling and Dee are my friends.'

'And Ishu isn't?' she asks.

'Ishu is...I mean...I've known Aisling and Dee for a lot longer. They've been with me through so much.' Aisling and I have been best friends since primary school. We met Dee in our first year of secondary school. We've been doing everything together for years. We have always supported each other...haven't we?

'That doesn't mean you should be unfair to Ishu.' Amma sighs. 'Do you believe Ishu would really cheat on her biology test?'

'Ishu is the most hardworking person I know,' I say. 'And the smartest. She could probably regurgitate our entire biology book if I asked her. But...why would Aisling lie?'

'I think you'll have to talk to her about that,' Amma says. The thought of confronting Aisling sets my stomach rolling. When

I say that to Amma she fixes me with a glare. 'If you and Aisling are really friends, you should be able to talk to her about this. Friends can talk about things. They can figure things out. Get past things. Do you want a friend in your life who you can never disagree with? A friend who you can't grow with?'

'I guess not.' I sigh. The thing is I don't even know any more what kind of friends Aisling and I are. And – if I'm being honest – I'm afraid of finding out.

Ishu is not at school the next morning. It's probably for the best because people are already talking about how she cheated on her biology test. They're wondering what else is true or false about her – if they couldn't even rely on her being the top of our classes. I know I should defend her – as far as everyone at school knows, Ishu and I are still together – but I can't bear the thought of going up to people I barely know just to defend Ishu. Especially when I don't even know what the truth is. Especially when it'll get back to Aisling.

'Hey, are you OK?' Aisling asks when she comes around to my locker. She even leans in and gives me a hug, like she feels sorry for me and everything I'm going through. 'Did you and Ishita talk?'

'Yeah,' I stuff the last of my books into my locker and close the door. It makes a satisfactory click. 'Ishita said she didn't cheat off you.'

'Obviously she would say that.' Aisling leans against the locker next to me and looks at me with pity in her eyes. 'But… well, the truth is the truth.'

'It is…' I say. 'I wish…I wish you'd tell me the truth, Aisling.' I say it softly, but the change in Aisling's face is immediate. Her soft and piteous expression hardens, like I've made an accusation. She stands up straight and shoots me a small glare.

'I am telling you the truth, Maira. I wouldn't lie to you. I've been trying to look out for you this whole time.'

I rub my elbows and look down at the speckled grey floor, wishing that it would swallow me up. I don't know how to have this conversation. I don't want to have this conversation. 'It's just…' I start. 'Ishita wouldn't—'

'You've been with Ishita for, like, a couple of weeks. We've been best friends our whole lives, Maira. Come on, don't do this. Sisters before misters, right?' Her hand presses on to my shoulder. When I look up and meet her gaze she's smiling sympathetically. 'Don't worry. Dee and I will find you someone way better than Ishita. Even a girl if you really swing that way.'

I step back from her grip, keeping my eyes steadily on her. 'What do you mean…if I really swing that way?'

'I mean…' Aisling rolls her eyes. 'Come on, you know what I mean. I figured you're still making up your mind. Whatever you want, is what I mean.'

I shake my head. 'Aisling…you know that I'm bisexual.

That's not swinging one way or another way,' I say. 'I don't know why you've been so weird about it.'

Aisling sighs and folds her arms over her chest. 'I don't know why *you're* being so weird about it. It doesn't have to be such a big deal. You're going to end up with one or the other at the end of the day, so.'

'That doesn't mean my sexuality changes. Is that why you've been calling Ishu and me lesbians, because you think two girls being together have to be lesbians?'

Aisling rolls her eyes again. 'Why is this even a thing? Everyone knows that you're going to be with a guy at the end of the day, and this whole bisexuality thing is your way of seeming interesting or whatever. Like you're so Muslim you won't even drink a drop of alcohol and you want us to think you're for real gay?'

'Wow.' I shake my head. I'm not even sure how to respond to her, or how to set her right about Muslims and gay people. I had thought that she and Dee were finally coming around, what with them actually spending time with me and Ishu, and actually seeming to get along with Ishu. It seems like the whole thing has been off-track from the beginning. Maybe Aisling and Dee were never going to come around, no matter what I said to them.

'I should go to class.' I swing my bag over my shoulder. Aisling just looks at me with that frown on her lips. For a moment, I think she's going to say something more, try to defend her position more. But as I turn and head away from her, she doesn't say another word.

chapter thirty-seven

~ishu

Nik and I don't talk during most of the drive. With each turn, I get more and more nervous. The road we're driving down feels disturbingly familiar.

'What exactly are we doing?' I ask.

'Fixing things,' Nik says, staring straight ahead. 'Don't worry, you'll feel a lot better after this.'

By the time we're taking the last turn, my stomach is in shambles and I'm pretty sure I'm going to throw up.

'Nik…I didn't come to school today for a reason!' I exclaim. 'Why are we here?'

'Trust me, OK?' Nik reaches forwards and takes my hand into hers. She gives my fingers a reassuring squeeze. 'I would not bring you here if I didn't know exactly what I was doing. Come on.'

It's two o'clock, so lunchtime has thankfully already passed. The hallways are deserted as Nik and I enter, Nik with her head held high and me all but cowering behind her.

'Hi…we have an appointment with the principal,' Nik

says, tapping on the secretary's glass separation.

'Oh…' Anna looks up from her phone. Her face transforms from confused to happy as soon as she recognises Nik. 'Nikhita!' she says. 'So good to see you!'

'Oh…same.' Nik puts on her best polite smile. 'Principal Gallagher?'

'Right…you can go ahead. She's in her office.'

'Perfect, thanks.'

'Nik…' I say as I trail behind her. She has a laser-focused gaze as she marches towards Principal Gallagher's door. 'I just don't know if—'

I don't get to finish my sentence, because the next moment, Nik has opened up the door to the principal's office. Ms Gallagher is on the phone, in deep conversation. She glances up at our arrival, her face darkening when she spots the two of us.

'I'll call you back. I have a meeting,' she mumbles into the phone while waving the two of us in. I take a seat, the same one that I was sitting on yesterday when my life got turned upside down. Nik stands, her arms crossed and her feet tapping loudly against the floor.

'Nikhita!' Ms Gallagher says as soon as she's hung up the phone. 'It's so great to see you again! How is UCL?'

Nik rolls her eyes. 'Ms Gallagher, I'm here about my sister. It seems she's been unfairly accused of cheating. By you.'

'Not…not by me,' Ms Gallagher recoils in feigned shock. Like she wasn't the one who ambushed me in her office with

Ammu and Abbu to tell me about Aisling's accusation.

'By a student, whatever.' Nik waves her hand like it doesn't matter either way. 'It's a false accusation. I know that Ishita hasn't cheated. You know that Ishita hasn't cheated. Prolonging this process with your ridiculous investigation while disallowing her to run for Head Girl is deeply unfair.'

'An investigation is just how the process works when a student has been accused of cheating.' Ms Gallagher's voice is full of sympathy, but there is none on her face. I suspect there's even a little glee dancing behind her eyes. Like she's beaten me and my sister down. After all, we have both been top of the class for our entire careers in this school. 'There's really nothing I can do about it. I'm sorry that you've come all the way here to—'

'Can I see the tests?' Nik doesn't even seem to be listening to her words. 'Both of them?'

'I'm not sure if—'

'You showed my parents,' I cut in. 'Nik is a guardian.'

Ms Gallagher heaves a sigh before walking to her desk and rifling around one of the drawers. Finally, she takes both of the tests and places them on the table. Nik is quick to swoop down and look through them, her tongue clicking as she flicks through the pages.

'And can we call the student in question to the office?' She asks, glancing up at Ms Gallagher once more.

'She would really prefer to remain anonymous,' Ms Gallagher says.

'Her name is right here on the test.' Nik holds it up, folding the sticky note up, so we can all see 'Aisling Mahoney' scribbled on to the top.

Ms Gallagher heaves a sigh. 'Is this really necessary, Nikhita? I understand that Ishita is your sister—'

'Ms Gallagher.' Nik's smile is forced, like it's really paining her. 'I'm just trying to save you time here. Please.'

Ms Gallagher presses the intercom on her desk. 'Can Aisling Mahoney please come to the principal's office? Can Aisling Mahony please come to the principal's office?' The announcement echoes for a moment before Principal Gallagher turns back to Nik.

'You know, Aisling really is a fantastic student. Liked by all her peers and her teachers. I can't see a single reason why she would cheat on her test. Nor why she would accuse Ishita of cheating if she hadn't. Really, she sounded quite distressed when she came to me about the situation. Said Ishita was a friend, and she really didn't want to make things difficult.'

Nik gives Ms Gallagher a tight smile. 'I guess we'll see.'

There's a knock on the door, and then it swings open. Aisling steps in gingerly, looking from me, to Nik, to Ms Gallagher. Her eyes are wide with concern.

'Um, you asked for me, Principal Gallagher?'

'Please, take a seat.' Ms Gallagher offers her a genuinely kind smile.

Aisling sits down right beside me and shoots me a curious glance. 'Hey, Ishita. I thought you weren't in school today?'

I look away, up at my sister, and purse my lips.

'Aisling…can you tell me what a scramble competition is?' Nik asks.

My heart thumps. I remember that question from the test. Aisling glances at Ms Gallagher, instead of Nik.

'Principal Gallagher, what is this?' she asks.

Principal Gallagher, for once, doesn't help her out much. She shakes her head and says, 'Aisling, please answer the question.'

Aisling glances at me now, like she thinks I'm about to give her the answer. Finally, she holds Nik's gaze and parts her lips.

'Umm…scramble competition. When people scramble and compete with each other?'

Nik's lips twitch and I can tell she's trying to hold in a triumphant smile. She swiftly turns to me with a raised eyebrow. 'Scramble competition?'

'Scramble competition is when organisms are all struggling for a scarce resource.'

'And what's a saprophyte?' Nik jumps to the next question, her gaze on Aisling once more.

Aisling doesn't even try this time. She stares down at the carpeted office floor and shakes her head. 'I don't know.'

'A saprophyte is an organism that feeds on dead matter,' I offer.

Nik looks back at Principal Gallagher. 'They both answered these questions correctly,' she says. 'But Aisling doesn't seem to know any of the answers.' Handing the test papers back to

Ms Gallagher, she says, 'I rest my case.'

Shaking her head, Ms Gallagher mumbles, 'I'm very disappointed.' Though she doesn't look particularly disappointed as she sighs and shuffles to the other side of the table.

Beside me, Aisling is blinking back tears, though she doesn't struggle for long before her loud sniffles fill up the room. She wipes at her tears, bending down like she's trying to hide the very obvious fact that she's crying.

'I'm s-s-sorry.'

Ms Gallagher leans forwards, passing Aisling the box of tissues on her desk. She even gives her a pat on her hand, like Aisling is a misbehaving pet and not a manipulative bitch.

'Aisling, I think you can go,' she says.

Aisling looks up at Ms Gallagher with wide eyes, wiping away more tears with the back of her hand. She doesn't waste any time. Mumbling a soft, 'T-thank you,' she darts out the door.

'So I'm assuming there will be an investigation into her conduct?' Nik asks. 'I mean, not only was she cheating but she was also harassing Ishita with this false accusation?'

'I don't think that'll be necessary,' Principal Gallagher says grimly. 'I think we've traumatised the poor girl enough. Ishita didn't cheat on the test, Aisling did. I will accept that and we will move on. Ishita can continue on in the election for Head Girl; she has our endorsement. Thank you for clearing everything up for everyone, Nikhita.'

'So, Ishita had to be scrutinised, embarrassed in front

of our parents…and Aisling gets off scot-free? With no consequences?'

'There will be consequences,' Principal Gallagher says unconvincingly. 'Detention—'

'Detention.' Nik scoffs. I'm already getting up from my chair. At least my name is cleared, whatever happens – or doesn't happen – to Aisling.

'We should go, Nik,' I mumble.

'Ishu—'

'Please?'

Nik heaves a sigh of her own, settling Ms Gallagher with one last glare, before the two of us slip outside.

chapter thirty-eight

'YOU COULD HAVE TOLD ME YOU WERE GOING TO DO that, you know.' I tell Nik back in the car. I don't exactly feel relief from the truth finally coming out, but at least some of the overbearing pressure weighing on me seems to have lifted. I feel lighter.

Nik smirks at me from the driver's seat. 'The fun is in the surprise.'

'Not when my school career is at stake…' I say. 'Where are we going?'

Nik is turning on to the wrong road, not the one that will lead us home.

'We should celebrate the fact that we've bested that fucked-up school, and – whatever that girl's name is,' Nik says. 'Lunch, on me.'

'Aisling.' The feel of her name against my tongue fills me with a kind of dread. 'I can't believe the school won't even do anything to her…'

'Let's not think about that,' Nik says. She pulls the car into park in front of Mao's. 'Thai food?'

Later on, as Nik forks pad thai into her mouth, her gaze rests on me – curiosity flickering in her eyes.

'What?' I ask, when she's been staring wordlessly for long enough to make me feel uncomfortable.

'Tell me what happened with Hani.'

'I don't want to talk about that.' I shove a forkful of noodles into my mouth to avoid talking. Nik just pokes me on my side.

'I flew all the way over here—'

"Oo can' juz' use tha' 'scuze.'

Nik rolls her eyes. 'I'm not going to stop bothering you until you tell me everything. Doesn't matter if you're eating. I'm your sister – I can help you deal with all of this.' She raises an eyebrow almost threateningly. I swallow down my noodles and heave a sigh.

'It's complicated.'

'Would it even be romance if it wasn't?'

I play with the noodles with my fork for a moment, before launching into it. 'The thing is…Aisling is kind of Hani's best friend.'

Whatever Nik was expecting, I guess it wasn't that, because she almost falls off her chair with the shock of it. The knife and fork she was using drops to the ground with a clatter. The other customers at the restaurant look over at us with glares. Nik shoots them polite smiles and bends down to pick up the cutlery, before setting it down on the table and staring me down.

'Hani doesn't seem like the type of person to be friends with her. I mean…I don't know…'

I shrug. 'I don't know why they're friends, really. Just that they've been for as long as I remember. Well…Hani was on her side, obviously.'

'Hani thought you cheated on the test?' Nik's voice goes up as she says it.

'Well…not exactly.'

'So…'

'She…I don't know. She kept saying she was confused. She didn't know who to believe.'

'And then you two broke up?'

Instead of answering, I put another forkful of noodles into my mouth and begin to chew. At least that's keeping the lump from my throat, and keeping the tears at bay.

'So…you broke up with her, huh?' Nik goes back to her pad thai. 'You know, Ishu – I know you're a lot of things… abrasive, closed-off, cold, a little mean-spirited sometimes, jealous, definitely, and for sure—'

'Nik!'

'Sorry.' Nik smiles. 'I just never thought you were a fool. Cleverness is something you've always had going for you.'

'What are you talking about?' I ask.

'Well…you just gave Aisling everything. You gave up the girl you care about and want to be with instead of fighting for her, or even explaining your side of the story to her. You sent her right to Aisling. Why would she believe you when you gave up on her so easily?' Nik isn't looking at me. She's just taking small bites of noodles as she speaks.

'We were never even together to begin with, Nik. The whole thing…it was all a lie. I thought at least she could be a friend, but…she's not even that. She was *never* going to believe me,' I say. 'I bet Aisling has already spun some lies to make Hani believe that she isn't actually at fault. That it's all me, actually. She's…she's different when she's with her white friends. She tries to change herself to be more like them, to fit in or whatever. I don't even know if I want to be with someone like that.'

Nik settles me with a glare. 'You can hardly be angry with her for that.'

'Yes, I can,' I say, settling Nik with a glare of my own.

'It's not like you're always exactly yourself. You do things just because Ammu and Abbu think you should. Would you have let Aisling and Principal Gallagher walk all over you like that if Ammu and Abbu hadn't been there?'

'Well, no. But that's different. They're my parents.'

'My point, dear sister, is that we all have people who we bend ourselves for the approval of. For you and me, it's Ammu and Abbu. For Hani, it's her friends. We all need to fit in, or need to be loved, or need approval. You and Hani aren't that different, if you think about it.'

Nik is wrong. I know she is. I'm not bending myself or being someone I'm not because of Ammu or Abbu. They've never asked me to be what I'm not, have they? They didn't ask me to be Head Girl, but…would I have tried to be Head Girl if I didn't think it would get me their approval?

The noodles suddenly taste like cardboard in my mouth. I gulp down the mouthful I was chewing and push the rest of it away.

'Anyway, I know you were more than just "fake dating" Hani,' Nik says matter-of-factly.

'I was *not*.' I cross my arms over my chest, but I guess my defensiveness is not convincing because Nik smiles.

'You obviously care about her,' she presses.

I shake my head, because yeah, maybe I do. But I don't *want* to. If all of this has proved anything, it's that Hani and I aren't a good fit. That I should have never given weight to my feelings. Maybe then, all of this wouldn't hurt so bad.

'Can we move on and talk for a second about you and this wedding? Are Ammu and Abbu really not going to come?'

Nik sighs, and pushes away the rest of her pad thai too. Like this conversation has immediately made her lose her appetite. 'Look…I told them that…I'm not going back to university. That was the last straw for them, I guess. They said they were never going to come to my wedding if Rakesh and I were veering my life off course.' She shrugs like the whole thing is no big deal, but I can see her hands shaking underneath the table. I reach forwards and take her hands in mine.

'Why aren't you going back to university? Is it…are you…'

'Ishu…I never told you this, but…I never wanted to study medicine. Or…maybe I did. I don't know.' Nik shakes her head. 'The thing is, I was so caught up in what Ammu and Abbu wanted that I never spent a second thinking about what I wanted. They convinced me that studying medicine and going to UCL would be the best thing I could ever do with my life. I wanted to make them proud, and I was so used to competing. With you, with other students at school. So I just went along with it, and it was only when I got there, when I was in university, that I realised I hated it all. That I hated everything that we had been doing, really.'

She heaves a sigh and gives my hands a squeeze. I think it's to give herself strength more than anything else. 'My first year at university was awful. I was doing terribly in all of my classes and after competing and winning my entire life it was like…everything was upside down. And I was so determined to succeed in something that I didn't even like or want that I became depressed, I stopped eating, stopped…taking care of myself, mentally and physically. Thank God I met Rakesh.'

'He helped?'

She nods. 'So much. I mean, at first we were just friends, and he helped me study and get back on track. His older sister is a doctor so she helped me out a lot. I passed my exams… barely. I didn't come back to visit because I was so afraid of disappointing Abbu and Ammu…which is awful, you know? I wanted to see them, I wanted to see you. I wanted to come back home, sleep in my bed, but I was paralysed with fear about what Ammu and Abbu would say if I showed up with my barely passing grades. So I just stayed in London. Rakesh and I started dating and the more time that went by the more I realised just how much I didn't want to do this any more. At first, I thought I would take a year off from university. That was when I came here and I…used Rakesh and our engagement as an excuse when I shouldn't have. He has nothing to do with it. He was just an excuse I was using to deal with Abbu and Ammu's disappointment.'

'So…what do you want to do then?' I ask.

Nik sighs. 'You know, I'm not really sure. I think what I want is a little bit of time just to figure that out. It's like…ever since I decided to drop out…a cloud has parted over my head and I'm finally coming to terms with who I am. It feels like when you get out of a bad relationship and you have to learn about who you are all by yourself, you know?'

'No, but…I guess?' I say.

Nik smiles. 'Right. I guess Hani was your first relationship.'

'First *fake* relationship…' I try not to think too much about the *was*, and the fact that so much of it felt real.

'You know you can still fix things with her.' Nik tilts her head to the side as she observes me. 'It's not too late.'

I shrug. 'It doesn't matter. I just want to focus on getting back on track. I can't let everything I've worked for fall apart because of Hani and her shitty best friend.'

Nik sighs. 'So…I wanted to talk to you about that. The whole doctor thing…that's really something you want to do?'

'Well. Yeah.' I blink up at her. I guess I never thought of anything else I could do, but it's definitely what motivates me.

'Because…if it's just Ammu and Abbu pushing you, there's still time for you to reconsider. I'd help you out, no matter what happened. I hope you know that. I'm only an hour's flight away.'

'Thanks, Nik.' I shoot her a smile. She clutches my hands in hers tightly, and the warmth of the touch sends warmth throughout my whole body. I can't remember the last time Nik and I spoke like this. I don't think we ever have.

It's kind of nice to have an older sister looking out for you.

chapter thirty-nine

THE NEXT FEW DAYS OF SCHOOL DRAG BY SLOWLY, BUT at home everything is a rush. The election is only a few days away and it feels like there's so much to do, and not enough time to do it. Abba goes to the mosque almost every day, praying shoulder-to-shoulder with the Muslims in the community before trying to smoothly convince them to vote for him.

I tag along with him whenever he goes, carrying a stack of his flyers as I stumble into the women's balcony all by myself.

The good thing about the rush of Abba's election is that it doesn't really give me a lot of time to think about Aisling and Dee and…Ishu. It's been days since I've spoken to any of them, even though I keep picking up the phone to text Ishu about every little thing. But I know it isn't right. I can't reach out to her when I haven't figured out where I stand. When I'm not sure if I can make up for the things that Aisling has done. When I don't even have the guts to call Aisling out for what she's done.

I've been avoiding Aisling and Dee like the plague too.

That's been a little difficult since we share almost every single class together and usually spend our lunches together. But I've changed seats in all our classes, sitting towards the front where I can feel Aisling and Dee's disapproving frowns. And during lunchtime I sneak outside, towards the front of the school. I sit with my back against the trunk of a tree and eat my lunch alone, trying to forget about the fact that in the past few weeks it seems that everything in my life has shifted. And I don't know how to make things better.

On Friday afternoon, I come home to find Abba in the sitting room with his head buried in his hands. Amma is sitting beside him, her hands moving in soothing circles on his shoulders.

I shut the front door behind me as softly as I can, but both of them look up at the click of it. Amma puts on her usual smile, and Abba contorts his expression into something that's definitely supposed to reassure – but doesn't. A smile that looks more like a grimace.

'Is everything OK?' I ask. I can't imagine what would lead to Abba being upset – unless something has already come out about the election.

'Everything is fine.' Amma smiles, but I must not look convinced because the next moment Amma and Abba share a look between them.

'Your Abba is just a little stressed about what tomorrow is going to be like,' she finally says with a sigh. 'But…we've done all that we can.' She looks pointedly at Abba as she says this.

Abba sits back and heaves a sigh. He doesn't seem convinced by Amma's words either but he nods and repeats, 'We've done all that we can.'

The words open up a pit in my stomach. *Have* we done all that we can? I never told Abba about how I skipped out on canvassing the other day. How Aisling and Dee convinced me to go into town and celebrate with their boyfriends instead. I've been so caught up with Aisling, Dee, and Ishu that for so much of this election, I've neglected Abba and what I should have been doing for him.

Amma stands up and claps her hands together. 'There's no point sitting around stressing about what may or may not happen tomorrow. How about I make us all a nice dinner?'

Abba nods in agreement, and Amma drifts off into the kitchen. I can tell that Abba doesn't really feel much better about everything, though.

I squeeze into the sofa next to him, even though I'm still wearing my school uniform.

'Something happened to make you stressed out now, didn't it?' I ask slowly.

Abba heaves a sigh. 'We got some poll results that…don't look very positive.'

'Poll results are wrong a lot of the time,' I point out. 'Things can still turn around.'

Abba turns to me with a smile. 'Your Amma tells me that you've been dealing with a few things yourself.'

I shift around uncomfortably on the couch for a moment.

The last thing I want to do is unload all of my problems on to Abba the day before his big election. 'I'm fine.'

'Hani…you know you can always talk to me about anything at any time,' he says. 'Your Amma…she's been a little worried about you.'

'And she's been worried about you,' I say.

His smile widens. 'So, if we help each other out, maybe your Amma will worry a lot less.'

Slowly, I fill Abba in on everything that's been going on with Aisling, Dee, and Ishu. 'I know that I need to do something to make it up to Ishu for everything that I've done, but…I don't know how to apologise to her. Not when I can't even really confront Aisling or Dee. I don't know how to… make things right with anyone.'

Abba looks at me thoughtfully for a moment. 'If you were Ishu in this situation, what would make things better?'

I have to think about that for a few minutes. It's not exactly easy to place myself into Ishu's headspace. We're so different. When I think of her now, all I can think of is that day she was sitting outside our door, looking small and broken. 'I think I would just want to know that…someone I considered my friend didn't think the worst of me.'

'So, you just need to find a way to show her that.' Abba says it as if that's the easiest thing in the world. But how can I *show* Ishu that she's important to me? That I haven't chosen Aisling or Dee over her? And when I think of what the answer to those questions might be, I'm not sure if I'm strong enough to show Ishu that she can trust me, that we *are* friends…and maybe more. Maybe Ishu is right…maybe we are too different from each other to be together. Maybe we're too different from each other to even be in each other's lives. Maybe the reason why the two of us haven't been friends all this time isn't because of our fear that we would be pushed together, but because of our differences.

I wake up the next morning to an overcast sky and drizzling rain tapping against my window. Amma makes porota and halwa for breakfast, and it's supposed to be celebratory but nothing in the atmosphere of our house feels celebratory.

Amma has a PTA meeting, so it's just me and Abba driving down to the polling station together. It's in a primary school only a ten-minute drive away, but it feels longer. For the first time in the past few weeks, I'm not really thinking of my friends or Ishu, but of exactly what this election could mean for us.

We barely have the chance to shuffle out of the car before Abba spots familiar faces from the mosque outside the school building. There are a few people that I recognise – like Salim Uncle – but most of the faces are unfamiliar. I can tell that most of them are not Bengali.

'Assalam Alaikum,' Abba says as he approaches them slowly. His glum expression slowly transforms into the polite, political smile he's developed throughout this election campaign.

'Walaikum Salam,' all the Uncles murmur back in unison.

'We were just talking about how this is a historic moment,' Salim Uncle says. 'One of our own is about to become a councilor!'

Abba's smile is strained. 'Well…Insha'Allah.'

'Sajib, you've really done an amazing job on this campaign,' one of the Uncles – a tall man with pale skin and a black moustache – says. 'I've been seeing your posters all over everywhere…and the people who came knocking on my door to convince me to vote for you? Phenomenal. If I wasn't already voting for you, they definitely would have convinced me.'

Salim Uncle's expression shifts slightly. He turns to Abba with a slight frown. 'You had canvassers?'

'A few,' he admits. 'It's difficult to coordinate too many over the course of the elections, but I managed to send out a few different groups. And…Hani.' At this, he turns to me, putting his arms all the way around my shoulders. 'She helped me out a lot. She convinced her friends to give up their Sunday afternoon to canvass…so who knows what other kind of convincing she's done?'

I try to smile, but all the while I can feel the gnawing guilt in my stomach. Abba didn't ask much of me during this election – this *historic* time, as Salim Uncle put it. But I didn't even do the bare minimum to help him.

Salim Uncle seems to consider me for a moment, before turning back to Abba. 'I think you should have probably targeted our neighbourhood too,' he says. 'I don't remember any canvassers in our area who were campaigning for you. But, well…what's done is done.' He heaves a sigh, as if it pains him that nobody came to his door to convince him to vote for someone he was already voting for. 'Let's go in, shall we?'

I take a photo of Abba with the polling station sign before he goes in with the rest of the men from the mosque. I tell Abba that I'll wait for him in the car.

As soon as Abba is inside, I pull my phone out of my pocket. I haven't spoken to any of my friends for so long that it feels strange to pull up the group chat with Dee and Aisling.

Hey…are your parents voting for my dad today?

I hit send before I can think about it too much. After all, just because we're in a fight doesn't mean that we're not *friends* any more. Right?

Aisling's reply comes almost immediately: **oh, so *now* we're OK to talk to?**

I heave a sigh. I don't know why I expected anything more from Aisling. I wait for her to say something more – yes, her parents were still voting for Abba, or no, they aren't. But there are no more messages.

hani

IT'S ALMOST TWENTY MINUTES BEFORE ABBA FINALLY comes back to the car. Waving goodbye to all the Uncles, he opens up the car door and slips inside. He lets out a sigh of relief as soon as the door clicks shut behind him and leans back in his seat with his eyes closed.

'I wish I could vote,' I offer when the silence stretches out for a few minutes too long. 'That would be one more for you.'

Abba finally blinks his eyes open, a small smile appearing on his lips. It's the first genuine smile I've seen on him all day. 'Hani, you've already done more than enough for me and for this election,' he says. 'I mean…going to the mosque with me all the time, getting your friends to come and support me during rallies, gathering up your friends to help you canvass… putting up with Salim Uncle.'

'He's not…that bad,' I say, trying to muster up a laugh. It feels hollow, because all I can think about is how Abba thinks that I went above and beyond to support him. When really…I could be the reason that he loses the election. And he won't ever even suspect it.

Abba's smile widens. 'I know that you and your Amma aren't exactly his fans, but…he's an important member of the community. Without him, I'm not sure I would even have a chance at this election. Though I guess, even with him, I'm not sure about my chances.'

I shift in my seat, pulling at my seatbelt and wishing that Abba would just start the car. That we could just go home so I can try and put what I've done out of my mind. Except…I don't know if I can. What if Abba loses this election? What if that's because of me?

The car jumps to life as Abba starts the ignition. His knuckles are white against the steering wheel as he pulls out of the car park and on to the road. All the while, my mind is whirring. For the past few weeks, I've been thinking about all the lies that I've told – to my friends, to Amma and Abba… and wouldn't things have just been better if I told the truth to begin with? I definitely wouldn't be in this mess if I had.

So by the time Abba parks the car in front of our house, I've made up my mind about what I'm going to do.

'Abba,' I say, unbuckling my seat belt as he puts the car in park.

'Hmm?'

'You know how I told you about my friends?' I ask slowly. 'The way that…they don't always listen to me. And…well, everything that's happened with Ishu?'

'Right.' Abba nods. 'Did something else happen?'

'Well…' I look out the window, at the rain rolling down the glass. It's coming down much harder than it was this morning, and I can hear the raindrops hit the gravel of the road. 'The other week…when you asked me to take my friends canvassing…I don't know what happened. I shouldn't have listened to them, but…I guess, I let them talk me into not doing it. I thought I'd make up for it later, but I…didn't.' It sounds worse when I say it. I can barely get the words out. Because I'm not even sure who's to blame here.

For a moment, there's only silence inside the car, punctuated by the sound of the rain outside. When I glance at Abba, he's staring straight ahead, his lips pressed into a thin line.

'Abba…I'm sorry.' My voice comes out in a whisper. Abba just shakes his head slowly. He closes his eyes and takes a deep breath.

'So, when Salim said that nobody canvassed around his house, it was because of you and your friends,' Abba finally says. There's a strange calmness to his voice that fills me with dread.

'Yeah…probably,' I say. 'I shouldn't have listened to my friends that day. I know. I know I let you down. I know that—'

'If Salim finds out about this,' Abba cuts me off, 'do you know how this will look for me? I've been telling him, telling everyone, that my family have been supporting me throughout this entire election campaign. I've been singing your praises, talking about everything that you've done for me and the campaign. But you've been lying to me this whole time.'

'Only about this,' I say. 'I haven't lied about anything else. And Salim Uncle never has to find out, nobody does. I just…I wanted to tell you because I know you're worried about what's going to happen with this election and…I know I should have been better.'

Abba shakes his head, like he can't quite believe the words coming out of my lips. 'I know you've been having trouble with your friends, Hani. But I thought you were better than this.'

'That's not fair,' I say. 'You've been lying too.' At this, Abba's gaze finally snaps to me, his eyebrows scrunched together as he takes me in.

'You said that if Salim Uncle finds out that *I've* lied it'll look bad but…what about you? You've spent all this time lying to him and pretending that you're someone you're not. Going to the mosque every other day, when you and Amma never went to the mosque before this. You've been trying to get votes from the Muslim community, but you don't even care about them and what they want.' I'm not sure where all of that comes from, but suddenly it's all out there. Abba is still looking at me, but I can't meet his eyes. Suddenly, this car feels uncomfortably warm, and the silence inside it is deafening.

'I said…I *am* sorry,' I finally say in a whisper, though it doesn't feel like much. The guilt is twisting in my gut but so is a bite of anger that I didn't even know I was carrying with me all this time. After all, aren't all of the things I've said true? I'm not the only person who's been pretending for the past few weeks. I'm trying to make things right, Abba. But you…if you win this election, your lie will just continue on. Salim Uncle and the rest of them…they won't know that you were never winning for them – you were doing it for yourself.'

I watch as Abba takes one deep, long breath. Then he pulls the keys out of the car's ignition, clicks open the door and steps outside into the pouring rain. He doesn't even wait for me to get out. Instead, he walks up to the house and pulls the front door open, disappearing inside.

There are tears fighting their way through me, but I blink them back. My phone buzzes in my pocket, and when I check the notifications, I see that I finally have another new message in our group chat.

Deirdre: my parents don't really support your dad's policies so nope.

And somehow that clears up my tears, unclogs my throat of the lump that's been slowly rising throughout my entire conversation with Abba. Because finally – finally – I know exactly what I have to do. And maybe I'm angry enough now to actually do it.

chapter forty-one

~ishu

IT'S DIFFICULT TO NOT THINK ABOUT HANI WHEN I seem to spot her everywhere in school. After the past few weeks, I know her schedule inside out. I know what classes she has, when and where. I know all the times she goes to her locker, and I even know her favourite spots on the school grounds for when she doesn't want to spend lunch with Aisling and Deirdre.

I know that I should try to avoid her, put her out of my mind. But I can't help staring at Hani when we're at our lockers between classes, or watching her from the window overlooking the tree she loves sitting underneath during lunchtime.

There have been way too many times that I've almost run up to her, to tell her everything happening with Nik and my parents, or all my plans for the Head Girl elections. I've always stopped myself at the last moment.

Because no matter how I feel about Hani, it doesn't change that she's still friends with Aisling and Dee. That she'll never stand up to them. She'll never choose me over them.

And there's nothing *I* can do to change that.

I wake up on the weekend determined to get everything back on track. Everything with Hani, Aisling, and Deirdre has made me lose sight of what's really important: Head Girl, Leaving Cert, getting into the best possible university.

When I call Nik on Saturday morning, she picks up after just two rings.

'Do you ever sleep in?' Nik groans as a greeting.

'Sometimes,' I say. 'But not the week before the Head Girl election campaign!'

Nik heaves a sigh. 'Of course not.'

'Look…I need your help. I want to win this thing, OK? And now it's going to be more difficult than ever. I don't have the popular girls on my side – in fact, I'm pretty sure Aisling's new goal is to ruin my fucking life…but I need to win. You need to help me.'

There's the sound of rustling on Nik's end of the line, and the creak of the bed. I try to picture her shifting around in her bed, but it's tough when I have no idea what her bedroom even looks like. I've never been to visit Nik in London, and now I'm not sure if Ammu and Abbu will let me.

'Ishu…' Nik finally says. 'You know that I *lost* Head Girl, right? They didn't even make me deputy Head Girl. I don't think I'm the person you want helping you.' She says it like there's a line of people waiting to help me and I just happened to choose her. Like she isn't the *only* person right now who I *can* ask for help. But saying that will definitely make me sound pathetic – even if Nik *is* my sister and probably already knows I'm a bit pathetic, especially after she had to rush down here to sort out all my problems. I definitely don't want to remind her of it, though.

So I just say, 'Please?' and to my surprise, she actually begrudgingly agrees to help me.

'So, tomorrow…we have to make a presentation to our year about why we want to be Head Girl, and why we're the most qualified candidate for the job,' I say. 'I was thinking I'll just go up and…talk.'

There's a pause on the phone line, before all I can hear is Nik's giggles.

'And what? You're planning to win them over with your charming smile and personality?'

'I can be nice to people,' I say. 'I've learned how to tolerate the people in my year. Hani…taught me. I've been to parties with them. I've had conversations with them.'

Nik is still laughing. 'Like…actual conversations? Not just glaring at them as they try to talk to you?'

'No, actual conversations!' I say. 'Though…obviously things are different now that Hani and I are broken up and… everyone thinks I've cheated.'

That, at least, sobers Nik up a little. 'Well, then this presentation is the perfect time for you to set the record straight. Tell everyone the truth…you didn't cheat! The teachers know the truth – they'll back you up.'

I know Nik is right, but I also know Aisling. She'll find

a way to twist everything around to make me out to be the bad guy.

'Maybe,' I say.

'Look…I can help you put something together,' Nik says. 'We can do a digital presentation. A PowerPoint of why Aisling is a bitch.'

I have to stifle a laugh. 'OK…a PowerPoint…that's a good idea. I can prove why I would do a good job as Head Girl. I can show all of the things I've already done…' But I'm having a hard time trying to think of anything I've done that proves I would be a good Head Girl. Sure, I consistently have the best results in the school, and with Hani's help I've almost become acquaintances with people in our year that I never would have spoken to before. But…does any of that show I can be a good Head Girl?

'Ishu? Hello? Did the line cut out?'

I shake my head. 'No, everything's fine. Just…thinking, I guess. About Monday.'

'No point thinking about Monday when we're not prepared for it yet. Come on, open up your laptop. Let's get started.' So, with one hand holding my phone up to my ear, I open up my laptop and Nik and I get to work.

hani

I SLIP INSIDE ONLY LONG ENOUGH TO GRAB AN UMBRELLA before stepping out into the rain once more. I catch the bus that drops me off right in front of Aisling's house, and all the while I'm thinking up all of the things I have to say to her and Dee that I've kept to myself. Conversations that I've practised in my head for far too long but never dared to speak out loud to them.

By the time I ring the doorbell, I'm revved up. I'm angrier than I've felt in a long time.

But then the front door swings open and Aisling's mam is standing in the doorway. Her face lights up at the sight of me.

'Humaira,' she says, reaching forwards and pulling me indoors. 'I didn't know you were coming over today.' She throws her arms around me, like she always does when we see each other. I can feel my anger slowly dissipate. Suddenly, all I can think of is the fact that I've known Aisling since I was a little kid. We've sat next to each other all the way from junior infants to now. Am I really going to throw all that away?

'Aisling and Deirdre are upstairs,' Mrs Mahoney says.

I climb up the stairs slowly, listening to the hum of Aisling and Dee's voices coming from behind her closed bedroom door and to the sound of my heart beating way too loud in my chest.

When I finally knock on the door, Dee throws it open.

'Oh, you're here,' she says, like she's been expecting me this whole time. She steps aside and I step into the bedroom.

Aisling is sitting cross-legged on her bed with her phone in her hand. 'Maira, *finally*,' she says as if I've kept her waiting. 'If we hadn't seen you this weekend, Dee and I would have had to send out a search party or something.'

I cross my arms over my chest. There are still a million things I want to say to Aisling – to both her and Dee – but the words somehow get stuck in my throat, refusing to come out.

'Dee and I were just talking about how Ishita *humiliated* me. We're going to come up with a way to do the same to her.' Aisling barely glances at me as she says all of this. Instead, she springs out of bed and begins pacing around the room. 'I'm going to make sure she is *never* Head Girl. By the time I'm done with her, nobody's going to want to sit next to Ishita in class.'

'Nobody wants to sit next to Ishita in class *now*,' I say.

Aisling looks at me, her eyebrows scrunched together like she's having a difficult time placing me. 'What?'

'Ishita won't care about that,' I say. 'She doesn't *want* people to sit next to her in class. She doesn't care about what other people think of her. She never has.'

'Ishita pretends not to care. *Everybody* cares.'

I shake my head. 'She doesn't. And how...how exactly did she humiliate you?'

Aisling exchanges a glance with Dee that makes me wonder if the next words out of her lips will be the truth or something she's made up. 'So she hasn't told you yet...'

'We haven't spoken...in a few days.' It feels like it's been an eternity, but I don't tell Aisling that.

The smile that spreads across Aisling's lips at my words makes my stomach twist. But of course – this is what she's wanted all along, isn't it? She was always trying to keep me away from Ishu.

'Well, you should know that Ishita and her sister dragged me into the principal's office the other day, and now Ms Gallagher thinks *I'm* the one who cheated. Which isn't even true. It was horrible, and now we're going to get back at her. Even better now that you're broken up and—'

'If Principal Gallagher thinks you cheated from Ishita's test...what's she going to do?'

'Mum spoke to her.' Aisling shrugs. 'I promised I wouldn't do it again so she just let me off with a little warning. No issue there. Just—'

'The humiliation,' I finish for her.

'She made a spectacle of me in front of Ms Gallagher, and if it gets out to the whole school—'

'Everybody thinks that it was Ishita,' I interrupt. 'Because you haven't bothered to tell anyone the truth.'

'The *truth* is that this was all Ishita's doing. It's her fault, so why would I tell anyone anything?'

But I can barely hear her words any more. Even if her voice is steadily rising with every single thing she says.

'Why did you do it?'

'What are you even talking about, Maira?' Aisling finally turns to look at me properly. I finally see anger in her eyes. But she's not angry about being falsely accused. She's not upset in the heartbreaking way that Ishu was outside my house last week, convinced that nobody would believe her, convinced that she had lost everything she had worked so hard to achieve. Aisling is angry because I'm not wordlessly believing her side of the story, not offering her sympathy for her plight, not offering her help on how she can take Ishu down further.

For a moment, all I can see is the Aisling I knew when I was younger. The one who sat next to me in junior infants, and shared her Friday treat with me every week. The one who stood up for me when my first-ever boyfriend turned out to be an asshole. Suddenly it's all too clear to me that the Aisling I knew then and the one I know now aren't the same person. They haven't been the same person for a while. And I've just chosen not to notice that.

'Why did you lie to Principal Gallagher about Ishita cheating from you? Why did you lie to me?' I ask.

'I didn't—'

'Aisling.' I'm surprised at how even my voice sounds, though my heart is beating a million miles a minute. So fast that I'm surprised it hasn't burst out of my chest.

Her expression finally changes from a glare to something softer. 'I didn't want to lose you. And neither did Dee.'

'So you planned it? Together?' My gaze goes from Aisling to Dee. Dee at least has the grace to look ashamed. Her head is bowed and she's staring at the ground instead of meeting my gaze. Aisling is almost defiant, like she has no regrets. I suppose she probably doesn't.

'We just saw what that girl was doing to you. She's a bad influence on you.'

'I don't understand.' I shake my head. 'What was she doing to me? How was she a bad influence on me?'

'Well, it started when we all went to watch that movie together, and you told us about the two of you. Obviously you wouldn't have decided you were bisexual if Ishita wasn't in the picture,' Aisling starts. I clench my fingers into fists, trying to keep my anger and frustration inside myself. 'Then, at the party you were *weird*. You spent the whole time hanging out with Ishita at the back and then left early with her.'

'We've barely hung out these past few weeks, since she came into the picture,' Dee adds. 'It was like you were choosing her over us.'

'And she makes you different,' Aisling says. 'Not yourself. I don't know.'

I clench my fingers together so tightly that they dig into my skin painfully. Still, it helps keep the anger at bay.

'Ishita didn't make me bisexual…that's not how that

works,' I say. 'I came out to my parents ages ago. Not to you guys, because…because I was afraid you would act just like this. And…I was weird at the party because you made me feel like I didn't fit in for not drinking. I guess I didn't fit in. The thing is…Ishita doesn't make me not myself. She makes me more myself than I ever have been with you guys. You don't even call me by my real name.'

'What?! Maira's a nickname!' Aisling sputters. 'Like Deirdre is Dee, and I'm Ash sometimes.'

'Literally nobody has ever called you Ash,' I say. 'And I'm Maira because neither of you have ever tried to learn how to pronounce my real name. I went with it because… because I wanted to be your friend. You know, my dad might lose the election because I kept letting you guys talk me into abandoning helping him. And…you couldn't even get your parents to vote for him.'

I take a deep breath, letting some of my anger out with it. 'I don't know if any of this is worth it any more.'

I don't bother waiting for them to say anything more. I turn around and thunder down the stairs and out into the rain once more.

I should never have come here.

I should never have believed Aisling over Ishu.

I should never have let Ishu go.

I hope it's not too late.

chapter forty-three

I SPEND WAY TOO LONG DEBATING CALLING ISHU ON the bus home. On the one hand, all I want to do is tell her about everything that's happened since the last time we spoke. About Abba and our fight, about how I might have lost him his election, about my guilt…and about Aisling and Dee.

But on the other hand, I keep thinking about what Abba told me yesterday. That I need to find a way to *show* her that I trust her. And I'm not sure if telling Aisling and Dee off is that. That's not going to make her believe me.

I open up our fake dating guide for the millionth time, scrolling through our ridiculous rules. We've broken every single one of them. All this time we thought our fake dating plan was going exactly the way we wanted it to, but instead my friends were just manipulating us both. I wonder if there was any way that our fake dating plan would have actually got us what we wanted…

But of course, now I'm realising that I'm glad I don't have

what I want. What I *want* is to be with Ishu. And maybe I can't even have that any more.

What Ishu wants...

My fingers pause scrolling through my phone. What Ishu wants is to be Head Girl. And with everyone at school believing she cheated, with Aisling and Dee completely against her, she must think she's got no shot. But maybe *I* can help her win?

By the time I get home, I already have a plan forming in my mind. And it's not that I think I can single-handedly get Ishu the win, but I *know* that I can help. That's one of the reasons why Ishu and I started fake dating, after all.

Our house is eerily empty when I step inside, slightly damp from the rain. I sprinkle the water off of my umbrella and leave it to dry by our back door before heading upstairs. I'm hoping Abba isn't home any more, mostly because I have no idea what to say to him. I know I've got to make things up to him too, but I'm not quite sure how to go about that yet.

I push my bedroom door open, only to find Amma sitting on my bed, her eyebrows scrunched together as she stares at her phone. She glances up when the door creaks, and her face softens at the sight of me.

'You shouldn't have gone out all by yourself in the rain,' she says. 'Your hair's all damp.'

'I took an umbrella,' I mumble. 'But...the wind didn't help with keeping the umbrella up.'

Amma sweeps past me, grabs a towel, and begins to dry me off, like I'm a kid and not seventeen years old. She does it so gently that it feels nice, but I feel a pit of despair in my stomach. I know Amma's not been sitting in my bedroom waiting for me just to help me dry my hair.

'Your Abba told me about what happened today,' she says slowly, like she's really picking and choosing her words. 'He wasn't expecting any of that. Not today of all days.'

'I said sorry,' I say, though my words sound hollow. What good is a 'sorry' when I might have lost him his election? What good is a 'sorry' when I followed it up by accusing him of manipulating people like Salim Uncle? 'I feel bad about it…I know I shouldn't have gone along with Aisling and Dee and abandoned canvassing. I know it's important to Abba, and it's important to *me* because it's important to Abba, but—'

'Hani.' Amma cuts me off. Folding the towel up, she sits down on my bed once more. 'I know you've been struggling with your friends, but it's not a reason to abandon all the things that are important to you. Your friends shouldn't have the power to dictate what you do…and how you support your family.'

'I know.' I can only hang my head in shame. I should have known better – but it was just so much easier to give in to Aisling and Dee's demands. It always has been. 'Is he home? I'll apologise again, and anything that he needs me to do to make it right, I'll—'

'He says you were right,' Amma interrupts. 'About what you said…about how he hasn't exactly been telling the truth either. He went to see Salim Bhai.'

'Oh.' I blink. Whatever I was expecting, it wasn't that. 'Did he…do we know the results yet?'

'The polls haven't closed yet, Hani.' Amma chuckles. 'We won't know for sure until tomorrow morning.'

'I didn't mean to make this day even worse for him,' I say. 'But…he was just talking about all of these things I had done to support him and the election and…it made me feel like the worst daughter in the whole world.'

Amma reaches up and takes my hands in hers. She pulls me down on the bed beside her and brings me close until I'm in her embrace, and I can smell the scent of her coconut shampoo. It feels like forever since the two of us have sat down together and really caught each other up on what's been going on in our lives. I got so caught up in my lies that I forgot all the important things.

'You made a mistake, and your Abba made a mistake too,' she murmurs. 'It doesn't make anybody the worst anything in the world. It just makes us human.'

Abba is sitting at the breakfast table the next morning when I come downstairs. There's a frown on his lips as he types away at his laptop. I haven't spoken to him since our awful conversation in the car – he didn't come home from Salim Uncle's house until late last night. Now I'm not sure how to break the overwhelming silence between us.

I don't have to worry for long though, because as soon as he glances up and notices me, his entire demeanour changes. His expression softens, and a smile spreads across his lips.

'Hani,' he says, like seeing me this morning is the best thing that's happened to him in ages. 'Did you hear the good news?'

'You won?' I ask.

'I won.' He looks happier than I've ever seen him when he says this, and it takes a lot for me to not just jump up and down with happiness.

'You won! Abba...that's...wow.' It feels like there aren't enough words to really express how amazing it is that he's won. Because Salim Uncle was right – it's historic that he's won. It's historic that he was even in this election to begin with. He's going to be the first ever Muslim and Bangladeshi person to have been elected as a councilor in Ireland. But my excitement is quickly clouded by our argument yesterday.

'Amma said you were at Salim Uncle's yesterday. Did you... talk to him about me? About what I said?'

Abba's smile dissipates and he nods solemnly. 'Actually, I'm working on something for him right now.' He waves me over so I can look at his laptop screen. I shuffle over to find a word document.

Islamic Centre Outreach Program it says at the top, and a picture of our local mosque is pasted towards the bottom.

'What's this?'

'Well...what you said, it made me think a lot about the people who were voting for me yesterday. Everybody I saw at the mosque, they were voting for me because they trusted in the fact that I'd represent them…as a Muslim.' Abba heaves a sigh. 'Hani, has your Amma ever told you about how things were like when we first came here?'

I shake my head slowly. Amma and Abba have been living here for more than three decades now. They know Ireland like the back of their hands – it's their home. Maybe even *more* than Bangladesh, since Bangladesh wasn't even an independent country when they were born. But neither Amma nor Abba have spent a lot of time talking about the past – except to rave about all the ways things have got better.

'Well, when we first moved here, it was…difficult. There were barely any Bangladeshi people here, and there were barely any Muslim people here. There was no mosque, nobody from our communities. For the first few years we were here, we couldn't even find any halal meat.' Abba has a faraway look in his eyes as he says all this, like he's remembering a time that he had all but forgotten. 'We both missed Bangladesh, and we missed our family. But…we had fought so hard to come here. And the money your Amma and I made here was putting some of your cousins at home through school and university. We couldn't give up.'

'You wanted to give up?' I can't imagine Amma and Abba ever wanting to give up on anything – especially not something as big as setting up their life here. But I also can't imagine how difficult it must have been for them to come to a completely different country where everything was unfamiliar and try to start a life.

'Sometimes.' Abba chuckles. 'But your Amma and I had each other, and then soon Akash was born. That helped put everything into perspective. Akash, Polash, you…you've all had more opportunities here than you ever would have had in Bangladesh. But…being here, it was always difficult to hold on to some things…and I guess one of those things was…Islam.'

'Oh…' I'd never thought about how something like immigrating to a completely different country could affect your faith. Of course I hadn't, because I had spent my entire life in this very house, with my exact same friends. With *everything* the exact same. How can I possibly understand the things that Abba and Amma have done to get us here?

'It was more difficult when there was no mosque to go to every Friday for jummah prayers, no family and friends to celebrate Eid with, nothing that…held us close to Islam, I suppose.' Abba heaves another sigh, like it's paining him to speak about this. 'I guess gradually it became easier to just forget about those things, to…distance ourselves. So when Clonskeagh mosque was built, when a community started coming together…it didn't feel like our place any more.'

'I'm sorry,' I say, mostly because it's the only thing I can think of saying. It has been so easy for me to find myself in Islam, to read the Qur'an, and go to the mosque every chance I get.

'Don't be sorry.' Abba shakes his head. 'You know, when you started becoming interested in Islam, when you asked your Amma and me about praying and fasting for Ramadan… all of those things made us feel a little closer to Islam again.

And…now I'm realising you were right. I shouldn't have used the people at the mosque for a vote when I didn't feel like I was a part of that community. When I'd never been a part of that community before.'

'But it's not your fault,' I say quickly. The last thing I want is to make Abba feel like he has anything to prove – to me, to himself, or the people at the mosque. 'It's easy for me because you've given me everything I need to make it easy. To study Qur'an, and pray, and go to the mosque. But…I didn't know it was so hard for you and Amma.'

'It was,' Abba admits. 'But I'm not completely blameless either. And…yesterday your Salim Uncle and I had a long talk about all of this. And…we made a decision together.' Abba points again to his computer screen. 'This outreach program is for the local South Asian mosque. With your Salim Uncle's help we're going to work on making it better. On making it into a proper Islamic centre, and more inclusive as well.'

I've never been inside the local mosque – since there is no space for women to pray. It's a small building that looks like an apartment complex, grey and sad, and the only people who go to pray there are South Asians – mostly Bangladeshi people.

'How are you going to do that?' I ask, because I'm having a difficult time imagining anybody getting excited about jummah prayer *there*.

'Well, I'm working on contacting the right people. We're going to figure out if we can make it a little bigger, or even consider relocating it. And your Salim Uncle suggested that when the mosque isn't being used for prayer, maybe we can get some teachers to teach Arabic, Qur'an, and even Islamic history.' Abba's face is lit up as he says all this. He looks happier than he has in a long time. I can't help the grin that stretches my lips as well.

'It sounds like it's going to be a pretty big project.'

'It will be…' Abba trails off. 'And it'll probably take a long time. Which is why I'll need your help with it too.'

He meets my eyes, and though he doesn't say anything about how I disappointed him with the canvassing, I can tell that's what he's thinking about.

'I'm sorry about how I…didn't help enough with—'

'Hani.' Abba cuts me off, reaching forwards to place his hands on my shoulders. 'That conversation wasn't about you not helping. It was because you lied, and you didn't tell me that you couldn't do it. I would have understood. But…I needed you and you let me down.'

'I know.' I look down on the tiled floor of our kitchen instead of meeting his eyes.

'But we both made mistakes.' Abba's hands squeeze my shoulders gently, and when I look up there's no disappointment in his eyes. 'And I'm proud of you. I wouldn't be working on this project without you, Hani.'

I feel the pinprick of tears behind my eyes, and for once they're happy tears. I try to blink them away as Abba wraps me in the warmest embrace.

After our conversation, Amma makes us the most perfect breakfast to celebrate Abba's victory: bhapa pitha. She makes a few with gur between the steamed rice, a few with minced meat, and some with cheese. I eat one of each, and by the time I'm done with breakfast I'm completely full.

More than the breakfast itself, though, it's sitting at the breakfast table with Abba and Amma, feeling content and happy, that makes everything perfect. Like everything is finally getting back on track. Everything…except Ishu. But I have plans for that too.

So, after breakfast I find myself pulling out the baking trays from the kitchen cabinets.

'Planning on baking something?' Amma asks with a raised eyebrow.

'I need to make things up to Ishu,' I say. 'Like you and Abba said…I want to show her that I'm in her corner.'

'And baking is going to do that?' Amma asks. Her question makes me pause in my tracks. It's not exactly the most ingenious idea, but it's all I have.

I take a deep breath and say, 'God, I hope so.'

chapter forty-four

ishu

I WAKE UP ON MONDAY MORNING TO A TEXT FROM NIK that reads **good luck today!** Instead of making me feel better, though, it makes my stomach drop. The thought of going into school and standing up in front of our entire year to tell them about why I should be Head Girl next year? It feels like too much.

Still, I climb out of bed and slip into my uniform. I shuffle down the stairs to find Ammu waiting for me at the table. For a moment I wonder if she's somehow found out about the Head Girl presentations. Maybe she heard from one of the other parents, or maybe the school texted her about it. The thought of her knowing fills me with dread. Because what if I don't win – and that seems like a pretty big possibility at this stage – and then I've disappointed my parents once more?

'Ishu.' A smile flickers on Amma's lips when she spots me. 'Do you want me to make you some breakfast?'

'Um, no,' I mumble. 'I'll have some cereal.' I grab the milk, bowl, and cereal and take a seat opposite Ammu. She's not even on her phone or anything. She just observes me, as if she's seeing me for the first time in a while.

'Your school called,' she says finally when I'm already halfway through my cereal.

'Oh?' I try to sound nonchalant but the dread in the pit of my stomach grows.

'They told us that the accusation that student made about you has been dropped. You're not being investigated any more.'

'Yeah,' I say, stifling a sigh of relief. 'Did I…not mention that?' I've become too good at avoiding seeing Ammu and Abbu. Since they're so busy all the time, it's too easy.

'Your principal said that Nik was the one who spoke to her and helped clear your name.'

I pause with a spoon of cereal halfway to my mouth. Ammu is looking straight at me, and there's a question in her gaze.

'Yeah…Nik…I…called her.' I drop the spoonful of cereal back into the bowl, and it makes a splashing sound. Suddenly, I don't feel so hungry any more.

Ammu shakes her head. 'Your Abbu wasn't happy to hear about that. You should have talked to *us*. We're trying to give Nik some space. We're trying to—'

'Cut her out of our family,' I say. 'I…talked to you two. You didn't believe me. Nik…she believed me. She knew that I would never cheat. I didn't even have to ask her for help. I didn't ask her to do anything. But she did help. She knew how to fix everything. She was there for me.'

Ammu takes a deep breath. 'Well, I'm glad that she helped you, I am. But you can't go running to your sister when you have a problem. She needs to know that what she's doing is wrong. We don't support her in her decision.'

'But she's happy,' I say. 'And she's…figuring things out.'

'Everything was already figured out.' Ammu's voice is cold and heavy. Like her mind's made up about Nik and there's no changing it. For a moment, I'm not sure if I should ask the questions I want to ask. I'm afraid of the answers that Ammu might give me. I'm afraid that maybe our parents don't love us the way that I've always thought they did.

But then, the words are suddenly out of my lips. 'What if Nik never goes back to university? What if she never becomes a doctor? You won't speak to her ever again?' The questions hang heavy between us, and Ammu's face shifts. From cold and hard to an expression of despair.

'That won't happen.' But the waver in Ammu's voice makes me realise that she thinks it might. Maybe the last time my family was whole was that day Nik came home. The day we sat together at this very table, eating our biryani. The day everything changed.

And I hadn't even taken the time to appreciate it.

Principal Gallagher calls me into her office almost as soon as I come into school. I'm half afraid that Aisling has made another accusation against me. I step into the office gingerly, wondering if this is another ambush. But Principal Gallagher just urges me to take a seat and shoots me a pleasant smile, which makes her look kind of constipated.

This must be what *I* look like when I try to pretend I like people that I actually detest – at least according to Hani.

'How are we doing this morning?' Ms Gallagher asks, clapping her hands together. Like we're old pals. Like the last time I was here my older sister wasn't trying to clear my name, and Aisling wasn't sitting in this exact chair crying her white woman tears to get out of trouble.

'I'm doing all right.'

'Wonderful. And are you all ready for your Head Girl presentation?' she asks.

'Yeah…Nik helped me prepare.' I hold up the thumb drive with my PowerPoint on it.

'Great…great.' Ms Gallagher's smile doesn't make it seem great at all. 'The thing is…I've spoken to Aisling Mahoney's parents. She's going to be punished, of course.'

'Of course,' I mumble, though I already know that whatever's going to come out of Ms Gallagher's lips next isn't going to make me happy.

'But…I think it'll be in everyone's best interest if we keep things discreet. Nobody has to know what happened with you and Aisling. There's no point dredging it all up. I'm sure you understand.'

'It happened last week.' The words are out of my lips before I can stop them. But I also don't regret them. 'Everybody at school thinks I cheated. That I…get the results I do because I'm a cheater, which isn't true. And you want me to keep pretending it is?'

'We'll tell everyone it's not true. Anyway, nobody thinks that—'

'Yes, they do!' My voice rises by an octave. I close my eyes and take a deep breath. Losing my temper last time didn't help. 'Principal Gallagher.' I try to use the calm, collected voice I've heard Hani use when speaking to her white friends. 'People already believed the worst of me. And Aisling *did* cheat. What's the problem if everyone finds out the truth? Just because her *parents* asked you to keep it quiet?'

'Because we don't believe in tarnishing people's image in this school, Ishita. And it's nobody's business what happened in this office. I'm sorry, Ishita, but especially at this presentation today, we will have no discussion of Aisling. She isn't even running for Head Girl or prefect, so it shouldn't be a problem. Understood?'

I have so many things I want to say to Principal Gallagher. Instead, I grit my teeth and say, 'Understood.'

hani

When I get to school on Monday, I have a single focus. Find Ishu. Talk to her. Fix everything.

I ignore my locker, which is right next to Aisling's and Dee's – and head right towards Ishu's. I find her with her locker door open, staring inside with a faraway look in her eyes.

She must be more nervous about the Head Girl presentations than I expected.

'Ishu?' I tap her on the shoulder.

She turns around and her gaze immediately shifts into a glare. I try to ignore the pain in my chest at Ishu looking at me like this.

'What the fuck are you doing?' She steps away from me, like my tap on her shoulder was too much for her to bear.

'I just…wanted to wish you luck on the Head Girl presentations,' I offer. 'And…' I pull out the box of red-velvet cupcakes Amma helped me make yesterday. 'I made these cupcakes, see?' I open up the box so Ishu can see, with their multi-coloured icing spelling out *VOTE ISHITA #1* in bright pink writing. I figured the best way to win people over was with sugar – everybody's weakness. 'So that I can help you get people to—'

'I don't want your help,' Ishu says. She slams her locker door shut, like it's somehow personally wronged her. 'I don't *need* your help.'

'Ishu, I'm just—'

'Ishita,' she says. 'And leave me alone.' She pushes past me and disappears into the crowd of girls from our year. I feel my stomach sink. I've been relegated to calling her Ishita, like someone who doesn't know her, hasn't spent time with her, hasn't held her hand or thought about her until the late hours of night with butterflies in my stomach.

Like we're nothing at all to each other.

When the bell rings at eight thirty, everyone but the fifth years shuffle off into their respective classes. I follow the rest of the girls in my year into the main hall, where everything has been set up for the Head Girl candidates to give their presentations.

There are rows of chairs filling up the space, and a stage set up at the very front. There's even a little podium with a mic, and a projector towards the back facing the screen set up on stage. Somehow, this feels even more official than all of the election events I've been to with Abba.

The rows of chairs fill up fast, and I spot Aisling and Dee sitting towards the front. They're both sitting slumped in their seats, looking like this is the last place on earth they want to be. And they're whispering to each other. My stomach drops at the sight of them, and I look away quickly.

I decide to choose a seat at the very back of the hall – as far away from Aisling and Dee as humanly possible. But I'm definitely not going to spend this time feeling bad about what happened with them yesterday. Just because Ishu hates me now doesn't mean I shouldn't help her the best I can.

I promised to help her become Head Girl, and that's what I'm going to do.

So, I pull out the box of cupcakes from my bag and turn to the group of girls sitting next to me: Hannah, Yasmin, and Sinéad.

'Hey,' I say in the brightest voice I can muster. 'Are you planning on voting for Ishita?' I hold out the cupcakes so they can see that they're for Ishu's supporters.

The three of them share a look with each other, before Sinéad turns to me with a frown. 'Um…hasn't Ishita been cheating in school? I'm not sure any of us should be voting for someone like that.'

I don't let my smile falter – though it's difficult to keep smiling. 'If Ishu really has been cheating, would she be let back into the Head Girl election?'

Hannah shrugs. 'Well, if she's capable of cheating, then who knows what else she's capable of doing? I mean…she's always been ambitious.' She says the last word as if ambitious is the worst thing anybody could hope to be.

'Ishita didn't cheat,' I say with the most definitive voice I can – while still sounding pleasant. 'Everything got cleared up. It was…it was…' I cast a glance at Aisling at the very front. She has her arms crossed over her chest, and she's glaring at Ishu up on stage. 'Aisling was the one who cheated.'

Hannah blinks at me slowly. They all do. Like the thought of *Aisling* being the one who cheated isn't possible. Though I'm pretty sure Aisling was the one who told them all about Ishu.

'You should vote for Ishita,' I say, thrusting the box of cupcakes in front of them once more before they can say anything else. 'She's the best person for this job, trust me.'

None of them look fully convinced, but they do each grab a cupcake from the box.

I manage to give out only a few more cupcakes – and tell a few more people that it wasn't *Ishu* who cheated – before Principal Gallagher strolls up to the stage. I shuffle back into my seat as she casts a sweeping glance over the stage, a smile flickering on her lips.

'Welcome, fifth years,' she says into the mic. 'This year you have the opportunity to make a very important decision in this school. You get to choose which student amongst these four will represent you, and the entire school, as our Head Girl next year. *And* you can decide who will serve as deputy

Head Girl. Two positions that are of immense importance in our school.' She holds our gaze for a long, tense moment. She's acting as if we're choosing the next president of Ireland, not just the two people who will spend most of next year organizing school photos and planning our debs.

'So, this is your opportunity to listen to what each of these students has to offer and make an informed decision.' Ms Gallagher glances at the four girls sitting at the back of the stage. Alex, Siobhán, and Maya smile down at the rest of us. But Ishu – sitting at the very edge, looks lost to this world. Her eyebrows are furrowed together and she's deep in thought. My stomach twists at the sight of her.

'We'll start with Alexandra Tuttle.' The room erupts into applause and Ms Gallagher takes her seat on the other side of the stage.

All of us listen attentively as Alex tells us about her experience in leadership, and how she's been at this school since first year, and wants us to graduate next year in the best way possible. Next, Siobhán says almost all of the same things as Alex but smiles a lot more. Maya spends way too much time talking about the debs, and how she's been dreaming of her own ever since she saw her older sister's debs dress a few years ago, so she will spend her time organising the best dance she can possibly put together. She even has a PowerPoint presentation with some ideas of what our debs might look like. When she walks away from the mic, there are whoops and cheers.

Obviously, leadership skills and love of the school are not

what the girls in our year are looking for in a Head Girl.

Finally, it's Ishu's turn.

'Hi everyone,' she says slowly. 'I'm…Ishita Dey.' Ishu takes a shaky breath that reverberates around the hall. 'I think you should vote me for Head Girl because…I'm the best person for the job, I guess. I've consistently been at the top of my classes, which shows I'm a hard worker, and—'

Ishu's speech is interrupted by a low cough that sounds distinctively like 'cheater.' It's followed by another which more clearly mumbles 'liar.' I glance at the top of the hall at Aisling and Dee, but the thing is I'm not even sure if it was them. It could be anyone – they all think Ishu is a cheater.

Ishu pauses in her speech and glances back at Principal Gallagher. I will Ms Gallagher to stand up and tell everyone here the truth. That it was *Aisling* who cheated, not Ishu. But Principal Gallagher isn't even looking at Ishu. She stares off into the distance, a blank expression on her face.

Ishu clears her throat. '…And on that note, I would like to formally take myself out of the running for Head Girl.'

Now, Principal Gallagher shifts in her seat. 'Ishita—' she begins, but Ishu is already at the bottom of the stage, rushing towards the exit. The previously quiet hall explodes into a rush of whispers and giggles as everyone watches Ishu make her exit. She's holding her head up high – though everyone thinks the worst of her.

I'm not sure where the motivation comes from, but one moment I'm sitting in my seat, looking after Ishu, and the next I'm rushing up to the stage.

'Ishita is *not* a cheater.' The hall descends into silence once more. Everyone's eyes are turned to me but I can't exactly stop now. 'You've all got to be daft to believe that she *is*. What, do you believe every single thing Aisling has said to you?' I glance at Aisling, who is glaring daggers up at me. There's a tug of discomfort in my stomach at her gaze. We're *best friends. We* were *best friends*, I remind myself as I turn away from her, and towards Principal Gallagher. 'Ms Gallagher, you know it was Aisling who cheated. She *told* me so. Why are you letting Ishita take the blame for this?'

Ms Gallagher finally stands, and shuffles over to the podium stand. And as if she hasn't heard a single word I've said, she speaks into the mic, 'Thank you to the *three* Head Girl candidates for their presentations. Voting will be next week. You can all return to your classrooms.'

Everyone shuffles to their feet and out through the double doors at the end of the hallway, stealing glances back at me the whole time. My bravery from a few moments ago is gone now, leaving me with an impending feeling of doom in my chest.

'Humaira,' Ms Gallagher finally turns to me as the hallway becomes emptier and emptier. 'You can't just get up in front of your whole year and say things like that.'

'But it's the truth,' I say.

'Ishita and I have an understanding about the situation with Aisling,' Ms Gallagher says. Somehow, I don't believe her at all.

'An understanding that Aisling can do whatever she wants?'

'She'll be punished. But…dragging her name through the mud in front of the entire school? We have a zero tolerance policy for bullying here, so I'd be careful. Now, why don't you get back to class?'

There are still a million thoughts scrambling around inside my head, but I know that speaking to Principal Gallagher is pointless. She thinks somehow Aisling is the victim and Ishu the perpetrator, and I'm not sure anything I say will change the way she sees the two of them. So, I step down from the stage, trying my best to not let my anger spill over.

~ishu

I dropped out of the Head Girl election.

I send off the text and heave a sigh. The bathroom stall I've decided to hole up in has the lyrics to an Ariana Grande song scribbled on to it in black marker. That makes me smile, thinking about any of the girls in our school spending their time carefully etching lyrics on to the bathroom door instead of going to class.

My phone vibrates with texts from Nik just a few minutes later.

Nik: ????

Nik: WHY???

Because all the girls were accusing me of—

I hesitate and erase the text. That's not *really* why.

Because I didn't know how to say—

I stop again, staring down at my phone screen, unsure of how to exactly explain to my sister why I made the decision when I'm not sure I completely understand it myself.

I don't have the time to think about it too much though,

because in the next moment my phone is buzzing with a phone call.

'Hello?' I whisper, hoping that no teachers come in here looking for me.

'What happened?' Nik asks. 'Do I need to come down there again?' She says it like it's a joke but I fully believe she would do it again if she had to.

'No...' I trail off, unsure of where to begin. 'I just...I got up there and I didn't have anything to say, Nik,' I say. 'Why do I want to be Head Girl? Everyone else was talking about class hoodies and debs, and how they have all of this leadership experience. I don't want to be a bloody leader of these girls; I barely even like talking to them half the time. I definitely don't want to spend half of the final year in school planning a dance where I'll probably have a miserable time.'

'Well, if you go with Hani, I'm sure you—'

'Nik.'

'Sorry,' she chuckles. 'Look...I could have told you your reasons for running for Head Girl were rubbish, but if it's what you want, it's what you want.'

'I never even thought about becoming Head Girl before... before you told us about dropping out of university.'

'So you want to be Head Girl...to show me up?'

'To...show Ammu and Abbu that I'm...not you,' I mumble. When I told Abbu and Ammu that I was going to be Head Girl, the decision to run had made sense. But now, my reasons make a knot form in my stomach.

'Trust me, Ishu…Ammu and Abbu don't think you're me. They've already written me off, but they still have faith in you.' Nik says this all breezily, but I can sense the hurt in her words.

'They haven't written you off,' I say, even though I'm not sure I believe that.

'That doesn't matter.' Nik sighs. 'Look…if you want to run for Head Girl for Ammu and Abbu, I get that. But…you don't *have* to do it.'

'I don't…think I want to be Head Girl. Also…it's not even possible for me to be Head Girl. Everyone still thinks I cheated.' I sigh. 'They're trying to protect Aisling, apparently.'

'God, that bloody school,' Nik mumbles under her breath. 'It's always been a fucking nightmare, but somehow it's got worse.'

'Hani stood up for me.' I don't know why I tell Nik that when I'm still trying to hold on to my anger at Hani. But it's getting increasingly difficult with her baking cupcakes and running up on stage to defend me in front of our entire year.

'God, I wonder why,' Nik says in the most exaggeratedly sarcastic voice possible.

'Shut up.'

'Look…Ishu…you don't have to ever do anything you don't want to do. You don't have to run for Head Girl if that's not what you want. And you don't have to forgive Hani if that's not what you want to do. I just…want to make sure you're doing things for the right reasons. So, not because of

Ammu and Abbu, and not because you don't want to give you and Hani a proper shot.'

'That's not why.' My voice sounds more defensive than I want it to, and I can almost *see* the knowing smile on Nik's face.

'OK, Ishu…whatever you say. I have to go. Are you going to be OK?'

'Yeah…I'm going to be fine.' And I try my best to sound fine, and not like I'm standing in an ugly green bathroom stall questioning everything.

chapter forty-seven

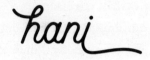

WHISPERS FOLLOW ME THROUGHOUT THE REST OF THE school day. I'm not sure if I've actually done much to help Ishu, or if I've just made things worse. But the worst part of everything is that I can't even find Ishu anywhere. She's obviously still avoiding me, and I'm not sure if I can even blame her. I go through the rest of the school day with my head bent down low, buried in my books.

When the final bell rings at the end of the day, I couldn't be happier. I rush to my locker before hurrying out of the school gates, like putting distance between me and the school building will somehow solve all my problems.

Still, somehow, Aisling and Dee manage to beat me to the gates. They're both waiting for me, their eyes boring into me.

'Maira, what the hell was that today?' Aisling asks as soon as I'm within earshot.

'I can't believe you would stand up in front of our entire year and accuse Aisling of—'

'The truth?' I cut Dee off before she has a chance to finish.

'It's not an accusation if it's the truth.' Shooting them both glares, I attempt to push past, but there's two of them and only one of me.

'Are you seriously going to do this over *one* fight?' Dee asks.

'It wasn't one—' I start, but Aisling cuts me off.

'I'm sorry.' Those words that I thought I'd never hear out of Aisling's lips slip right out. I stop in my tracks to take her in. She has her head bent down low and she's speaking slowly, as if this is all incredibly painful for her to say. Even Dee is looking at Aisling with wide eyes, so this must be unplanned.

'You're sorry?' I scoff. 'For what?'

'I'm sorry for…well, all of it, I guess. I shouldn't have…' Aisling sighs. 'I shouldn't have been so judgy of you for being gay—'

'Bisexual.'

'Bisexual, yes. And…I shouldn't have been…jealous of Ishita.'

'That's why you did all of this? Jealousy?' I ask.

Aisling shrugs. 'We've been friends since primary school…I just didn't want to lose you.'

I nod slowly. 'You're going to apologise to Ishu?'

'Are we friends again?' Aisling finally meets my gaze. There's so much hope in her eyes, but none of it makes me feel anything. How can I ever trust her again, after everything she's lied about? Everything she's done?

I shake my head. 'I don't know. I need…time.'

She glances at Dee instead of me. 'I can't believe you won't even accept my apology. I don't know what you *want* from me!' She exclaims.

'I want you to give me time,' I say. 'Everything you've done…it's a lot, Aisling. It's a lot to forgive.'

'It was a mistake,' Dee says. 'Aisling regrets it.'

'How are lying and manipulating mistakes?' I ask. 'And I'm not the only one who needs an apology. You know that.'

Aisling chews on her lips. It's the most nervous I've ever seen her, I think. The most human I have seen her in a very long time. Then, she shakes her head.

'Forgive me, don't forgive me. I'm definitely not apologising to Ishita Dey.' She waits for a moment, like she's expecting me to say something – to take back what I've said. Then, she turns on her heel and begins her ascent up the steps and out the main gates. Dee glances between me and her for a moment, like she's trying to make up her mind about who to choose. Like she hasn't already done that. Then she's gone too.

And it's just me.

chapter forty-eight

ishu

I KNOW I SHOULD PROBABLY FEEL BAD FOR eavesdropping on Hani's conversation with her friends, but as Aisling and Deirdre rush away from Hani like she's worth nothing, I couldn't be more glad about my decision.

I watch as other people push past Hani, casting curious glances. I have no doubt that within hours Aisling will have filled their heads with propaganda about Hani – even if they're friends. Though I'm not sure if they're friends any more. Not after this.

As I watch Hani stand there on her own, looking after her awful friends, it's as if all my confusion, all my questions wash away to nothing. Because Nik was right. I'm ready to forgive Hani, but maybe I haven't been ready to know if Hani and I could really work.

I slip out of the side of the secluded corner of the school building and walk towards Hani.

'Wow,' I say. Hani turns to me with unshed tears in her wide eyes. She tries to blink them away as soon as she spots me.

'Hey…what are you…' She gulps, like it's taking some effort to quell her tears. Aisling and Deirdre are definitely not worth her tears. I guess Hani still has to learn that.

'I was just going home when I saw this all blow up, so…I stayed behind to see how it all turned out.' I shrug. 'You held your own pretty well.'

Hani lets out a little sniffle, tears rolling down her cheeks slowly. She wipes one away almost aggressively. Maybe they're angry tears rather than sad ones, but somehow I don't think so.

'I…f-feel…silly.'

I chuckle. Step forwards. Brush away another tear from her cheek. Softer than she had done it. The touch of her skin again mine is hot. I want nothing more than to touch her again, but I don't.

I say, 'They don't deserve you. They never did.'

'I-I've been f-friends with…th-them m-my who-whole l-life.'

I wipe another tear away from her cheek, tucking a strand of hair away from her face. Then, I cup her cheeks in mine, holding her face up so we are eye-to-eye. She blinks. Hiccups. Then, sniffs.

'There will be other friends,' I say. 'Other people. Who… will appreciate you. Who will mean it when they say sorry. Who will be able to say the word 'bisexual' without cringing.'

Hani lets out a soft chuckle, and the hint of a smile on her face makes me smile as well.

'I'm sorry,' she says in a whisper. 'I shouldn't have—'

But I'm already kissing her, so the words are trapped between us. The apology dances between our lips and our tongues, and in her hands in my hair, in my hands on her back. We only pull apart to the sound of the rain against the pavement, and I'm not sure how long it's been raining for. From the look on Hani's face, neither is she. Both of us are smiling – grinning, actually – and clutching each other's hands like they're lifelines and if we let go we will drown. We're both already soaked, but we lean forwards again, pressing our foreheads together, and Hani trails a line down the nape of my neck with her fingertips.

'So…you forgive me?' she asks, her eyes bright with hope. Instead of responding, I lean in and kiss her once more.

'Come on.' I take her hand in mine and tug her away from the school gates. The rain is cold against our skin but there's something almost cleansing and wonderful about it.

'Where are we going?' Hani asks, letting me pull her along.

'Anywhere we can be together,' I say.

chapter forty-nine

It's the hottest day of the summer, and I'm glad that schools closed last week. There's no way any of us would have been happy being stuck inside a classroom in the scorching heat.

I'm sure that most Irish people are out at the beaches or parks sunbathing. But Ishu and I are outside our tiny local mosque – having a barbecue.

'I feel weird,' Ishu whispers in my ear, tugging at her salwar kameez. It's a cotton kameez that is soft yellow in colour. Nobody should look good in yellow – but Ishu does.

'Why?'

'Everyone else here is Muslim.' She casts a glance around her, like if somebody hears her confessing to not being Muslim, something bad will happen. 'They keep saying 'salam' to me, and I don't know if I should say it back or not.'

'You know if somebody says 'salam,' they're just saying hello in Arabic?'

'Yes, but—'

'If someone says "Dia dhuit" to you, which by the way means "God be with you," do you say "Dia is muire dhuit" or do you just—'

'OK, OK,' Ishu concedes, rolling her eyes. 'I just…meant, are you sure it's OK for me to be here?'

'Yes, obviously.' I reach over and slip my fingers into hers for a moment, giving her a gentle squeeze. She takes a deep breath, and that seems to calm her down a little at least.

'Hani?' Abba waves me over from where he's standing by the grill. He's surrounded by the Muslim men from the mosque that he's got to know more and more over the past few weeks. In fact, I've been seeing more of Salim Uncle nowadays than I have of even Ishu. It seems he's at our house all the time.

'I'll be right back,' I tell Ishu, before slipping away from her and towards Abba and his friends.

'Hey, Abba,' I say as I approach, casting a wary glance at Salim Uncle.

'We wanted you to meet someone,' Abba says, pointing to a girl standing beside Salim Uncle. She has long, wavy black hair and she's wearing a baby blue summer dress that goes all the way down to her ankles. She's also almost as tall as Salim Uncle himself.

'This my daughter,' Salim Uncle says.

'Hey, I'm Aisha.' She waves.

'I'm Hani.'

'Her bhalo nam is Humaira.' Salim Uncle beams, like he

couldn't be prouder of the fact that I'm called Humaira.

'Oh…like the nickname Prophet Muhammad gave to Aisha!' Aisha exclaims.

'Nobody really calls me Humaira though.'

'Her girlfriend is over there.' Salim Uncle points to where Ishu is standing by herself, looking a little lost and out of place. 'I thought maybe Aisha could keep the two of you company.'

'Oh…sure,' I agree. 'Come on over.' I turn and begin to lead Aisha towards where Ishu is standing.

'So…girlfriend,' she says thoughtfully. 'Brave of you to bring her here.'

'Honestly, I didn't think we were even telling people that,' I say. 'I mean…not hiding it but not exactly showcasing it. But my dad must have told yours.'

'You know, when Leo Varadkar became Taoiseach I thought my dad's head might explode – a gay prime minister: he couldn't wrap his head around that. But I feel like he's really come around to a lot of stuff since then,' she says. 'I mean, he's sort of had to, I guess, because my brother's gay.'

'Yeah?' The thought of another queer Muslim in this community makes my heart fill up with joy in a way that I hadn't quite expected.

'Yeah! And I mean, we wouldn't go around advertising it to everyone, you know. But my dad really likes *yours*…and he must really like you too.' Aisha casts me an appraising look. 'My brother is about your age, I'd say. He's going to do his Leaving next year.'

'I'm doing my Leaving next year too!'

She grins. 'Well, I'd introduce you if he were here, but he somehow managed to wrangle his way out of coming to this thing. I think he feels a little weird sometimes…he's still figuring things out, being Muslim and gay.'

'Oh…well. Maybe we can talk some time. I mean, I'm…' I trail off, unsure if I want to finish that sentence. The last time I told someone I was bisexual didn't exactly go well. But back then, with my friends, I had so much to lose. I've only just met Aisha. 'I'm bisexual, so maybe it won't be the same, but…'

'Honestly, I know when I tell him about you, he's going to lose his shit. He's going to be so annoyed he didn't come today.'

'Hey…' Ishu says hesitantly when we're within earshot. She smiles at Aisha – and her smile doesn't look constipated. She's been working on that.

'Ishu…this is Aisha, Salim Uncle's daughter,' I say. 'This is Ishu.'

'Nice to meet you,' Aisha greets Ishu with a smile. 'So, how long have the two of you been together?'

Ishu glances at me, like she's asking permission to talk about us. I guess nobody's really asked us this question before – everyone at school thinks we've been together since the time we started fake dating, Abba and Amma finally know the truth now, and Ishu's parents still think we're just friends.

'Well…' I hesitate, unsure of how to answer her question. 'I guess we've only been together for about three weeks. But…

technically we might have been together for much longer than that.'

Aisha raises an eyebrow at the two of us. 'I'm not sure I understand.'

'Hang on, let's see,' Ishu mumbles, slipping her phone out of her pocket. She taps for a few moments, and I can see the fake dating guide open on her screen. 'We technically started dating six weeks ago,' she says, looking at that first picture of the two of us on our 'first date.' We both look horribly awkward. 'But it was fake.'

'But our fake dating led to us realising we liked each other for real,' I add. 'And…we got together for real about three weeks ago.'

Ishu glances away from her phone and up at me, meeting my eyes. She smiles for real this time – that smile that I'm sure is what made me fall for her in the first place. The rare one she only seems to reserve for the special people in her life.

'Wow.' Aisha chuckles. 'I thought that only happened in the movies.'

'The movies, and us, I guess.' I loop my arm through Ishu's, and pull her close.

~ishu

DATING HANI FOR REAL IS WEIRD. IT'S DIFFERENT THAN dating Hani for pretend.

Maybe because I know when Hani holds my hand now, it's because she *wants* to, not because she's trying to prove something to her friends. Because I know that Hani cares about me in the same way that I care about her. She's also forced me to spend less time shut up in my bedroom, poring over my books and exam papers this summer – even though I keep telling her this is our *last summer* before the Leaving Cert – and to spend *more* time hanging out with her in all of the places that I have never hung out before.

Which is how I've found myself at events like her parents' mosque barbecue, and today I find myself in St. Stephen's Green park with ice-cold bubble tea in my hand. We're in the middle of a heatwave and there are way too many people around with their shirts off. Normally, this would annoy the fuck out of me, but with Hani in my arms, I don't even care. I don't want to sidle back home to the company of my books.

'We should try crocheting!' Hani exclaims, like she's figured out the solution to world peace. 'Amma does it, and she says she finds it so calming. Plus, she always crochets me the *best* things.'

'I don't think crocheting sounds…like me,' I say. For the past few weeks, Hani has been trying to cajole me into picking up a hobby. I agreed, mostly because Hani says whatever I agree to do, she'll do with me too. But it's definitely not going to be *crocheting*.

Hani lets out a gasp, like she's suddenly got the best news of her life. She points towards the entrance of the park, where a group of musicians are setting up. 'I wonder what they'll play,' Hani whispers. There's wonder in her eyes – as if there aren't a bajillion buskers in Dublin at any given time, playing all kinds of music.

They set an empty guitar case in front and begin playing an upbeat, folksy tune. Hani bobs her head side-to-side, as if this is the best music she's heard in her entire life.

I stifle a groan, and a roll of my eyes. I mean, the music isn't *terrible*, I guess.

'What if we started our own band?' Hani asks.

'Can you play an instrument?' I ask.

Hani glances at me with a little frown. 'No…'

'It's kind of important to have musical talent to start a band.' I point out. 'I mean…I can play the guitar, but—'

'Shut up!' Hani turns to me now, and her jaw is practically on the floor.

'I can play the guitar…badly,' I finish. 'I learned a long time ago, when I was a kid. My sister and I wanted to start our own band. I don't even know if I can play any more. Plus…Nik was obviously a million times better than me.'

'So, you'll start a band with your sister but not *me*?' Hani sounds mortally offended at the idea.

'Yeah, when I was a *kid*, Hani.' I sigh, leaning back to watch the band change into a new song. A woman with a mass of curls tosses them a coin as she passes by.

'Did you like it?' Hani asks.

'I guess…' I trail off, trying to remember what it felt like. It has been years and years. In that time, I've moved on from any fascination I had with the guitar, or music in general.

My phone buzzes with a text in my pocket. I slip it out and read Nik's text, an automatic groan escaping my lips. 'I have to tell her,' I tell Hani.

A smile flickers on Hani's lips. 'Well, you've been putting it off for a long time. It's not going to get any easier – maybe harder, actually.'

I lie back on the grass, feeling the heat of the sun on my skin. Hani shifts beside me until she's lying on the grass too. Even without turning sideways, I can see the way her long, black hair spreads out all around her.

'Imagine you tell Nik that you've picked up the guitar again…' Hani says after a long pause. 'You'll be better than her.'

I grin. 'You're not going to let this go, are you?'

Hani threads our fingers together until I can feel the

warmth of her skin against mine. 'At least not until I figure out exactly how terrible you are.'

Ammu is in the kitchen preparing dinner when I get home. The aroma of what she's cooking – chicken curry and rice – fills the entire house.

'Ammu…'

She glances up with a raised eyebrow. 'You're home. Out with Hani again?' She doesn't sound angry exactly, but there's an edge to her voice. I guess she doesn't like me spending so much time with my 'friend' when I could be studying. But I don't let the edge in her voice bother me.

I take a deep breath, and dive right in. 'Ammu, you know Nik is getting married in two weeks, right?'

Her eyebrows furrow together at the mention of Nik's name. I don't think they've spoken in months now. 'Yes,' she says with a tone of finality in her voice. She goes back to her cooking.

'You're really not going to go to her wedding?' I ask. 'She's your daughter…you're going to regret it.'

She keeps stirring the chicken curry, though I'm not sure it even needs to be stirred. I chew on my lip, trying to figure out how to say the next thing, when Ammu stops and turns back to me.

'If I could go, I would,' she says slowly. 'I can't always do the things I want to. Your Abbu…' She shakes her head. 'And anyway, he's right. If we go now, if we support her in these ridiculous decisions, she's going to think it's all right. She'll never go back to university to finish her degree.'

'She's not going to go back because you decide to punish her for following her own path,' I say. 'She's just…doing what makes her happy.'

Ammu shakes her head. 'We can't always do what makes us happy. If we did, the world would not function. Do you think we came to this country because it made us happy?'

I sigh. 'It's different, Ammu…you know it's different…and I'm going.'

Ammu turns to me with a glare. 'No, you're not.'

'Nik already bought me a ticket…and Hani. We're going together,' I say. 'You don't want to go…OK. But I'm not going to miss my only sister's wedding, Ammu. You shouldn't ask me to.'

She's still glaring at me. I'm preparing all of the arguments in my head. Hani and I have been practicing them together for weeks now – ever since we decided that I couldn't miss Nik's wedding, even if my parents did everything in their power to cut her out of our family.

But then, Ammu says, 'Fine,' turning back to her chicken curry. 'Did you eat out? Or do you want to eat with us?'

'Um…I…I ate,' I say, not sure if I've heard her correctly.

'When is your flight?' She doesn't look at me as she says it, like she's afraid to be seen approving of my decision.

'Friday…evening.'

'I'll drive you,' she says. 'I'll handle your Abbu.'

I can't help the smile that tugs at my lips, or the tears prickling behind my eyes. I feel like I've picked this up from Hani – too many emotions. I'm not really a crier, but ever since becoming friends with Hani…

'You can come too, you know,' I say. 'If you want to. Nik wants you to. She *really* wants you to.'

Ammu just shakes her head. I'm not sure if it's coming from her or from Abbu, but I know there's nothing I can say or do to change her mind.

chapter fifty-one

~ishu

NIK'S HOUSE IS LIT UP LIKE A CHRISTMAS TREE. IT'S A tiny apartment just outside of London, and its sparkling with fairy lights streaming down the front and back. It's actually a little difficult to look directly at it.

'This is such a pretty house,' Hani says, even though she's squinting her eyes so much that I'm not sure she can see the house at all.

'Thanks…' Nik sighs. 'We're hoping to move out of London to somewhere a little more affordable soon. Once all the wedding stuff is over and done with.'

She helps us pull our suitcases inside the house and then takes us in with bright smiles. 'I'm so glad you're both here,' she says finally. 'It's nice to have…family here for the wedding. Rakesh has such a big family in London and it's just nice to have some—'

'OK, don't get all sappy.' I cut her off, rolling my eyes. 'Are we sleeping on the couch?'

'It extends out to a bed, actually.' Nik leaps towards it in two quick steps and demonstrates how it becomes a bed big enough for two people. 'See?'

'Nice.' I nod. It's a lot roomier than it looks at first glance.

'You guys aren't sleeping here together, though. Only Hani,' Nik says. '*You* are sleeping in bed with me.'

'What? Why?' I turn to Nik with a frown. 'I didn't think *you* were going to be weird about this, of all people.'

Nik sighs. 'I'm not being weird. I just…wanted to talk and spend some time with my sister after not seeing her for a long time! But if—'

'OK, OK.' I give in. Mostly because I know that if I don't, Nik is going to keep pushing and pushing until I *do* give in. She's been doing so much for me over the past few months, the least I can do is sleep in bed beside her. Like when we first moved to Dublin as kids and only had a tiny one-bedroom apartment.

'You're OK to sleep on the couch all by yourself?' Nik asks Hani. Because obviously *she* gets a choice.

'Of course, no problem. Looks comfy, really.' Hani is all smiles, and I have to stop myself from rolling my eyes again.

I settle myself down on the couch, and when Hani sidles in next to me, I wrap an arm around her. It's like it's become second nature to me. Before all of this started, I didn't even know what being in a relationship was, but now I'm sure I can write a guide to *real* dating. Hani would probably say I can't, but I'm sure I'm pretty much a dating expert by now.

'So…when is your holud?' I ask Nik. In India, whenever we had weddings, the holud was my favourite part. It was always so intimate and fun. Full of family, food, and an outpouring of love. Also, a lot of music and dancing.

'I'm not having a holud.' Nik sighs. 'Didn't you hear what I just said? You're the only family attending!'

'But you have friends coming.'

'Like…a few. Half a dozen. It's going to be such a small wedding that a holud seems…pointless.'

'You *have* to have a holud,' Hani says. 'Holuds are supposed to be small. With family and close friends…and it'll be fun. When else are you going to get your mehndi done after all?'

'We'll plan it!' I exclaim, even though I've never in my entire life planned a party. There's a first time for everything, I guess. 'We can have it tomorrow. Just invite your friends, and Hani and I will take care of everything else.'

Hani glances at me hesitantly, like she's not sure she thinks we can do this, but I know that we definitely can. So I ignore her gaze.

'Are you *sure*?' Nik asks, looking at us with narrowed eyes.

'Yeah, we're sure. I'm not going to let you have a wedding without a holud, Nik.' Especially not when she's already having a wedding without Ammu and Abbu.

Nik finally smiles. 'Thanks, Ishu.'

We spend all of the next morning preparing for the holud. Hani strings up flowers on the walls of Nik's sitting room. Nik and I push the couch to one side and lay down a throw, pillows, and cushions on the floor to make a seating area. With the mattress and an old bedsheet, Hani and I create a makeshift stage just in front of the seating area. We decorate the wall of the back of the stage with flowers and glitter and balloons.

While Hani prepares the turmeric paste and mehndi and creates a holud playlist, Nik and I work together to cook a large pot of biryani.

'You have to go get ready,' I tell Nik once the biryani is done. 'The guests will be here soon…make sure you wear holud, OK?'

'You guys have to get ready too,' Nik says.

'We *will*. You're the bride though – you're kind of more important.'

'OK, OK,' Nik concedes, before finally disappearing into her bedroom.

Hani disappears into the bathroom to get changed, so I pull out my own set of clothes: a delicate yellow and green lahenga. Lahengas are not usually my thing – but you can't really go wrong with them during a wedding. I even slip on some green churis that jingle with every movement of my arms.

When Hani steps out of the bathroom, I feel like my lahenga can't compare. She's wearing a dark red kameez that's as long and wide as a ballgown. There are subtle hints of green splashed on to the dress. The two colours shouldn't go together

– but they do. And it makes Hani's bronze skin look more beautiful than ever – though that might also be the makeup.

'You look amazing!' I exclaim. Stepping forwards, I take her arms in mine. Both of our arms jingle with churis. That sound has never sounded better to me.

'So do you,' Hani says.

I reach up to brush back a lock of her hair before leaning forwards until our lips touch. Hani leans into me, and I thread my hand through her hair and—

'Ow!'

I jump back.

'Your churi…' Hani says.

My bangles are caught in the strands of her hair. I lean forwards, trying to unclasp the churi.

'Bengali clothes are really not designed for kissing, are they?' I sigh. This isn't the first time we've been caught up in each other awkwardly while wearing Desi clothes. You would think we'd learn by now, but I suppose we're determined.

'How does Bollywood make it looks so effortlessly romantic?' Hani asks, pulling at the threads of her hair.

'I guess we're no Deepika and Ranveer, huh?' I sigh.

Thankfully, we don't have to be a Deepika and Ranveer to take a picture together in front of the stage we decorated. A photo where we're pressed together a little too close and Hani is kissing my cheek. After all of our old fake photos together, we've got pretty good at taking the cheesiest real couple photos together.

Nik's guests start pouring in by seven o'clock. They're mostly her friends from university, but also a few friends from outside university. They *ooh* and *aah* at the décor, and I can't help but feel pleased that the three of us have pulled this all off in just a few hours.

When Nik comes out of her bedroom, dressed in a bright yellow salwar kameez that makes her glow, the room descends into silence. She blushes a pretty pink and comes over to greet everyone and give them huge hugs and thank them for coming.

'OK, OK.' I step in when the hugging has gone on for a bit too long. 'We need to get started. Come on, Nik. Up on stage.' I guide Nik on to the mattress. Someone dims the light, and a kind of fairytale glow descends on to the room. The music comes on, and the speakers begin to thump out a Bollywood song: 'Mehndi Laga Ke Rakhna.' I can't help the grin on my face – Hani couldn't have chosen a more perfect song to start off the evening.

It's not until hours later that I finally manage to find my way back to Hani. She's standing at the edge of the room, leaning against the wall, watching as Nik's friends dance to 'Bole Chudiyan.'

'Hey,' Hani says, resting her head on my shoulder as I wrap an arm around her waist.

'This is nice, huh?'

'It is. Nik looks…happy.'

I watch Nik smiling and laughing with her friends. She looks happier than I have seen her in a long time. I just wish

Ammu and Abbu were here to see this too.

'This has been a tough few months for her,' I say in a low voice. 'I just…wish I could have convinced Ammu and Abbu to come, you know?'

Hani picks her head up off my shoulder and turns to me with a frown. 'You're not allowed to think about that stuff today,' she says. 'Or…well, for this entire trip. We're here to celebrate your sister and her wedding. Not to think about all the stuff that's gone wrong.'

'I just—'

'Shh.' Hani reaches up her finger and presses it against my lips. 'It's easy to get caught up on the negative stuff. But *this*. This is a *good* day. We deserve to enjoy it.'

'You're right.' I nod, because she *is*. We do deserve to enjoy this day. Hani slips her fingers into mine and, for the umpteenth time, I'm surprised at all of the ways the two of us fit together. All the ways I never expected us to fit together in a million years. 'I'm glad you're here to share it all with me.'

'The good and the bad,' Hani says.

'The good and the bad,' I agree. She squeezes my hand, sending a jolt of electricity through me.

Gathered up in her arms with the beat of Bollywood music all around me, everything feels strangely right. Like none of the bad stuff even matters any more. Because as long as Hani and I are side-by-side, everything will be all right.

acknowledgements

It almost seems like there is a never-ending list of people who helped make this book possible. Thank you to each and every one of you.

Thank you, first of all, to my wonderful agent, Uwe Stender, for your endless support and belief in my work. I hope that we can bring many more books into the world together.

Thank you to my editor, Lauren Knowles, who pushed this book to be the best that it could be and always understood my vision. I get to write books that are unapologetically Bengali, Muslim, queer, and many other things, all thanks to you.

Thank you to everyone at Hachette Children's Group, particularly Katherine Agar, Rachel Boden, Nicola Goode, Siobhan Tierney, Laura Pritchard, Bhavini Jolapara and James McParland. Thanks also to Halimah Manan, Aashfaria Anwar and Becci Mansell.

A massive thank you to Nabigal-Nayagam Haider Ali. I could not have dreamed of a more fitting cover for this book. Thank you for bringing these characters to life.

Thank you to my Bengali squad, Tammi and Priyanka, for always being there when I need a listening ear or (more often) a question about Bangladesh or Bangla. This book would not exist without the two of you.

Muita obrigada to my friend Gabhi. I've spent countless

hours complaining to you about this book, about writing, about revisions…and you've always been there to listen. I cannot believe how lucky I am to get to call you a friend.

Thank you to my friends Aleema and Faridah. You basically held my hand through the first draft of Hani and Ishu, and listened to so many hours of me trying to figure out plot and character problems. You never complained, and you helped make this book into what it is today. This book would be worse off without the two of you.

A huge thank you to my debut buddy, Anuradha. You were such a source of light and support while debuting at a very difficult time, and I will always be grateful for that.

Thank you to all of my friends who have been immensely supportive throughout the years: Amanda, Gavin, Lia, Ramona, Alyssa, April, Kristine, Shaun, Timmy, Alechia, Maria, London. I appreciate all of you so much.

Thank you to my brother, and my sister-in-law, Biyut Apu, for hosting me in your house for two weeks while I wrote the large majority of this book. Thank you especially for taking me out for some amazing biryani at Dum Biryani and Dishoom. I'm not saying that all of the biryani scenes in this book were written as a result of that, but I'm also not not saying that.

I debuted during a strange time, and I'm immensely grateful to all of the people who helped me navigate everything at a difficult time. First of all, thank you to my two very talented friends Fadwa and Vanshika. I feel very lucky to know the both of you. And a huge thank you to Saajid and Carmen for all you support. It was such a pleasure to get to work with you.

Thank you to every single person who supported my debut, who showed up to virtual events, who messaged me or sent an email to share how they connected with my work, who tweeted out their support, who drew fanart, or made an aesthetic or edit. All of this helped me keep going and motivated me to work on bringing this second book out into the world. If I wrote down everyone's names it would be a never-ending list. But there were a few people who have been immensely supportive of me, and it would be unfair to not shout them out here. So, a huge thank you to Fanna, Gargee, Mis, Lili, CW, not just for your support of my work, but for all you do to uplift diverse books and voices. The book community is incredibly lucky to have all of you.

Lastly, and most importantly, thank you to you, the reader, for picking this book up and giving it a chance.

about the author

Adiba Jaigirdar was born in Dhaka, Bangladesh, and has been living in Dublin, Ireland, from the age of ten. She has a BA in English and History from University College Dublin and an MA in Postcolonial Studies from the University of Kent. She's the author of *The Henna Wars*. All of her work is aided by many cups of tea and a healthy dose of Janelle Monáe and Hayley Kiyoko. When not writing, she enjoys reading, playing video games, and ranting about the ills of colonialism. She can be found at adibajaigirdar.com or @adiba_j on Twitter and @dibs_j on Instagram.

Have you read *The Henna Wars*?

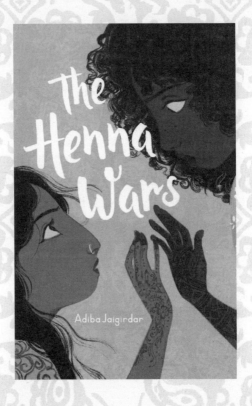

'Impossible to put down'
Kirkus